Where There Is Smoke, There Is Fire

MONIQUE FISHER

To my husband Joe and my two beautiful kids Michael and Alexander. I love you all so much and couldn't have done this without you!

Mentions of cancer, infidelity, difficult childbirth and death.

Where There Is Smoke, There Is Fire

Seated on the edge of her bed, Kara shoves a foot into one of her Nike running shoes. She stands and looks at herself in the full-length mirror. Her grey sweats pants hug her slim but curvy frame. Her naturally curly hair is pulled back into a ponytail without a hair out of place, her lips are glossy and full, and her brown skin glistens thanks to her shea butter lotion. She's so put together one wouldn't think she's going out for a jog.

Kara runs her fingers along the red letters of her white Lakeside High School t-shirt. The Fighting Rams. She stares at the illustration of the school mascot for so long it appears to be moving. The shirt takes her back in time to when things were simpler. It was only two years ago, but it feels like a thousand lifetimes. The plan to go cold turkey and throw out all traces of her high school track career hasn't worked. The truth is Kara can't bring herself to get rid of any of it.

She rolls her eyes at her misplaced nostalgia. If her classmates could see her now, they'd think she was one of those pathetic losers who couldn't move past their high school glory days, but that wouldn't be fair. Kara never even got to experience any glory days.

Her eyes travel to the framed photo booth pictures on her vanity table. The memory of the carnival years ago makes her smile. While taking silly pictures in the booth, Bryan told her he loved her for the first time, and they had only been dating for a month. A warm feeling surges through Kara's body. This warmth has been one of her main sources of strength lately. She picks up the picture and runs her fingers across Bryan's handsome, silly face. The edges of the photos are getting worn. She can barely make out Bryan's eyes. To unsophisticated high school girls Bryan's physical combination of being dark skinned with light eyes made him unique and exotic, but not to Kara. She loves him for who he is not what he looks like. Though she'd be lying if she said she never noticed how fine he is. He basically looks like Tyrese but with green eyes.

If she gets the good news she's hoping for, she'll ask Bryan if they can have some new pictures taken. The last time she mentioned it, he rejected the idea, insisting that a camera could never fully capture her beauty.

"Why waste time with a picture when I can just stare at you all day?"

Dating in high school should have been a nightmare. Countless unsuspecting girls had their reputations sacrificed every other day, all so some average, mediocre guy—of which there were many—could feel like a man around his boys. Bryan wasn't even close to being anything like those assholes. He was never average or mediocre. Nope! Her man has always been a rose amongst a shitload of thorns.

The two of them found each other junior year and fell in love. This was nothing short of a miracle as far as Kara was concerned. Her belief in miracles was shaken a year into their relationship, but it now held firm thanks to Bryan's patience and love.

They're literally the only couple from Lakeside that is still together. That might not mean much in the grand scheme of things, but it means the world to Kara.

She kisses photo booth Bryan, then gives herself a once over. Confidence exudes from her every pore, and she desperately needs it. Every day for the last three months, she's repeated her routine from when she ran track. Wake up, shower, get dressed, do a quick jog, recite affirmations with her mom, meditate, then have breakfast. Some may call it superstitious, but this same routine resulted in her winning most of her races. And she's determined to continue doing it until her bones are dust.

Back in February, Kara filled out her application to USC. Her old track coach, Mr. Lewis, assured her that his contact at the school would personally look at her application and help her find an on-campus job. It's a simple assistant job for the athletics department involving answering phones and responding to emails, but it would be hers.

Twenty-year-old Kara is dying to have a life that doesn't revolve around her parents' split. Being Evelyn's linchpin for the past two years has been a sacrifice Kara happily made, but it also came with a lot of stress. Being forced to become her mother's caretaker at the age of eighteen is one of about a million reasons why Kara despises her father. Other reasons include him cheating on her mom for years, getting his mistress pregnant, and abandoning them both to be with her. Kara's mother suffered greatly after learning about Stephen's affair. Things only got worse when he left shortly after and Evelyn was forced to hide to avoid the humiliation. Their neighbors tried to pry any info they could from her whenever she left the house. And when it finally became too much of a hassle, Kara became the head of their household.

Growing up overnight was not fun. Bathing Evelyn and forcing her to eat became another part of her daily routine. As was comforting her mother nightly as she wept in Kara's arms. This was all happening at the worst possible time. Kara's senior year was right around the corner. It was supposed to be *her* year. She was popular, dating one of the finest guys in school and USC was well within her reach, but thanks to her selfish asshole of a father, she was forced to put it all on hold. The scouts that were once vying for her quickly moved on after she had to turn them all down, and Kara watched helplessly as her dreams were set aflame and turned ash.

One of the few bright spots during this whole ordeal was having Janae move in with them. Kara and Janae had been tight since meeting in homeroom sophomore year of high school. Janae had on press-on nails with cute rainbow designs, and Kara complimented her, causing Janae's face to light up.

From their outward appearances, most folks probably have a hard time seeing them as friends. Kara is five foot, eight inches, with a slim, curvy figure; an athlete always wearing designer labels. Janae is six feet without heels, with a rotund body, and can often be seen in tight jeans and t-shirts, representing her love of all things geek. She distresses her shirts so they can be worn in her unique style. When she's not wearing interchangeable wigs, she wears her hair natural in afro puffs and corn-rows, her go-to hairstyles.

Janae is also the biggest nerd. She loves sci-fi and horror movies—all movies really, gaming and math. Basically, she's the coolest fucking person on the planet and Kara's sister from another mister. The two bonded over being organized neat freaks with good grades and later bonded over having selfish bastards for fathers.

Janae was kicked out by her parents after coming out as trans. She currently attends USC as a mathematics major— of course and has already made the dean's list.

She's about to enter her sophomore year and just started a new job as a student assistant. Kara's happy for her but can't help but feel a little jealous. Make no mistake, Janae deserves all the happiness in the world after surviving her asshole parents, but Kara can't help but envy her freedom. Janae often reminds Kara that her freedom comes at a price, so she needs to stop tripping. She also promised Kara that she wouldn't move out until they both could. That type of loyalty has meant everything to Kara and her mother.

Janae and Evelyn are bonded like superglue and have been since day one. They connected over a shared love of Diahann Carroll. When Kara suggested Janae move in with them, her motives were selfish, but it quickly turned out that helping a dear friend and giving her mother someone else to rely on has been a win-win for everyone.

Kara heads downstairs relieved to find the house empty except for Trixie. Trixie licks Kara's hand, and she smiles before giving her favorite girl a pet. Trixie may be a big ass pit bull and mastiff mix, but she would always be Kara's little love muffin. After grabbing her essentials—her keys, earbuds, iPod, and phone—Kara heads out the door. She starts out at a steady pace, only slowing down when she approaches a crosswalk. She turns on "Survivor" by Destiny's Child. It's become her theme song throughout this waiting period.

Kara's mind wanders back to Janae. She loves Kara and Evelyn but is certainly not obligated to stay like Kara is. And the last thing she wants is for Janae to become stressed out and resentful like she has. If Janae decides to leave before Kara does, she'll understand. Hell, Evelyn wouldn't even put up a fight. Evelyn's need for Kara's constant support has resulted in her becoming very overbearing. She's protective of Janae, too, but worries about Kara far more. And while incredibly annoying, it's also a little understandable. Janae is tougher because she didn't grow up being coddled like Kara.

Bryan has argued against Kara staying home insisting that she move in with him and his dumbass roommates. His parents pay for his off-campus apartment while he attends Cal State, Northridge. That's all well and good for him but Northridge is an hour away from USC, whereas Ladera Heights is only twenty minutes away. If her mom needs her, Kara can get to her with a lot less hassle.

As she jogs across the baseball field of a nearby park, Kara's mind shifts to her dad. He offered to pay her full tuition. Being the head of mortgage lending for one of the nation's largest banks made him a pretty penny. Being an idiot who cheated without a prenup made him a chump. When it was all over, her mother received a nice settlement, the house, the car, and monthly alimony. As far as Kara's concerned, she deserved more after all he took from them.

Stephen has left Kara countless messages asking her if she's heard anything. Once she does, she'll send him a quick text, so he knows when to send in the tuition money. After which, she'll promptly go back to ignoring his ass. He, of course, will continue to reach out and send gifts, claiming to want to reconnect. Apparently, his side-hoe turned second wife, Paige, is dying to meet her and introduce her to their new baby. They already have a two-year-old named Jase. God, that's such a stupid fucking name.

Stephen has even sent Kara pictures of his "replacement" family. As if leaving them wasn't hurtful enough. He's trying to create one big happy family when Kara has zero interest in being a part of one.

What Kara can't wrap her brain around, even after two years, is what went wrong? Did her parents argue? Yes! All fucking married couples do. But they were also a real-life fairy tale. Stephen would bring Evelyn flowers just because. He never once forgot her birthday or their anniversary. He sold her mother and Kara on the idea that true love was real, only to snatch that away from them. Bryan carefully restored Kara's faith, an act for which she'll be forever indebted to him.

The big picture is that no matter how many times he invites her, Kara will never, ever spend a single minute with that man, his wife, their loud ass tiny human, or their brand-new squishy pile of flesh that poops all day. Fuck him, fuck Paige, and fuck their kids too.

A half-hour later, Kara makes her way home and is greeted by her mother. She notices how much healthier her mom looks. Her skin is back to being a luminous, rich brown hue. Her hair is shiny and thick, worn flat ironed and down. She looks like the Black mom from a

HOA newsletter. She even joined a divorce women's group and has made some new friends. Kara still does a good bulk of the weekly errands, but Evelyn has done some on her own recently. She has come far in two years, and while Kara couldn't be prouder, her mom still has a long way to go.

Evelyn smiles, her face as bright as the sun. "How's that endorphin high?"

"It's good, mom," Kara giggles.

Evelyn always tries to use exercise lingo like a trainer, much to Kara's amusement. Kara knows Evelyn wants to make up for all the sacrifices Kara has made, so she has become an even bigger cheerleader for her daughter than before. Along with making friends and leaving the house more, she initiates all daily affirmations, checks in with Kara a lot more, and each morning makes smoothies she knows Kara will like.

"Ready to do the affirmation?" Evelyn asks, handing her a kale and apple smoothie.

Kara takes a sip before replying. "Ready when you are."

Kara feels the pride beaming from her mother, and she vows not to think about her dad anymore today. Evelyn is the only parent she needs, and they will find their way back to before. Kara knows it.

Mother and daughter make their way to the bathroom. Evelyn turns on the light, and they grin at each other's reflection in the mirror. Evelyn's much healthier appearance makes Kara notice their resemblance more.

She has her mom's honey-colored eyes, dark hair, dewy brown skin, and features. Aunt Geri has often joked that Evelyn gave birth to her twin.

"Okay, baby. Repeat after me. I am Kara Jacqueline Matthews."

"I am Kara Jacqueline Matthews."

"I am smart."

"I am smart."

"I am capable."

"I am capable."

"And I am strong."

"And I am strong."

Evelyn smiles, and hugs Kara tightly. "Go get 'em, baby girl."

"There's nobody to get. Either I got in and got the job, or I didn't. I'm not really up against anybody."

"And once you get into school and get the job, you'll go get 'em. You're going to take the world by storm, sweetheart."

"Thanks, mom."

As they embrace, Kara cell phone buzzes. It's Coach Lewis. Kara immediately accepts the call.

"Hello, Mr. Lewis."

"Hello, Kara."

Mr. Lewis's voice is even. Kara can't tell if she's about to get good news or bad news. Her stomach clenches, and she suddenly regrets drinking that smoothie.

"Do you have good news for me?"

"I sure do. You're in. I mean, for school and the job. You did it, kiddo."

Kara hears the smile in his voice before she hears his words. Once they register, the tears stream down her cheeks as she grins so wide her face hurts. Evelyn jumps up and down cheering, and Kara hugs her mom, unable to let go. She thanks Mr. Lewis, who congratulates her again before hanging up.

The front door opens, and Kara runs to greet Janae. She catches her just as she leans down to pet Trixie.

"J! I got in. I have the job, too," Kara screams.

Kara runs up and leaps, and Janae catches her and hugs her tightly.

"Kare Bear!" Janae screeches. Her voice goes up a couple of octaves, which is impressive since Janae's regular voice is husky.

Janae puts Kara down and hugs her some more, her spiked heels adding to their already significant height difference.

"Girl, I knew it. I knew you could do it."

Janae busts out into her happy dance, and Kara joins her. It's a mix of the cabbage patch, WAP, and the robot.

"I have to call Bryan."

"Do you though?" Janae playfully cringes.

"Be nice."

Bryan and Janae don't mix. At all. That's underselling it. They hate each other. Things came to head between him and Kara last week during a date at their favorite froyo place.

"I'm excited about this fall, Kara. Once you get to SC, we'll have more time together."

"Fingers crossed, baby. I can't wait."

Kara bounces up and down in her seat like when she was a kid, and Evelyn would pull into a McDonald's. Bryan chuckles at her exuberance.

"You are goofy as all get out."

"Thank you, suga," Kara says with a southern drawl and winks at him.

"Seriously, though. There's no need to be nervous. You got this, baby."

"Aw. Thank you, Bryan. You're the best boyfriend ever."

Kara grabs him by the collar, pulling him forward and crushing her lips against his.

After breaking the kiss, Bryan has a delirious smile on his face as Kara takes a bite of her cookies n cream.

"Thank you," he says, shaking his head to bring himself back down to Earth.

Kara giggles. "Now, who's goofy?"

"You still are."

Bryan blows her a kiss, and she blushes before blowing one back.

"God, I can't wait. And since I already know someone who goes there, it'll make the transition easier." Kara takes another bite.

Bryan snorts out a laugh. "And if anyone knows anything about transitions..."

"Do not finish that sentence," Kara warns.

Way to ruin the fucking moment, Bryan. Kara is so sick of the two of them being at each other's throats. And she's even more tired of playing referee.

"Ugh," Bryan rolls his eyes. "I'm sorry, but I don't get why you two are friends. You're way too smart and classy to associate with *her*."

"Okay, first, Janae is at the top of her class. Second, she always has my back…"

"So, what? So do I."

"Can I finish?"

Bryan lets out a sigh that tells Kara he doesn't want to hear it, but she doesn't care.

"Go ahead," he says sounding bored.

"Janae is sweet, funny, kind, and like family to me. That's all that should matter to you." There's a sharpness in Kara's tone that she hopes sends a clear message, *Don't talk shit about my sister.*

Bryan doesn't get the message.

"She's loud, obnoxious, and annoying. You really need to think about who you're running around being friends with."

"I think you've said enough," Kara snaps.

"Oh, so you can talk, but I can't?"

"No, not when you're talking shit about someone I love. You see me saying anything about your knucklehead roommates?"

"Fine. Whatever," Bryan grumbles.

The rest of the date was frosty, to say the least, but Bryan did apologize and agreed not to bring Janae up anymore. Kara forgave him, and they've been good ever since.

Kara can't wait to hear his voice. He's going to be so excited and happy!

"Hey. How's my girl?" he asks, and the warmth returns, making her feel more tingly than ever.

"Baby, I got in!"

"I knew it! That's what I'm talking about. I knew you could do it, baby."

"Thank you."

"We have to celebrate. Pizza and froyo, tonight, on me," he says.

"Okay. I'll pick you up at seven."

"See you then, Beautiful."

Evelyn takes Kara's hands and offers what Kara has deemed her "please don't say no" face. Evelyn breaks it out whenever she wants to ask Kara for something. It's caused her to break dates with Bryan a few times, but not tonight. Please, not tonight. She needs to be with him. To celebrate this win with him. His love and support played a huge part.

"I was hoping me, you, and Janae could have a girls' night? I was even going to invite your Aunt Geri and the girls."

Kara hides her disappointment and chooses her words carefully.

"Could we please do it tomorrow? We'll spend the whole day together—I promise."

While Kara loves her mom's fun-loving older sister

and her new crew of girlfriends, playing chaperone to a group of forty-something divorcees isn't her idea of a fun time.

Evelyn playfully sighs in annoyance and rolls her eyes.

"Okay. I know I'm no match for a boyfriend. Have fun."

"Thank you, mom." Kara sees the hurt in her mom's eyes. "I'll tell you what. I'll come home by eleven, and the three of us will have a movie night tonight."

"Cool. We'll watch Black Orpheus," Janae says smiling.

Kara chuckles at her friend, but not mockingly. She always believed Janae was born in the wrong era.

"Sounds good."

Kara's in her room putting the finishing touches on her makeup. When she's done, she hangs her black Chanel purse on her shoulder to complete her look. The bag is one of the few recent guilt gifts from her dad she accepted. She may hate the man, but she's no fool. She gives herself a once over. Her ensemble for the evening consists of a sexy, black asymmetrical off-the-shoulder blouse with a pair of tight blue jeans that make her ass pop. Kara completes the look with some cute as hell black suede ankle boots. Damn, she looks good!

Kara comes down to show off her look to Evelyn and Janae. They've been in the kitchen putting away all the junk food Evelyn bought for movie night. Right now, they're making snickerdoodles and singing along to "Sweet Love" by Anita Baker, Evelyn's favorite singer.

Kara clears her throat to get their attention, and both ladies turn around and applaud.

"Look at you!" Evelyn squeals.

"Thank you, ma'am. Do you think I could borrow the car for the night? I'll fill the tank."

Evelyn looks at Janae like they both have a secret, giggling like schoolgirls.

"What? What is it?" Kara smiles along with them though she has no clue what she's smiling about.

"You could take my car, or you could drive your own?" Evelyn says, tossing a pair of car keys to Kara.

Kara stares at the keys in shock. She runs to the driveway, only to find a fresh off the lot 2007 black Jeep Wrangler wrapped in a red bow. Evelyn and Janae have joined her. She looks back at her mom, and Evelyn winks. Kara wraps her arms around her, squeezing her tight.

"Jesus Christ, child. You and your bear hugs," Evelyn laughs.

"Oh, my God! Mom, thank you!"

"You're welcome, sweetheart."

"How did you know? How did you know that I'd get accepted today? How did you have all this ready?"

"I got the ball rolling on this a while ago. I told Coach Lewis to let me know about the USC decision first so I could call your dad, and he could drop the car off."

Kara's smiles fades replaced by a hate fueled frown.

"Dad was here?"

"He was. Your car was towed behind his. He

promptly dropped yours off, then left. He wanted to congratulate you, but I told him that wouldn't be wise. He wasn't happy, but he'll survive."

Evelyn is calm, her eyes clear and not filled with sadness

"Are you okay?" Kara asks.

"I am. I swear. And don't worry, I'm the one who picked the car out."

"That goes without saying. Stephen would pick out something boring, like a sedan."

Kara runs her fingers along the hood of her new car and smiles. This is a complete surprise. Evelyn's always been an expert at those. Every birthday and Christmas, without fail, her mother would pull off a huge surprise without anyone having a clue. It's her superpower.

Janae suddenly snatches the keys from Kara.

"You're going to let me borrow the car, right?" she asks.

"If mom says it's, okay?"

Kara chases after her and quickly retrieves her keys. Janae's legs may be longer, but Kara's faster. She blows a raspberry at Janae, who responds with a silly face.

After a few more hugs and a quick goodbye to her family, Kara hops in her car and drives off, even more excited to see her man.

Kara and Bryan arrive at Papa Guidos for dinner. They stand in line, waiting to order, hugged up on each other. Kara's arms are wrapped tightly around Bryan, and she can tell he loves it by the way he kisses her forehead. She gazes at him, smiling like a fool. He's always been her safe space.

Kara was acutely aware of how her peers at school saw her. She was the goodie-goodie, straight A student and popular athlete. That's it. Nothing more. She might as well have been a one-dimensional Black character on a popular sitcom. Very few people knew her. The real her. Aside from her mom and Janae, Bryan was the only person to really see her.

Kara pulls Bryan's face to hers and kisses him. When they break away, he shows his appreciation with a toothy grin. God, he has the most perfect set of pearly white teeth. Kara imagines what their kids will look like, their whole future playing out in her head. She's even hopeful that with some time and maturity, Bryan will come to see Janae as family. They will never grow apart like her parents, only growing closer and stronger as a couple.

"You look like you have something on your mind," Bryan says.

"Just thinking about us and our future."

"Is that right?"

"Yes. Do you think about that often?"

"All the time, baby."

Kara rests her head on his chest, and he twists one of her curls around his finger.

"I was surprised when you offered to come pick me up, and even more surprised when you pulled up in that Jeep. Can you do me a favor? Have your mom talk to my mom about buying me a new car."

"I'll see what I can do. Now, kiss me."

Bryan obeys Kara's orders, and soon they're full-on making out with his hands cupping her ass. Several customers look at them disapprovingly. Others giggle. Kara doesn't care. This day couldn't get any better. She's floating on air.

"Mmmm," Bryan moans, "that was fun."

When they get to the front of the line, Bryan orders three slices of pizza with extra cheese and all the meats, while Kara opts for three slices of veggie, easy on the cheese and sauce with thin crust. They take a seat at an outdoor table and wait for their food which arrives ten minutes later, and Kara lets out a grateful sigh. Papa

Guidos always has a long line, but they're cheap and fast. Her stomach grumbles as she eyes Bryan's slices. The scent of pepperoni, sausage, and ham overpowers their table. He holds a slice up to her face.

"Go on, Kara, take a bite. You know you want to." He smiles. He is such an asshole! Kara giggles and throws an olive from her pizza at him.

"No, thank you. I'm fine."

Kara may no longer be an athlete, but she's still diligent about what she puts in her body, and Bryan knows this. He loves to tease her endlessly for it. Eating pizza isn't exactly a smart dietary choice, so she always makes sure to order it with as little of the bad stuff as possible.

"I have a surprise for you." Bryan smiles.

"What is it?" Kara asks.

Bryan takes out a decorative box. When he opens it, Kara sees the most beautiful gold necklace she's ever laid her eyes on. It has a heart pendant with *K & B* engraved on it. Her eyes sparkle as he walks behind her seat and puts the necklace on her. Overcome with joy, Kara leaps out of the chair and hugs Bryan so hard she almost knocks him over.

"Thank you, baby," she squeals.

Bryan holds on to her and laughs at her excitement. Kara stares at the sparkly object as she runs her fingers over the engraving. Kara has never loved him more. This necklace symbolizes their love and commitment to each other. Bryan truly wants them to have a future just as much as she does.

"Anything for my girl."

After they're done eating, Kara and Bryan get in her Jeep. Before she can start the car, he reaches over and strokes her cheek.

"You want to go somewhere private before we get yogurt?" he asks.

"That sounds good," Kara purrs, her voice light and breathy. She smiles as she spies movement in Bryan's pants, and he adjusts himself.

"You got to stop doing that voice, baby. You know what it does to me."

Bryan grabs the crotch of his jeans and Kara chuckles, enjoying the power she has over him.

"Where did you want to go?" she asks.

"The bluffs in PV are pretty secluded."

"Let's do it," she replies in her breathy voice.

Bryan groans, throwing his head back for dramatic effect. Kara sends him a wicked grin before throwing her head back and cackling like a witch.

Bryan looks at her like she's gone mad, obviously not wanting to play anymore. Kara chuckles. He reminds her of the kid who loses, then takes his ball and goes home.

"See, you can never just leave it alone. You always gotta add extra shit when we're goofing around."

Kara knows she shouldn't do it, but she can't help herself. She really needs to stop testing Bryan's limits, but it's just too much fun to tease him.

"I have no idea what you're talking about," Kara says in a British accent.

"A witch cackle and now an accent. Funny." Bryan rolls his eyes.

His expression grows weary. Is...is he serious? That's weird. She always thought Bryan liked her silly side, but judging by the look on his face, he must have just been tolerating her this whole time. If he doesn't like this side of her, maybe there are other parts of her personality he doesn't like either. Her worries are clearly etched on her face because Bryan lets out a sigh and leans his head back. Neither says anything for an eternity, and Kara wonders if they can fix whatever has caused this sudden rift between them. Kara touches the necklace. She was so sure only moments ago that this was a symbol of their everlasting love. Now, she's not sure what to think. Is that what this is? He gives himself to her forever, but only if she changes things about herself? Kara looks over at Bryan and sees a Cheshire grin spreading across his face. He winks and laughs.

"You asshole!" Kara screams.

Catching him by surprise, Kara repeatedly slaps the shit out of him all over his face and body.

"Whoa, whoa! Come on now. It was just a joke."

Bryan blocks Kara's slaps while laughing his trifling ass off.

"What the hell is wrong with you?" Kara shouts. How the fuck is this funny? Tears sting her eyes. Bryan reaches out and wipes them away.

"Kara, baby. I was just kidding. I love you. You know that. Witch cackle, British accent, and all. Come on, baby. We're supposed to be celebrating. Don't be mad at me, and don't cry."

Kara looks up at him, and he looks so apologetic and kind. The weight pressing down on her stomach dissolves, and she leans over and hugs him. Bryan presses his lips to her ear.

"It's okay, baby. It was just a joke."

By the time they arrive at the bluffs, all is forgiven, and Kara is ready to be his. They may not always agree on everything, but that's how all relationships are. In the end, they love each other, and that's all that matters.

Bryan takes off his seat belt.

"Come here." He smirks.

Kara giggles as she takes off her seat belt. She tingles with anticipation at the thought of his touch. The one thing she and Bryan do agree on is that sex is vital to a relationship. Kara fucked Bryan after their first date. She knew the risk, but she also knew and trusted Bryan. They have sex almost every time they go out. The only time they didn't was recently after their fight about Janae.

"Take your dick out."

"Yes, ma'am."

After Bryan obeys Kara's command, she squirts some flavored lube on his dick and jerks it slowly.

"Do you love me, Bryan?"

"You know I do."

"Take off your pants and boxers."

"I'm liking this bossy side."

"Good. Now, are you ready to make up properly?"

"More than ready.'

Kara massages Bryan's balls and leans down, sucking the tip of his dick.

"Fuck, Kara. That feels good."

Kara loves the sounds Bryan makes when she pleasures him. It makes her feel powerful knowing she can bring him to the brink of losing it every time. She takes in more of his dick until she's deep throating him.

"Fuck, baby. I'll never play a prank on you again. I promise."

That's what she wants to hear, and for that, he gets something special. Kara sucks harder which is not an easy task. Bryan's dick is fucking big.

No matter, she makes her mouth into a vice grip around his dick.

"Fuck!" Bryan shouts.

Kara pulls back and goes back to sucking his tip, and their eyes meet. It's intense and unyielding. She can feel his soul colliding with hers. Letting him out of her mouth with a pop, Kara wraps her hand back around his dick and jerks him off some more. Bryan thrusts his hips up, fucking her hand with slow strokes.

After five minutes, Kara's wrist starts to ache, and after ten, it's practically numb. Honestly, as much as she loves her new car, this is not the most ideal vehicle to be doing this in. In hindsight, it would have been better if her mom had picked her an SUV. Kara switches hands back and forth multiple times. Bryan doesn't even notice. His eyes are closed in ecstasy. Kara attempts to go faster, and Bryan takes her wrist, squeezing it.

"No, baby. Slow down. Do like you were doing before," Bryan whispers.

"Of course."

Kara blocks out the discomfort and concentrates on pleasing him. She strokes him slower. Bryan's dick throbs in her hand. She blows on the slit, and some pre-come drips down.

"Slower," he whispers again.

She goes even slower. No matter how much her wrist aches, Bryan's pleasure is all she cares about.

An hour and a lot more lube later, they're eating frozen yogurt, laughing and talking.

"You want to see a movie later?" Bryan asks.

"I can't. After I drop you off, I'm going home to movie night with mom and Janae."

"Baby, you can do that any night."

"I know, but I kind of promised her. I'm doing movie night tonight and girl's day tomorrow in exchange for spending tonight with you."

"You know that's kind of fucked up, right?" Bryan says.

"Bryan, I don't want to fight again."

"I'm not picking a fight. I'm telling you that as a twenty-year-old grown-ass woman, you should be able to spend time with me whenever you want. That shouldn't come with conditions where your mom manipulates you into spending time with her."

"I like spending time with my mom."

"Look, baby. I know you and your mom are close, but she's been in a funk about your dad for two years and has made that your problem."

"It is my problem."

"Not really. You're not a shrink. You're her kid. She dumps way too much on you."

That's it. They need to find a new favorite froyo place because this one is cursed or something. This is the second time they've had a disagreement about someone in her family while coming here.

"Spend tonight with me." Bryan kisses Kara's knuckles one at a time.

"I'll think about it."

Kara offers him a sweet smile. She'll give him another blow job to tie him over before coming up with an excuse to go home. Her wrists and jaw still kind of hurt, but she doesn't want him going home mad at her.

"See that you do. Now, if you'll excuse me."

Bryan goes to the men's room. Kara feels shitty basically ditching her boyfriend, especially since he's right about everything concerning Evelyn. But she doesn't want to disappoint her mom. Evelyn was clearly hurt that Kara picked going out with Bryan tonight. Watching one of Janae's movie picks and keeping divorced ladies' wine glasses full is a very small sacrifice to make to keep her mom happy.

Kara takes out her compact to check her makeup when she sees a girl approaching her from behind. She looks pissed. Kara can hold her own in a fight—one of the few useful things her father taught her—but the anger emanating from this girl tells Kara she may need to run. These boots may be cute, but they could prove problematic even for a former track star.

"Hello," Kara says as the girl sits across from her. She sizes Kara up, carefully studying her face. Not knowing what else to do, Kara does the same. She's incredibly pretty even though she is currently frowning so hard Kara thinks her face might crack down the middle. She has engaging brown eyes, smooth cedar-colored skin, long, flowing, flat ironed brown hair with light brown highlights, and a figure that you'd find on BET Uncut. Her lips are shimmering, and if she wasn't being so bitchy, Kara would ask her where she got her lip gloss from.

"Hey. I'm Denise," she *finally* says.

"Kara."

Kara holds out her hand. Denise looks at it like she's not sure whether to shake it or slap it away.

"No offense, but if you don't mind, I'm going to hold off on shaking your hand until Bryan's bitch ass returns, and I get to the bottom of this."

Kara takes back her hand. Okay...this is a new development. How the hell does she know Bryan? God, please, no. Don't let him be a cheater. Not after everything they have been to each other. Not after everything she's been through with her parents.

"Get to the bottom of what? Who are you?"

Kara's voice is shaky, she tries to recover, but it's clear Denise heard it. Her expression softens a bit.

"I'm Bryan's girlfriend. Or at least, I thought I was."

Denise pulls out a necklace that's tucked under her blouse and shows it to Kara. It looks exactly like the necklace Bryan just gave her, only with the initials *D & B* engraved.

What the fuck? No! This cannot be happening. Bryan's been cheating on her? How? They spent more than enough time together that she would have noticed something was off. Wouldn't she? Just a few hours ago, Kara was daydreaming about forever, and now reality has punched her in the gut, stomping on her heart.

"You okay?" Denise leans in showing concern.

"I think I'm going to be sick." Kara braces against the table.

Bryan comes back from the men's room. He takes in the scene before him and looks like he's seeing a ghost. All the color leaves his face. If Kara didn't know any better, she'd swear *he* was about to take off running.

Kara gathers her bearings, taking a deep breath, and stands up. Anger rushes through her like lava. All this time, wasted. She fell for Bryan hard and fast, and thought they were on the same page. Was he just pretending to be the man of her dreams? Kara's rose-colored glasses instantly become clear.

"Bryan. Denise says she's your girlfriend, but that can't be possible because I'm your girlfriend. So, which one of us are you dating?"

Bryan looks down for a second seemingly full of shame. Kara can't wait to hear how he plans to weasel his way out of this. Unfortunately, that doesn't happen because once Bryan looks back up, he's a different person. The expression he wore on his face when he was pranking her is back. This time there's no light in his eyes. Instead of regret, he exudes indifference. He carelessly shrugs at both women. What kind of sociopathic bullshit is this? Over an hour ago, Kara had forgiven him and had his dick in her mouth. Her stomach turns at the thought.

"What do you want me to say? I was fucking both of you," he says, completely blasé.

That's it? That's his response? Before she has time to react, Denise throws Kara's cup of froyo at him.

"You bitch ass nigga! You were fucking her while we were supposed to be going together, and you gave her the same janky ass necklace you gave me."

"What the fuck, Niecey? Yeah, so what if I did? I'm not even trying to deal with this bullshit. I don't owe either of you a thing. Hell, the truth is, I've been thinking about ending things with *both* of you for a minute."

He points at Denise.

"I know for a fact that you got some weird ass incest thing going on with your cousin. My boy, Trey told me he saw y'all making out a few weeks ago."

"What?" Denise yells.

Who the fuck is this guy? Kara feels like she's in the damn Twilight Zone. This can't be real. Denise must feel the same way because she's stunned into silence, her mouth opened in shock.

He then brings his attention to Kara.

"And where do I even start with you? Let's see, there's the corny ass, goofy shit you do, which is annoying as fuck. You clingy as hell, too. Shit. You hug up on a nigga so tight I can barely move."

Bryan's eye light up with a cruel sense of glee. Kara uses her meditation techniques to control her breathing. She cannot give this asshole the satisfaction of seeing her lose her shit in any way.

"And to top it all off, you let your lonely ass momma control your life. You're pathetic, Kara."

He lets out a humorless chuckle.

"Shit, you're so fucking insecure about being friends with real girls that you fuck around with a goddamn tr...."

This motherfucker just insulted her mother and he's about to call her best friend the t-word. Oh, hell no! Kara sees red. She gets all up in Bryan face.

"What? What the fuck you gon do, Kara? Your boujee ass is too fucking soft to do shit. Just like your soft ass momma. That's why your dad left."

This asshole must have a death wish. And yes, it's true Kara grew up in a nice cushy neighborhood with a father who made so much money that her mom didn't have to work. Hell, Evelyn still doesn't have to work, but Bryan made the grave mistake of letting the "boujee" fool him into thinking Kara wasn't about that life. He quickly learns otherwise when she punches the shit out of him so hard, he stumbles. Denise takes the opportunity to jump in, and soon, both are punching and kicking Bryan into next Tuesday.

"Ow! Shit. Get the fuck off me." Bryan manages to free himself from their onslaught. "I oughta press charges against both of y'all crazy bitches."

"Go ahead. Go to the cops and tell them you got your ass kicked by two girls. See how quickly that shit spreads around. What do you think will happen when your boys find out?" Kara says.

Bryan's jaw ticks. She hit a nerve. Good. Kara knows he knows what will happen. Bryan's stock will plummet. He's basically the leader of his friend group. And just like in nature, the alpha male can always be usurped. And as sexist as it sounds, the minute his friends find out he was jumped by two girls, he won't recover.

"Fuck this shit." Bryan walks off heading towards a bus stop a few blocks away.

At least he wasn't stupid enough to think he was getting a ride home.

"I'm out of here." Kara heads to her car but stops and turns to Denise. "Do you need a ride home?"

"Naw, I'm good. I was at the movies across the street with my girls when I saw y'all."

"Okay. I'm really sorry, Denise."

"Me too, Kara."

Denise holds out her hand. Kara shakes it feeling like

she may have just made a new friend amongst all this wreckage.

Kara hops in her Jeep and heads home. After driving a few miles, the adrenaline of the night's events wears off, and the sadness seeps in. Kara pulls her car over and weeps. More than being hurt, Kara is disappointed, mostly in herself. After her parents split, Kara read one article after another on what to look for when a man is cheating. She committed the signs to memory. Even on his worst day, she never recognized a single sign in Bryan. Now that the glasses are clear, her mind is inundated with one bad memory after another. Hell, tonight's date was a perfect example. Past Kara—as in Kara from two hours ago—would have thought that she and Bryan were as close as ever. Yeah, he made a mistake, but he apologized, and they moved on. Only, he never apologized for the prank, and he barely apologized for judging her mom. She feels like shit that she even agreed with him.

Fuck! How could she be so foolish? Kara shakes her head at the realization that she took the dreams of forever she had for her parents and dumped them on her and Bryan. This must be a record for the best day turning into the worst day in someone's life.

Two days later, word spread on the Lakeside alumni Facebook group that Bryan and Kara broke up. She ended up being one of those girls she used to pity. Her reputation was sacrificed, and she's not even in high school anymore!

Kara knew better than to look, but her dumbass read

every comment. They ran the gamut from the truth to the most outrageous of lies. Some of the most ridiculous ones are that her and Janae were a couple and Bryan was her male equivalent of a beard, and that she fucked all of Bryan's friends behind his back. All of it was enough to make her head spin. It shouldn't have surprised her given the mentality of her peers, who are only a couple of years out of high school, but she's still shocked at how, with each rumor, the blame was placed squarely on her shoulders. She wants to stay in her room forever, but Evelyn won't have it, and makes her continue her routine over the next two days. Evelyn reminded her of how hiding after the break-up just makes things worse. The neighborhood went buck wild with speculation when Evelyn stopped leaving her house.

Luckily by the end of the week, the Facebook group is all abuzz because Ebony Smith was caught fucking her very married PolySci professor. As gross as it sounds, Kara's relieved that the focus is now on someone else, though it doesn't temper the pain Bryan caused.

A week after the break-up, she lays on her bed listening to "Brokenhearted" by Brandy on repeat for the thousandth time. Kara's love for 90's and 2000's R&B came from Evelyn. She would blast it when Kara was a kid, so it holds a special place in her heart. Right now, though it's only adding to her pain. The pit of sorrow and despair that she's currently in is unending, so she's figures, why not lean into it.

There's a knock on the door.

"Come in," Kara groans.

Evelyn enters alongside Janae. Evelyn turns the music off.

"Honey, I think you need to leave your room," Evelyn says, concern etched on her face. "You haven't left at all today."

It's true. Kara has rebuffed Evelyn's attempt to do the routine today. She's been doing it reluctantly all week and still doesn't feel any better. Smart, strong or capable are not how she feels now.

Janae sits behind Kara and lets her lean on her for support while wrapping an arm around her.

"I don't want to leave. Besides, I have nowhere to go," Kara replies in a zombified stupor before more tears stream down her face. "Love is a lie."

"Sweetie, love isn't a lie. It's very much real." Evelyn wipes her tears away.

Kara looks at her mother like she's a pod person.

"Who are you, and what have you done with Evelyn Matthews?"

"Very funny."

Evelyn picks up a brush from Kara's vanity table and hands it to Janae, who proceeds to brush Kara's hair.

"Kare Bear. Don't let that sorry ass nigga make you feel this way. He's not worth it."

"Amen. Look, baby, I know it hurts. Trust me, I know. But just because your dad and Bryan are selfish assholes doesn't mean all men are." Evelyn kisses Kara's cheek.

"That's not how it feels right now."

Kara's phone rings, and Janae answers it.

"Kara Matthews phone, her best friend, Janae, speaking."

Seconds pass then Janae speaks again.

"Yes, she's here, but she's currently wallowing in self-pity."

Janae laughs before she replies. "I'm coming, too, just in case you two decide to do something silly, like egg Bryan's car or something."

Kara offers a weak smile. Janae must be talking to Denise. She and Kara exchanged numbers.

"Where are we meeting you?" Janae asks then listens. "Okay. We'll meet you there in an hour."

Janae hangs up, and hands Kara her phone.

"Come on. We're meeting Denise in an hour at Burger Barn."

"Why?"

"She wants to drown her sorrows in cheese fries and invited us to come with."

Kara sighs. "Cheese fries do sound good."

"Then get up, and let's go. We'll go out and have some fun."

"Don't waste your time being sad over someone who doesn't care about you. It's useless. Go out and have fun with your friends." Evelyn cups Kara's face in her hands.

Kara nods and gets up.

"Come on, J. Help me pick out something to wear."

"Yes!"

An hour later, Kara enters Burger Barn. Janae drove her jeep and is currently looking for parking. She's convinced Kara to dress up. Or at least dress up as much as she could for a burger joint. Janae helped Kara wash and condition her hair before straightening it and adding waves. She has a part down the middle, and her edges are perfectly laid. Her outfit consists of a black turtle-neck crop top with a yellow and black plaid pleated skirt and knee-high boots. Her makeup is light, just gloss, lip liner, and mascara, but it's enough. She looks like a million bucks. Janae's motto is "when you look good, you feel good," and Kara's trying her best to take her sister's words to heart.

Kara sees Denise who waves her over.

"Hey. Cute outfit." Denise smiles.

"Thanks." Kara smiles back.

Denise looks much calmer and happier than the last time Kara saw her. She even gets up and hugs Kara, but there's an inner sadness Kara recognizes. It's well hidden, but Kara can see it because she's just spent the past week desperately trying to hide her own.

Janae enters and joins them.

"Denise, this is my best friend/sister Janae. You two spoke on the phone."

Denise takes a good look at Janae. She has on black pleather jeans and a bright red T-shirt worn off the shoulder and shredded on the bottom with the symbol for Virgo on the front. Her look is completed by four-inch lace up stilettos. Tonight, she has on her Janet Jackson circa the Velvet Rope wig with bright red curls. Her makeup is flawless. Red lips, light blush, lashes—the works.

"Wow. Sorry, I didn't mean to stare. It's nice to meet you," Denise says.

Janae laughs. "It's all good, sweetie. I do look amazing. Nice to meet you, too."

Denise chuckles. "Thank you both for coming," she says, fiddling around with a napkin.

"No problem. Are any of your girls coming?" Kara asks.

"Nope, I didn't invite them. They didn't say anything, but I think they're tired of hearing me bitch about Bryan." Denise offers them a sad smile.

Yet another reason Kara's thankful for her friendship with Janae. She's always there to listen no matter what. Kara wants to do the same for Denise.

"Go ahead and vent. We don't mind," Kara says.

"Before we get started ladies, who's having what? My treat," Janae says.

"You don't have to do that.," Denise replies.

"It's no problem. Y'all both got dealt a big blow and can use a pick-me-up."

"Thanks. I'll have a bacon burger, cheese fries, and a cherry coke," Denise says.

"Same, but I'll have Dr. Pepper. Thanks, J."

"Coming right up."

Janae heads to the counter to order their food.

"Okay, let it out." Kara places her hand on Denise's.

"Honestly, I just wish I could stop thinking about him."

"Me, too. Fortunately, my thoughts have gone from sadness to homicidal rage."

Denise has a dreamy look in her eyes. "I been planning how I could kill him and get away with it for the past week."

"Do tell." Janae returns with a plastic order number.

Before Denise can respond, the front door opens, and Kara instinctively looks. The most handsome Black man she's ever seen enters, and he heads straight for their table. His melanin-rich brown skin is smooth and flawless. His eyes look like dark brown pools of liquid, and she can only describe his body as mouthwatering. He has on a plain white T-shirt, grey sweatpants, and a pair of white Air Force Ones. His dark hair is cut short with three sixty waves and a line-up.

"Niecey, you left your phone in the car," he says as he hands it to her.

"Thank you." Denise retrieves it and gestures toward Kara and Janae.

"Kara, Janae. This is my cousin, Smoke."

Smoke offers Janae a friendly smile and a nod. He looks at Kara as if he's the Big Bad Wolf and she's Little Red Riding Hood.

"What's up?" he asks.

Heat, raw masculine power, and SEX. That's the

only proper way to describe Smoke's presence. He stands before Kara like a king amongst his subjects, yet he doesn't exude arrogance. His aura is overwhelming but also strangely comforting. From his appearance, it wouldn't be hard to believe that he isn't to be fucked with—and he probably isn't—but at the same time, Kara can easily see him helping an old lady cross the street. This piques her curiosity.

"Hi." Kara smiles.

Her greeting is met with a warm smile. Kara squeezes her legs together in a pointless attempt at keeping her pussy from throbbing.

"So, you're the chick Bryan was tipping on Niecey with?" he asks, examining Kara's face carefully.

Kara shifts in her seat hoping that will make a difference. It doesn't. Smoke looks at her like he's memorizing every inch of her face. Kara damn sure is memorizing every part of his. His body too. She makes a mental note to check out his ass when he turns around.

"Yeah, but she didn't know that." Janae asserts.

"I figured as much," he replies.

He looks over at Denise, and Kara takes notice of how his benevolent energy shifts into something familial and protective. It's sweet.

"You sure you don't want me to beat his ass?"

Good lord, he would probably fuck Bryan up with no problem.

Let him do it, Denise. Let him! Kara thinks.

"Yeah, I'm sure. I don't want you getting into any more trouble."

"What chu mean, anymore? I haven't beat down a nigga in years."

Kara wonders how many niggas Smoke's beat down? She's sure he's won every fight too.

"Exactly. You really want Aunt Paulie going in on you?" Denise gives him a playfully stern look.

"Good point."

He looks back over at Kara and Janae. A king addressing his subjects.

"It was nice meeting you two."

"You, too," Janae says.

"Nice to meet you." Ever the competitor, Kara offers him a sweet smile that turns into a bite of her bottom lip.

Smoke's self-assured stance wobbles for a split second. He quickly recovers but not before Kara notices. She licks her lips hoping to make him wobble again. Instead, he gives her a look that says if she does that again, he'll *punish* her. So, of course, she does it again. He smirks and keeps his eyes on Kara while addressing Denise.

"Niecey, let me know when you need me to come get you."

"Are you sure you and Kara don't want to fuck each other before you leave?" Denise mocks with a goofy grin.

Damn Denise, really? Janae snorts out a laugh. *Et tu, J?* Kara is almost knocked off her game thanks to the two trifling heifers next to her, but no worries. She's got this.

She's smart, strong, and capable, and this time she believes it.

"I'm game if she is," Smoke teases.

He clearly thinks Denise's question has left her tongue tied.

You wish, you sexy motherfucker. Kara thinks.

"Sounds good to me," She purrs

This makes his chest rise and fall as he lets out a deep breath. Never has the simple act of breathing been so enticing.

"Maybe next time. Bye, Kara."

"Bye, Smoke."

As he turns to leave, his ass comes into view. Kara stares at it like she expects the power of x-ray vision to kick in at any moment.

Holy shit! Bryan, who?

Three

S moke chills on the front porch of his house smoking a blunt.

Kara.

Just thinking about her bright, beautiful smile brings a wide ass grin across his face. He heard her name mentioned over the past week because of the whole Bryan thing, but none of that could have prepared him for what he saw when he entered Burger Barn. While Smoke is used to women finding him attractive, there is something about the way Kara looked at him that makes him feel ten feet tall. From the way her sweet golden-brown eyes lit up when she first saw him, to the way she never broke eye contact as they went toe-to-toe flirting. His curiosity has never piqued this much with any woman he's ever encountered.

Kara.

And now his dick is hard. Time to go inside and take care of that. He takes one last pull before going inside.

Smoke enters the house and sees the state in which he and Tone left it. Jacking off is no longer necessary because the mess makes his dick immediately deflate. Empty pizza boxes and beer bottles are spread out around the living room. The regular weekly cleaning—vacuuming, dusting, dishes, etcetera—hasn't been done in two weeks. Smoke takes in the mess and starts with the trash in the living room. It's a good thing it's not the beginning of the month, or else his mother would be here to collect rent. If she saw how her mother's house looked right now, she'd kick Smoke and Tone's asses.

Kara.

Yep, that's better. He can feel himself calming down. Funny how she has that effect where she can calm and excite him. That's new.

Smoke rolls his eyes as he cleans up more trash. Why in the hell is he thinking about Tone's free-loading ass or how pissed his mom would be when he could be thinking about her? What he needs to do is figure out a way to see her again. She and Denise are becoming tight, so it will be tricky. Niecey's made it plain that she does not want Smoke anywhere near her friends. And it's not like none of them haven't tried.

Smoke's interactions with girls started at a young age. From the time he was twelve, girls came to him. He barely had to try. The old adage of girls asking for nice guy but really wanting a bad boy proved to be very beneficial for him. Smoke got into fights at school. A lot. Typically, it was because some dude thought Smoke fucked his girl—which he usually did—but it was also because he was protecting Niecey. She's a pretty girl and attracts a lot of dudes who see her as nothing but a conquest.

Niecey is three years younger than Smoke, and as far as he's concerned, she's his little sister. They were raised together by their moms: Sheila and Pauline Tompkins, two sisters who found themselves becoming single mothers around the same time. Smoke thinks about how hard the two of them worked to make sure neither he nor Niecey knew how much they were struggling financially. It's not easy to get child support when one father is in jail, and the other has vanished without a trace.

The only male role model Smoke and Niecey had was their uncle Duke. He was their moms' younger brother. Duke had a way with women starting with his own mother, Grandma Lou. She would outwardly favor him, and this caused a rift between him and his sisters that never fully healed. Despite their tense relationship, Duke made sure to spend time with his niece and nephew, Smoke more so. They were particularly close. Duke made furniture and could fix practically anything. When Smoke was eight, Uncle Duke started taking him on jobs with him. Duke worked as a freelance repairman and taught Smoke everything he knew. Smoke was so adept at fixing and building things that, by the time he was fifteen, his woodshop teacher recommended him for a trade school program for high school students. He landed his first job not long after he graduated and has been working steadily ever since.

Fixing stuff wasn't the only thing Duke taught Smoke. When Duke would take him on a gig where the customer was woman, her plumbing wasn't the only thing that needed fixing. And a good number of these women were married.

During those excursions with Uncle Duke, Smoke learned three valuable lessons about being a reliable repairman and satisfying women.

Lesson one, if you're good at your job, you will get repeat business. Smoke puts a great deal of pride in his work. Both kinds. A lot of dudes like to hit it then move on to the next. This is because they're only interested in their own pleasure. Smoke found that if he concerned himself with how a female's body responded to his touch, she was more likely to come back for more. This belief has never steered him wrong, and it's the main reason why he's always swimming in pussy.

Lesson number two, when you do quality work, word-of-mouth will follow. Most of his customers were referred to him. This goes for the girls he fucks around with, too. On more than one occasion, he's found himself at a party where some chick will approach him and tell him that her friend was bragging about how good his dick is. Next thing he knows, he has her bent over a sink in the party host's bathroom, covering her mouth to muffle the noise.

Lesson three, never forget your tools. Smoke has never been caught slipping and isn't about to be. He makes sure all the tools he needs for a job are in his truck. There are plenty of repairmen that will "forget" an important tool for a job. This leads to them having to come back and charge another fee to the customer. Yeah, you'll get more money, but you'll also look unprofessional and probably won't get called back. As for women, Smoke uses condoms every goddamn time. He is twenty-two and has no interest in becoming a father. He's way too young for a responsibility that big. And having fire shoot out his dick when he pees isn't something he'd like to experience, either. Luckily, he has yet to catch anything.

This lesson came from a pregnancy scare Duke had with a married woman. Her husband found out and showed up at Louella's house, where Duke was playing a game of spades with Smoke. The man barged into the house and punched Duke before he could react. Louella was screaming for him to stop. Smoke was only fifteen, but he was already strong. He jumped in and started throwing punches. Smoke and Duke overpowered the husband, who then left with his tail between his legs.

Bonus lesson, confidence is key. After Smoke fought a grown-ass man—at least that's what folks were saying—his stock went up at school and elsewhere. Soon it wasn't just girls his age noticing him. Adult women were too. It didn't hurt that his voice was deeper than most teenage boys. Hell, when he was thirteen, folks would often mistake him for Duke over the phone. It was one of these encounters that made him realize that while being good-looking helped and having a strong body was a bonus, it was his self-assured attitude that proved to be impressive.

One of Pauline's co-workers called the house one day. She couldn't see Smoke's face or body, but the minute he answered the phone, she was putty. Smoke had no interest in fucking his mom's co-worker, but he had fun flirting with her. Unfortunately, Pauline walked in on them and promptly took the phone. Pauline proceeded to tell said co-worker that if she ever spoke to her son again, she would swing by her house and beat her ass. Smoke was seventeen at the time.

Unfortunately, this incident put him on his mother's radar way more than he already was. Pauline had always approved of him spending time with his uncle, but after Duke passed away, the parallels between Smoke and his late uncle became blurred. That's when Pauline stepped in and told Smoke that he needed to stop messing around with all those girls. Being a rebellious teenager, of course, he didn't listen. A few weeks later, Smoke fucked LaTisha Hawkins. She was fine as all get out and wanted to get revenge on her boyfriend, Rashad, who got her best friend pregnant. None of that was Smoke's business. LaTisha was pretty, and she wanted to fuck him. What was he supposed to do? Say no?

LaTisha saw Smoke at a party, and they began to flirt. A couple of hours later, she and Smoke were fucking at her house. Her mother worked the graveyard shift, so they were alone...or so they thought.

"Fuck! Smoke."

Smoke had LaTisha in the flat doggy-style position. He pounded his dick into her relentlessly. She gripped the sheets so tightly, her knuckles turned white.

"Shit! Oh, my God!"

"You want me to go faster?"

LaTisha was unable to reply as she bit into the pillow. That wouldn't do, so Smoke smacked her ass.

"Answer me!" Smoke ordered.

"Yes! Fuck yes."

Smoke pulled his dick out.

"Too late. Get up."

LaTisha obeyed Smoke's command. After ripping the condom off, he placed his dick on her lips. Without hesitation, she opened her mouth taking in every inch of him.

"That's right. Suck that shit. You gon swallow every drop of my nut, too. You hear me?"

"Mmmhmmm," LaTisha nodded, and sucked harder.

"Arrrghh!" Smoke groaned. Goddamn, it felt good. He thrusted his hips forward and fucked her mouth.

"Fuck! You about to make me come."

LaTisha pulled away, opening her mouth, ready to accept Smoke's load. He gripped his dick and jerked it. When his come spilled out, LaTisha licked it up, taking his dick back in her mouth to suck down every drop like he'd told her to. When she was done, she pulled away again and opened her mouth to show him she had swallowed.

"Good girl," Smoke smirked down at her.

After a few more rounds of fucking, Smoke headed out around three in the morning. As he walked to his truck, there was an outline of someone heading toward him. He paid them no mind until a fist came crashing into his face, sending him to the ground. Rashad, LaTisha's boyfriend, stood over him.

"What? You thought you could fuck my bitch, and I wasn't gon find out?"

Smoke got up and wiped the blood from his mouth. He took off his jacket and rolled up his sleeves. All he wanted was some pussy and to grab some food on the way home. Now he had to beat this nigga's ass. Which meant his homies were going to try and retaliate, and he'd have to beat their asses too. Contrary to what many believed, Smoke didn't enjoy fighting niggas. It just became the price of having a good dick.

"I'm standing right here, 'Shad. What the fuck you wanna do, nigga?"

Rashad threw another punch, but Smoke blocked it, throwing one of his own. It landed squarely against Rashad's jaw. That punch clearly hurt because Rashad shook his head like a fucking cartoon character. Rashad charged at Smoke, who used Rashad's momentum to throw him against the truck, then proceeded to pummel him into next week with a series of jabs. When the smoke had cleared, Rashad's face looked like a bloody pulp, and Smoke merely had a busted lip. Not wanting to embarrass himself any further, Rashad told everyone that he got jumped. Pauline wasn't so easily fooled though. Between Smoke coming home way past his curfew and having a busted lip on the night in question, she knew something happened between him and Rashad. When she confronted Smoke, he confessed. Thinking his mom would be pissed and go off on him, Smoke was not prepared for how she responded. He remembers how tired and weary she looked.

"I can't do this with you anymore. You want to be grown and not abide by my rules—then you need to live somewhere else."

"I'm eighteen; I'm not old enough to rent an apartment. Where am I supposed to go?"

"You'll live in Lou's house. And since you've found work, you'll pay me rent each month. I've done everything I could to prevent you from ending up like Duke, but you're determined to follow in his footsteps in every way. I'm not going to watch you do it."

Smoke packed his bags and moved into Grandma Louella's old house that night and has been here ever since.

As he finishes up the last of the vacuuming, Smoke sees headlights pull up in front of the house. He goes out and stands on the porch. Denise hops out of a black Jeep and heads toward the house.

"I thought I was picking you up?" Smoke says.

"I know, but Kara offered to drive me home, and I remembered that I left my charger here the other day." Denise goes into the house to retrieve it.

Smoke runs in the house and grabs a clean shirt. He wants to talk to Kara again. He wishes Janae weren't there so they could talk alone, but beggars can't be choosers. He puts the shirt on and jogs over to her car.

"Hey," he says.

"Hey," she smiles.

"Nice ride."

"Thank you. A congratulatory gift from my mom."

"What was she congratulating you on?"

"Getting into USC."

"Congratulations, that's impressive."

His eyes darken and he makes his voice huskier. Janae or no Janae, he's prepared to continue the back and forth they had earlier.

"Thank you."

Denise is on her way back to the car, and not wanting Niecey to tease him or talk shit again while he talks to Kara, he makes his intentions known before she gets to the car.

"Feel free to stop by sometime. By yourself. As blunt as her suggestion was, Niecey wasn't wrong. I would like to see a lot more of you, Kara."

Kara grins showing that big, bright, beautiful smile. "I'll think about it."

"Okay, well, when you're done thinking, give me a call"

Smoke takes out a business card and hands one to Kara. He always carries them, just in case.

Kara bites her lip again as she takes the card. *Fuck.* He's going to have to make her pay for doing that so much.

Smoke bids everyone good night just as Niecey hops back in the car. He makes sure to walk slowly back into the house so Kara can get a good look at his ass...again. Yep, he's definitely going to need to jerk off now.

Four

Kara lays on her bed listening to Glenn Lewis sing while looking at photos of Smoke on Facebook. She keeps going back and forth about calling him. This whole Bryan thing left her feeling raw and exposed. She doesn't want to put herself in a situation like that ever again. But would that even happen with Smoke? He doesn't do relationships, according to Denise. She gave Kara a rundown on all things Smoke after he left Burger Barn. He has God knows how many girls in his phone, and hearing that upset Kara. It shouldn't have, but it did. The image of Smoke butt naked pleasuring some girl made Kara jealous. She felt a strange possessiveness over him—like he was hers.

Wow. She needed to get a grip. Smoke is fine, but not the type of guy she could be with long-term. This could make him a perfect rebound, though. Still, Kara isn't interested in being one of Smoke's regulars, or anyone's. If she makes that clear upfront, how would he respond? She doubts he'll want to give up any of the girls he already has. And there she goes again! She can't stop going back and forth with this shit.

Denise also shared that Smoke works as a repairman and knows how to build furniture, which of course made him even more appealing. She grew up in a household where if anything broke, a call was made, someone came by, and it was fixed. Kara doesn't think her father even knows what a wrench is. And Bryan? Ha! There were times when she had to open jars for him.

Kara knows she shouldn't even be looking at Smoke's pictures, but she can't stop. This is Denise's fault. She knew what friending Kara would mean. Of course, she was going to visit her cousin's page. Now, she's stuck at home daydreaming of his smile, wondering what it feels like to be in his arms, and remembering his scent. Nautica Voyage. It invaded her nostrils at Burger Barn, and now every time she remembers their interaction, his scent is never far behind. Constantly thinking about him is overwhelming, but she can't call him. Can she? No—at least, not yet. Kara decides to give herself a "Smoke" break. She turns off the music, puts down the laptop, and decides to do some yoga. Right as she pulls out her yoga mat, Janae walks in.

"I can think of something else you could be doing that involves bending and it's a lot more fun."

"Wow. That was corny."

"Fuck you. I thought that was clever." Janae tosses a pillow at her. "Come help me find something to wear."

Kara gets up and follows Janae to her room. Kara opens her closet and pulls out a blouse paired with a wrap-around. Janae vetoes it.

"I want to look cute and fun. That feels like too much."

Kara gives it some thought.

"Got it."

She pulls more outfit choices from the closet and hands them to Janae, who goes behind the folding screen in the corner of the room to change. Janae found it at an antique store and had to have it. It does give the room a certain vintage flair.

"Where are you headed off to?"

"This guy, Tony's crib. I met him at a café, and we hit it off. Turns out we both love Battlestar Galactica. He's having me over to watch season one, and he's making us lunch."

Kara grabs a few pairs of shoes and some more shirts before handing the options to Janae.

"What does he do?"

"Don't know, but he left the café in a Benz."

"Be careful. Going to a guy's house after you just met him is a little iffy."

"Aren't you considering going to Smoke's house after you *just* met him?"

"Point taken."

Janae comes from behind the screen in a cute

vintage Battlestar Galactica t-shirt that she ties into a knot at the bottom and a pair of jeans with high-heeled converse sneakers. While she doesn't need glasses, Janae has taken to wearing them with fake lenses. Each pair is a different color. Today's pair is a dark blue to match her jeans. She puts on her makeup and lashes and styles her hair in her signature afro puffs.

"You look super cute," Kara smiles.

"Thanks. I have some time before my date, so let's talk about what's going on with you."

"What about me?"

"Talk to Smoke."

"I will. I just don't want to seem too eager."

"But you are eager, Kare Bear."

"All the more reason not to seem so."

"I guess."

Janae grabs her purse and heads out, stopping short at the door. She turns to face Kara.

"Kare Bear, what time is it?"

"One o'clock."

"Cool. By the way, I friended Smoke on Facebook and gave him your number. He's going to be calling you shortly."

"What? Why did you do that?" Kara screeches.

"Because I knew you'd be going back and forth about calling him. So, I took matters into my own hands. He's going to call you during his lunch break. Okay, see you soon. Smooches!"

This time, Kara throws a pillow at Janae but misses as she runs away laughing.

Right on cue, Kara hears her phone ring. She runs back to her room and checks her hair in the mirror until she realizes Smoke can't see her. It's a shame, really. Her hair looks luminous today.

"Hello?" she answers.

"Hello, Kara," Smoke replies.

Sweet Jesus, that voice. Kara falls back onto her bed from the sheer force of it.

"Hello, Smoke."

"I wanted to see if you weren't busy, maybe you could swing by later?"

Kara should end the phone call. This is all too soon after Bryan. And she doesn't want to become one of Smoke's many girls. She should tell him she's not interested and ask him not to call her again. But she can't, and she won't. Kara gathers her thoughts before she replies.

"I don't know."

"What about this are you having trouble with?"

"All of it."

"I'm going to need you to be more specific, baby."

"I don't want to get hurt, I don't want a relationship right now, and I don't want to be part of your harem."

"My harem?"

"Denise told me about all the girls in your phone."

"And you think I want to make you one of them?"

"Yes."

"I assure you, Kara, I don't want that."

"Then what do you what from me?"

"Simple. I want you. All of you, but obviously, you're not ready to give me that. So how about I offer myself, instead?"

"As?"

"As whatever you'd like me to be. A friend or more; the choice is yours."

"Okay," Kara says with butterflies in her belly. She could only imagine what "more" meant.

"Is that something you'd like from me?" he asks.

As if he doesn't know. With all the flirting they did and Denise's goofy-ass comment, it's all been put out there. Besides, Kara's an adult, and so is Smoke. This doesn't need to be complicated.

"I wouldn't be opposed to hooking up with you."

"Alright. I'll be home by five. You want to swing by?"

"Can we make it tomorrow?"

Kara needs to coordinate with Janae first.

"Sure. Does seven work?"

"Yes, that works. Smoke?"

"I love the way you say my name."

"Thank you. I love the way you say mine, too."

"Kara," he says her name as if he's letting out a long-held breath.

"Jesus, stop that..." Kara giggles.

Smoke chuckles. "You okay, baby?"

"Yes. Just a little..."

"Wet?"

"Tingly."

"Tingly is good. I don't mind making you tingly."

"Okay, stop saying tingly."

"Tingly," he growls.

"Asshole," Kara smirks

Smoke laughs. "Sorry I interrupted you. You were going to ask me something?"

"Right. You said that you want me."

"I do."

"Why? I'm curious. We only met yesterday. How can you be so sure you want me? You don't know anything about me."

"I know enough. Besides, you intrigue me."

"What about me intrigues you?"

"Everything. Your beauty, your intelligence, and you're incredibly sexy and confident. And frankly, I can't stop thinking about you."

Damn him. He's so...nope. Stop doing that. He's not an option. She'll stop by tomorrow and maybe a few more times, but she can't handle anything more. They can meet up for now, but once Kara starts school, they'll go their separate ways, and that will be that.

"You look just like your mom," Smoke says, disrupting her pep talk.

"I'm sorry, what? How do you know that?"

"I peeped your Facebook page."

"Oh, so you're stalking me."

Okay, so she's a fucking hypocrite. So what? He can't see what she's doing.

"That isn't stalking, and like I said, you intrigue me.

And don't act like you haven't looked at mine. I know you're friends with Niecey, and she follows me."

Wait. Could he see what she's doing? Kara's face becomes flushed. She hasn't just been ogling his Facebook page; she's also masturbated to his pictures a couple of times when her mom and Janae weren't home. Kara swallows a lump of embarrassment, suddenly feeling hot. She really needs to end this phone call.

"Your silence speaks volumes, Miss Kara. Tell me which picture of mine is your favorite."

Fuck it! Might as well tell him. Maybe he'll post more.

"The one where you're building something."

"Oh, right. I was building a doll house for a neighbor's kid."

Kara almost squeals at the thought of tough-ass Smoke handing a kid a homemade doll house.

"How many trophies do you have? That, by the way, is my favorite picture of you. You're smiling while holding a trophy," he asks.

Kara smiles. Wow, Smoke sounds genuinely interested. Kara has come across her fair share of guys who asked her questions about running track. A few questions in and it usually turned into a weird competition with some of them even challenging her to a race. She's not getting that feeling from Smoke at all.

"How many trophies from high school or all together?" Kara sits back and gets comfortable. She's enjoying their conversation. Turns out, Smoke is easy to talk to.

"Damn, it's like that?" he laughs.

"I won all but three of my races during my track career, and I started running when I was twelve."

"So, do you have a track scholarship for USC? Are those given to athletes after they graduate?"

Kara's jaw ticks, and her anger rises at his questions. She needs to chill. It's not his fault. He couldn't possibly have known this was a sore spot for her. She takes a deep breath before answering.

"No. My dad is paying my tuition, and I got an on-campus job."

"That's great. You don't sound so happy about that, though."

"It's a long story."

"No need to tell it if you're not ready. I look forward to hearing it when you are."

"Thank you."

"Alright. I've bugged you enough. Imma let you go."

Kara wants them to keep talking but she doesn't want to force them into a longer conversation. Besides, he must have spent most of his break talking to her.

"I'll see you tomorrow, Smoke."

"Counting down the minutes, Kara."

Five

Smoke begins his last set of bench presses while Tone sits nearby, drinking a beer.

"So, did you ever fuck the uppity chick you was telling me about?"

Smoke wishes Tone wouldn't bring Kara up, but unfortunately, he made the mistake of telling him about her. Now he won't shut up. Smoke has been vague about his interactions with Kara because he knows Tone wouldn't understand. His idea of getting to know a girl boils down to charming her, fucking her, and moving on to the next. Admittedly, this has been Smoke's MO as well, but he doesn't want to do that with Kara. Smoke is supposed to see her in a couple of hours. He's excited and kind of nervous. This is all new to him, and he wants to make sure he doesn't blow it.

"No."

"For real? That's not like you, nigga. You should have been hit that by now."

"We've talked for a bit, but that's it."

Tone bursts out laughing. "Talked? Motherfucker, what is this? Junior high? No, scratch that. I was doing more than talking in junior high."

Tone laughs at Smoke's expense. Smoke wishes Tone would take his Black ass home, but unfortunately, he doesn't have one...kind of. Tone's mom kicked him out for the millionth time, and since he has nowhere to go, and Smoke's his only friend, he's stuck with him for God knows how long.

"I got to admit, my nigga, you losing stripes with me."

Is this motherfucker serious? He has no job, a "rap career" that's going nowhere, and *he's* losing respect for Smoke.

"You haven't stopped working out since yesterday. You all pent up, fool. Call one of your bitches to help you release that tension."

Smoke gets serious. He is not in the mood for Tone's bullshit. Not today.

"Tone, Imma say this only once. I can't have Kara coming through here feeling uncomfortable. Which means by the time she gets here, and anytime she comes over; you need to be gone."

Tone nods in agreement. "Aight, nigga. Damn. I'll leave and let you guys have some privacy. Gotta say, I ain't ever seen you hung up over a chick this bad."

No kidding.

~

Kara pulls up to Smoke's house. She and Janae spent close to two hours picking out something for her to wear. She was nervous as hell. Like she was about to lose her virginity again. Janae, of course, calmed her down. Once she was in the right head space, she ended up picking a cute ensemble comprised of tight, white jeans and a cute soft yellow and floral midriff top. A nice casual look that shows a little skin.

Kara gets out of her car and is surprised to see a guy covered in tattoos with cornrows sitting on the porch. He must be around Smoke's age, but he looks older, like life dealt him a bad hand and aged him by about ten years. His attention goes to Kara as she approaches the front door.

"You must be that uppity chick, Kara?" he asks as he grabs her hand.

Uppity? Is that how Smoke described her? Kara's starting to have second thoughts about being here.

"My name is Kara, but I'm not uppity," Kara replies. She tries to pull away from his grip, but it's too tight. "Let go of my hand," she commands.

Instead of doing so, he gives her a lecherous smile. "I'm Tone."

"Don't care. Let go of my fucking hand."

He lets go and gives Kara another unsettling look. "Smoke is back out by the garage, *Kara.*"

Kara ignores him and enters the house. The screen door is unlocked, and the front door is open. The way he said her name made her skin crawl. She rubs the hand Tone grabbed. Kara walks out the sliding door that leads to the garage and backyard. The garage door is open, and one side of the garage is set up as a workspace for repairs and carpentry, and the other side is a gym. Smoke is currently using the gym, doing chin-ups with his back facing Kara. Right now, he's shirtless, and she finally notices he has tattoos. The day they met, she was so hung up on his face and body that she somehow missed all his ink. And when she stopped by his house with Denise, he'd had on a long sleeve shirt.

On his left shoulder blade is the West African Adinkra symbol for Good Fortune, and on the right shoulder blade, the symbol for Unity. Kara moves to get a closer look and sees "RIP Duke" on his outer left forearm and the name "Louella" is on his right shoulder. He has headphones on, so Kara's reluctant to say anything to him. She doesn't want to bug him, and she doesn't want to stop staring at him.

She works up the nerve and taps him on the shoulder. He takes off his headphones and turns around. Sweat drips all over him. Good God, this man is an Adonis. Smoke looks pleased to see her.

"Hey, sorry, I must have lost track of time," he says in his low, seductive tone. There's an added hint of adorable embarrassment. "I apologize. I tend to get into a bit of a trance when I work out."

"A meditative state."

"Yeah."

"I get it."

She spots another tattoo on his upper right pectoral. It's his name, Smoke.

He catches her staring. "You got any?"

"Any?"

"Tattoos."

"Nope. My mother would not approve, and I hate needles. Um, listen your friend grabbed my hand and wouldn't let go and it made me really uncomfortable."

"Tone's still here?" he asks, his voice rising. Smoke's nostrils flare, and his eyes heat up with anger.

Okay, that was not the reaction she was expecting. She thought he'd be a little annoyed, not ready for battle.

"Yeah, he's sitting on your porch."

"Fuck! I'm sorry. I asked him not to be here when you arrived so we could be alone."

"Maybe I should leave and come back later."

Smoke places his hands around Kara's waist and gives her a little squeeze.

"No, please don't. I'll get rid of him."

Kara smiles. It's sweet he's so determined to spend time with her.

"Okay."

Smoke winks at her before turning towards the front of the house to confront his friend. Kara follows but hangs back a bit, watching from a nearby window in the living room.

"Nigga, I asked you not to be here. You knew she was coming over."

"I know, but I wanted to meet her—see what all the fuss was about. She is fine. Got a bit of an attitude, though."

Seriously? Kara can't believe her ears.

"Motherfucker! You grabbed her. What the fuck did you think was going to happen?"

Thank you! Who the fuck does that?

"Alright, nigga. Calm down. I was just fucking with her. I'm leaving anyway. I'm hooking up with that Puerto Rican chick I was telling you about. Imma stay with her for a bit."

Kara sees the look of relief on Smoke's face as Tone enters the house and grabs his stuff from one of the bedrooms. He gives Kara a mocking smile.

"Bye, Kara," Tone chuckles.

Kara shoots daggers at him. She would love to kick him in the balls, but that would just prolong his leaving.

"See what I mean, Smoke? Attitude."

"Whatever, nigga. Just leave."

"Alright, alright. I'll catch you later."

Tone finally leaves, and Smoke comes back into the house.

"Again, I'm really sorry about that, Kara."

"Thank you. I'm sorry, but I have to ask this. You

seem like a nice enough guy. Why are you friends with that asshole?"

Smoke lets out a sigh as if he's been asked this question his whole life.

"I know Tone can seem..."

"Sexist, rude, aggressive? I can go on."

"I'm sure you can. But he's a good guy. We've been rolling together since we were in high school. We both didn't really know our fathers, both got kicked out by our moms—hell, he still gets kicked out by his—and we've always had each other's back. He has his issues, but he's, my boy."

"You're friends with him because you both have tragic backstories?"

"I guess. Why are you friends with Janae?"

"Because she's amazing. She's funny, kind, loving, and always honest with me."

"In his own way, Tone is all those things too."

"I don't see it, but I'll take your word for it."

"That's fair," he says, and they share a laugh.

Suddenly nervous, Kara looks away. Casual hookups are all well and good, in theory, but now that she's here, her nerves are getting to her. She tells herself to chill and turns her eyes to meet his.

"So, what are your plans for us tonight? What does the Smoke experience feel like?"

The Smoke experience, huh? He likes the sound of that, and Kara has no idea how much she's about to find out. Smoke takes her by the hand, leading her to his bathroom. He gestures to her to take a seat on the closed toilet. She sits, gazing up at him with a look of hunger and curiosity.

"What's your real name?" she asks.

Smoke removes his shoes and socks. Kara watches his every movement.

"Why?" he teases, removing his sweats.

She stares at his legs, and he's grateful for the dead-lifts he did this morning. Her eyes travel to his crotch, and his dick throbs. He notices her face heat up and sends a wicked grin her way. Their eyes meet. This is about to be the best sex she has ever had. He will make sure of it. She's expecting an experience, and Smoke will make damn sure to deliver. She must see his thoughts cross his face because it takes a full two minutes of them looking deeply at each other before she realizes she hasn't spoken.

She finally answers, "Because I...I don't want to yell 'oh, Smoke' when I come. I'd much rather say your name."

"Fair enough. It's Aaron."

Kara smiles. "Aaron, I like it."

"Thank you." He smiles. "You want to join me?"

Aaron removes his boxers then turns the shower on.

Water cascades over his naked body as he waits for Kara's response.

She sighs deeply then smiles. He can tell she likes what she sees.

"If you don't mind, I'd like to watch you."

"I don't mind at all."

Aaron washes the sweat off his body. Soon the room is filled with steam and the smell of sandalwood. He stands under the water with his head back and his eyes closed. He can hear Kara take in a breath as he strokes his dick. When he opens his eyes and looks at her, she smiles at him. Bright and beautiful as ever. She bites her lip causing Aaron to let out a low groan. He turns the water off and steps out of the shower. He takes her hand and leads her to the bedroom.

Kara takes off her clothes while Aaron stands dripping wet, watching her. Goddamn. She has some pretty ass titties. They're full and round. She lays on the bed and beckons for him. He lies beside her so they're facing each other. Aaron runs his fingers through her soft, wavy hair, releasing another deep sigh from her. When he traces his fingers down the side of her neck, she giggles.

"You ticklish?" he asks.

"A little," she replies, smiling.

As fun as it would be to tickle her, that's not what he's planned for her. Aaron runs his hands over her ass, and is about to smack it, but holds back. He should warn her first.

"Before we get started, I need you to know something," he says as he rubs his hands over her breasts, squeezing them. He leans down and flicks his tongue over a nipple.

"That your tongue feels amazing?" Kara scratching her fingernails over his head.

Aaron looks up at her. "Thank you but seriously, I need to tell you something."

Aaron sees a flash of concern in Kara's eyes. It's quick, but he caught it. Hopefully, this doesn't scare her away. Kara doesn't seem like the type to shy away from anything, but you never know.

"Okay," she says. The apprehension in her voice isn't hidden, coming through clear as day.

"Don't be scared, baby. I just need you to know that when I get going, I can be dominant. I like being in charge."

All apprehension leaves, a huge smile spreads across Kara's gorgeous face.

"Okay. Do we need a safe word?"

"If you'd like we can have one, but I'm pretty confident you're not going to want me to stop."

"Okay." Kara's eyes sparkle with anticipation.

Those last two "okays" were way more upbeat than the first one. Between that and her bright-ass smile, Aaron's on cloud nine.

Aaron leans back down and takes her nipple into his mouth, and sucks. Kara's body is more beautiful than he could have ever imagined. He moves on to the other nipple and sucks on it harder, giving it a gentle bite.

Aaron goes back and forth between each breast, sucking and licking while his hands roam all over her body. The only sounds are the moans of satisfaction coming from them both. Aaron's sure his heart is about to burst out of his chest. He's insatiable. He cannot get enough of her soft skin, her scent, her moans; he wants more.

Kara lifts his head up and kisses him. Aaron rolls onto his back and brings her with him so she's on top. They stay like that with her on top of him, kissing while he rubs his hands all over her ass. This goes on for a while before he gently pushes her off—which is not easy. Having her in his arms feels euphoric but he's ready for more. Aaron opens the nightstand drawer and pulls out a condom.

She helps him roll it onto his dick, then climbs back on top of him. They stare into each other's eyes, and she looks hungrier than before. Just the thought of all the shit he's getting ready to do to her makes his dick twitch. She obviously feels it because she giggles before pushing herself down on it.

"Shit, Kara," Aaron whispers breathlessly.

That's what she does—she takes his breath away. That's her superpower, and he's more than willing to give in to her.

They start off with a quick but steady rhythm. As Aaron quickens his pace, Kara keeps up with him. When she slows down, Aaron keeps up with her.

"Aaron, please. Shit, you feel so good," she moans.

"So do you, baby. Your pussy feels so fucking good."

With every pant, moan, and move that Kara makes, Aaron listens and takes in what she's communicating. He grabs ahold of Kara and, in one fluid movement, rolls her onto her back. Pushing his dick deeper, he's dying to hear her beg again. That aching need in her voice is addictive. He craves it, and she doesn't disappoint.

"Aaron! You're so deep."

"Yes, I am. I'm deep as fuck. Now, tell me you like it."

"Oh, shit!" Kara cries.

Aaron thrusts harder, his lips against Kara's ear, and he takes the opportunity to lick and suck on her ear lobe.

"Tell me, Kara. Tell me how much you like this dick."

"I love your dick, Aaron," she whispers.

And she's about to get more of it too. Aaron pulls his dick out, flips Kara over again, and raises her hips. He takes her wrists, holding them behind her back, then proceeds to push every inch of his dick deep inside her wet pussy.

"Oh, my God!" Kara whines.

"You like that, Kara?"

"Yes."

"You want more, baby?"

"Yes. Yes, Aaron."

Aaron takes Kara's wrists and holds them over her head.

"I'm going to let go of your wrists. You gon' keep

your arms up above your head and not move them. You heard me?"

"*Yes.*"

Aaron lets go of her wrists, and like a good girl, Kara keeps her arms where they are.

Aaron pulls out slowly then thrusts his dick harder and faster, gripping Kara's hip with one hand and smacking her ass with the other.

"Fuck, Kara. You're so damn tight, baby," Aaron says through gritted teeth.

"Aaron, oh, shit. I'm about to come," Kara moans.

Keeping her arms above her head and gripping a pillow to keep her steady, Kara moves her body, matching Aaron's rhythm.

"Oh, fuck, Aaron. Aaron!" she says as she comes.

Hearing her scream his name is all it takes.

"Fuck, fuck, fuck!" he roars.

Kara collapses on the bed, and Aaron moves to gather her into his arms. Kara plants gentle kisses on his lips before resting her head on his chest as they continue to lay wrapped in each other's embrace. He could do this forever. In that moment, Aaron decides that he will. He meant for things to go slow, but after tonight, he's more than ready to give Kara all of him, and he will do whatever it takes to make sure she feels the same.

wo months later, Kara is still having her casual thing with Aaron, though she isn't sure how casual it is anymore. She walks Trixie with Janae as she replays the night before in her head for the millionth time.

It was incredible.

Aaron is incredible, and that scares the ever-loving shit out of her. This was just supposed to be about sex, but he's surprised her by cooking dinner—something he's not very good at, but he tries so hard—taking her to movies and remembering things she's said to incorporate them into their evenings together. It feels like a real relationship, and that's not what she signed up for, but she can't stay away from him. And after last night, she may never be able to.

She met him at his house after he got off work like all the other times, and when he opened the door, there was something different about his energy, but not in a bad way. He had on a navy-blue Henley with a pair of dark jeans and a pair of Jordans. His hair had been freshly lined up, and his waves... He looked sexy as hell! Kara could not wait to devour him.

As she walked up the porch stairs, he headed down to meet her, smiling at her look of confusion.

"If you don't mind, I'd like to take you somewhere. Then we can come back here, and I promise to make you scream."

"Are you going to do that thing that made me scratch up your back?"

"I was planning on it."

"Okay, we'll do things your way, but this better not take too long."

Aaron smiled. "Yes, ma'am."

As they rode in his truck, Kara noticed how nervous Aaron was. His usual intensity wasn't coming off as strong. It was still there but only halfway.

When they pulled into the parking lot, Kara smiled. They were at Willow Creek Park. She absent-mindedly told him she used to go there as a kid. He opened the door for her and offered her his hand. Walking hand in hand, she looked at him, and he appeared calmer. She was sure Aaron noticed her smile when she realized where they were at. It must have been a huge relief to him, and she wondered what else he had planned.

The park was more beautiful than Kara remembered. It now had gazebos right by the large pond. The baseball field and track had been updated, and the playground had new equipment. It felt familiar, yet new. Still holding her hand, Aaron led her to an ice cream vendor and bought them two ice creams. He had an ice cream sandwich and ordered her the strawberry shortcake bar, yet another thing he remembered. They made their way to a gazebo and enjoyed their frozen treats. Somebody in one of the nearby apartments was playing music. Kara swayed to the sounds of Atlantic Star's "Send For Me." Aaron stood up and offered her his hand, which she took. He was so close and smelled so fucking good. Being held by him felt right. Like it was where Kara was always meant to be.

After ice cream and dancing, they made their way to the pond, where they walked around watching people feed the ducks.

"Tell me about Janae," Aaron said, suddenly breaking the silence.

"Why?" Kara asked. She was aware of how protective her tone sounded, and she was sure it wasn't lost on Aaron, too.

After all the anti-Janae bullshit with Bryan, she promised herself that the next guy would not only have to be accepting but loving to every member of her family. Truth was, Kara felt tremendously guilty for not ending things with Bryan sooner. A lot of the stuff he said about Janae was downright disrespectful, but he would always apologize, and Kara would forgive him. As if it was her place to forgive someone on Janae's behalf. Kara simply didn't want to let Bryan go. She was in too deep. Believing that she and Bryan would be the couple her parents were supposed to be had made her ignore some glaring signs. She wasn't doing that again.

"I was looking at your Facebook pictures again, and the ones with you and her stuck out. I was curious how you two came to be friends."

Kara looked at Aaron like he was a gift. Not once did Bryan ever ask anything close to that. He simply met Janae and proceeded to bad mouth her once it became apparent that she didn't fall for his charms. That should have been the first red flag.

"We met sophomore year. She was in my homeroom. I liked her nails, and we started talking. We've been tight ever since."

"How did she come to live with you?"

"Her parents kicked her out after she came out as trans."

"I see."

"No follow up question?"

"Not really."

"I'm sorry, it's just that most people..."

"I get it, but most people haven't been exposed to someone who's trans and I have."

"Really, who?"

"Her name was Wanda. My Uncle Duke knew her... very well. Their relationship started off with him going to her house to fix something, and as always, he brought me with him so I could learn on the job. I was about nine years old at the time. Whenever we went over there, it was the same thing. He'd fix something for her, she'd feed us, then they would send me to a nearby arcade with a shitload of quarters. It didn't take me long to realize why they were sending me away. Anyway, Wanda was always nice to me. And goddamn, she could cook. I still miss her salmon croquettes to this day."

"What happened to her?"

"Don't know. One day, Uncle Duke just stopped going to her house. I asked him why, and he didn't want to talk about it, so I never asked again. I should have though. I hope she's doing okay."

Holy shit! Stop. He needed to stop because Kara couldn't take it. He was handsome, sexy, funny, thoughtful, strong, and protective. And the sex was mind-blowing. He needed to stop, or she might just be forced to have his baby.

"Could I get a lemonade?"

Kara pointed to the nearby lemonade stand set up by the baseball field.

"Sure."

Aaron bought her a strawberry lemonade and himself a raspberry one. They went over to the track and continued their walk. Kara looked around and let out a sigh. She missed it. The crowd, her opponents, the sound of the starter pistol, the beads of sweat as she inched closer to the finish line, and the call of her name when she won.

"You want to race?" Aaron suggested, throwing away their empty cups.

"Seriously?" Kara looked at him and smirked. He had no idea what he was in for.

"Yeah, it will be fun."

"I don't race for fun. I race to win."

"Winning is fun."

"Okay. Prepare to get smoked. No pun intended."

Aaron laughed as they took their mark. Aaron's starting pose was a mess, so Kara walked up behind him and lifted his hips.

"Thank you," he smiled.

"You're welcome."

"We're going right into the 'get set' portion of the position, as in 'on your mark, get set, go.' Since this isn't a real race," Kara smirked.

"Not a real race?" Aaron looked offended, but she could see the playfulness in his eyes.

"Not really. I've been doing this for a minute, and you've been doing this for a literal minute."

Aaron chuckled. She'd discovered quickly that she enjoyed making him laugh. She'd toned down her silliness considerably, thinking it safer to make silly comments than do any accents. She wondered if Aaron would call her corny, too.

"We'll go on three," Aaron suggested, and she nodded.

Once she took her position, she closed her eyes and centered herself, freeing herself of all distractions. Her mind relaxed, she heard him say, "three." It was all a blur after that. Her legs moved as if on their own. She cut through the air like a knife through butter. As she turned the corner, she looked up at the stands like she did with all her races, except instead of seeing her mom or Janae, she saw him. Aaron. He was seated and watching her. And the look on his face was one she wouldn't ever forget.

Kara comes back down to earth, but she can't get it out of her head. His face. The look he had on his face. He was so amazed by her. Thinking about it makes her want to cry. Kara wipes a tear before it falls. No! She can't do this again. She fell for Bryan too soon. She will not do that again. What she and Aaron have is a strong physical attraction. Nothing more. Yes, he's funny and sweet and charming, and he makes her feel like nothing else matters, but there cannot be anything more. She needs to focus on school and her job, which will be starting soon.

"Kare Bear!" Janae shouts.

"Jesus! Yes, why are you yelling?"

"Because heifer. I've said your name five times. Trixie needs to pee, and you keep walking."

Kara looks down at her poor dog. Shit. She kneels and pets Trixie.

"I'm sorry, Trix. Go ahead and make your pee."

Trixie relieves herself while Kara and Janae patiently wait.

"Still thinking about Smoke?"

"Yes. I am so confused. Do I want something more with him? Or should I keep it simple and just about sex?"

"I vote for that latter. You don't have time to pursue something more serious right now. If this thing you have with Smoke turns into something more, cool. If not, that's fine, too. Keep it casual so you don't end up blind-sided and heartbroken again."

"Janae, you're a genius."

"I know."

Later that day, Kara thinks more about what Janae said. If things get deeper between the two of them, she needs to know that there's no one else. She knows how silly it sounds but she can't take the chance. She takes out her phone and calls Aaron.

"Hello, Kara."

How? How does he make her knees weak with just two words?

"Hey, are you busy?"

"I'm working right now, but I'm heading out in about an hour."

"Can I come by?"

"Of course."

"Good. We need to talk."

～

We need to talk.

Not the words Aaron wanted to hear today. The past two months have been filled with great sex and apprehension on both their parts. Having Kara in his space has been amazing, but whenever he tries to steer the relationship toward something more serious than sex, Kara is always hesitant. She seems to want more but is being really wishy-washy, which causes him to rethink his approach. He wants to give her space, but he also wants to make her his. This has left him feeling confused. He hoped that after last night, his chances of getting with her were getting stronger, but based on how she sounds right now, he's not so sure. It had been an amazing night—the slow dancing, the ice cream, watching her run—he loved all of it and wanted more. He can only hope she does too.

"Come by my place at 7:30. Sound good?"

"That works. Bye, Aaron."

"Bye."

At 7:15, Aaron parks his truck in the driveway. He's exhausted both emotionally and physically. The whole thing with Kara left him feeling defeated. Aaron is not used to feeling this way when it comes to women; it's left him questioning whether he should even continue seeing Kara. Maybe he should just leave her alone and let her heal, but what if that means losing her? As much as it hurts, having her in his bed is better than not having her at all.

Or so he thought. This mental tug-of-war is wearing on him. As if that weren't enough, work has been stressful as hell, too. His freelance jobs have been piling up, and while he's grateful to have the work, some of his clients are really testing his patience. It's gotten so bad that he put in an application with WELCO properties to work as a repairman. If he gets the job, it will mean doing repairs for the various apartments and office properties WELCO owns. It also means a steady paycheck with benefits, but he won't have control over who he accepts work from. He lets out a humorless chuckle at the thought. He barely has control over that now. Being freelance means taking whatever work you can get. Bills, rent, and food aren't going to pay for themselves, and Tone's most recent stay with him took a huge hit on his budget. This has resulted in Aaron taking every job he's been offered.

Today's job was extra hellish. He spent close to twelve hours working on a playhouse for an eleven-year-old. The kid's obnoxious parents were breathing down Aaron's neck the whole time, and if that weren't enough, they seriously tried to lowball him on the price. With the materials, labor, and time he would put into this project, it's easily a fifteen-thousand-dollar job. So why did these motherfuckers only offer Aaron five hundred bucks? That wouldn't even cover gas driving back and forth from Inglewood to Hidden Hills, where the assholes lived. Their reasoning being that the dad did most of the work, and all Aaron had to do was "some finishing touches." Finishing touches? That motherfucker did such an awful job that Aaron had to tear the whole thing down. The structure was so weak that if his kid had set even one foot in the playhouse, the whole thing would have collapsed on top of him. After they quoted their bullshit price, Aaron almost introduced them to Smoke, but instead, he informed them that they weren't going to find anyone who would accept such a low offer. His demeanor must have made an impression because they changed their tune real quick.

Aaron lays his head on the steering wheel and loses all sense of time until he's startled by a knock on the driver's side window. It's Kara. Seeing her makes him feel a weird mix of elation and sorrow. He gets out of the car, and they greet each other with a hug. She smells like jasmine. The scent hits Aaron like a freight train before calming him. It makes him not want to let go of her. Instead, he pulls away from her, not wanting to crowd her.

"Hi," he says, trying to keep his voice even so she doesn't suspect what he was thinking.

"Hi," her voice is sweet and chipper, like she's trying to hide how nervous she is.

They enter the house, and Kara sets her purse down before taking a seat on the couch while Aaron grabs something to drink for them, then joins her. The energy in the room is thick. No doubt, a good deal of it is from him and his mood. As if tracing his thoughts, Kara takes Aaron's hand and squeezes it.

"Aaron, I came by to talk to you about us and what we're doing."

"Okay."

Aaron isn't sure where this is going, but he hopes he's happy with the result.

"In a few short months, I'm going to be starting school, working towards building my future. I want that future to include you."

This is promising...

"But not as my boyfriend."

Fuck!

"At least, not until I have a clear sign of where this is headed."

Um...he's hasn't beaten her over the head with what he wants, but he has been incredibly fucking clear about it too.

"I have a question," she says.

Aaron's starting to think he should have grabbed something stronger than water from the fridge.

"Hopefully, I have an answer," he jokes.

"Have you been hooking up with other girls since you and I...?" she trails off.

"No."

"Are you interested in hooking up with anyone else?"

"No, I'm not."

"Do the other girls know you're kind of seeing someone?"

Aaron lets out a breath. He feels like he's taking a lie detector test.

"No. Why would they?"

Aaron's uneasy with all this questioning, and there's a slight annoyance in his voice. But Kara either doesn't get the hint or ignores it altogether and keeps going.

"Do you plan on telling them?"

"No."

"Why not? You don't think they should know."

"I haven't spoken to most of them in a while. Kara, 'the harem,' as you call it, aren't my girlfriends. They are girls I would occasionally hook up with. They would contact me, or I would contact them whenever we were horny. They are not a threat to whatever you and me are doing."

"I think you should tell them. Keeping them in the dark doesn't seem fair."

She has got to be kidding. What the fuck would that accomplish?

"Kara, what you're asking me to do makes zero sense. These girls know what the deal is between me and them. They don't need to know about us. They're used to not hearing from me for long periods of time, and vice versa. Hell, some of them I haven't seen in a year. Besides, there's like fifty of them in my phone. You really want me to call fifty people right now?"

"Fine. Which one have you seen the most recently?"

"I don't know. Reynisha, maybe. She and I hooked up three weeks before I met you."

"Okay, call her."

What in the...? Aaron is at a loss for words. He takes

another deep breath. He's trying to be understanding. Clearly, this insecurity is because of her ex, and maybe if he wasn't in such a shitty mood, he would be more receptive to what she's asking, no matter how harebrained it is. Aaron looks deeply into Kara's eyes. In them, he sees pain and fear. She obviously needs this, and it's not like Reynisha will trip and show up at his house, so if this is what it will take to get her to trust him, he'll do it.

"Fine. I'll text her."

Aaron pulls out his phone and starts typing a text to Reynisha.

Hey, I know you haven't heard from me in a minute but just letting you know, you don't need to come over anymore.

Okay. Everything cool?

Yeah, it's fine. I'm seeing someone.

And what? You want my blessing or some shit?

No, my girl thought I owed it to you to let you know.

LMAO!!!!

Why is that funny?

Because you sound whipped, and she sounds insecure. I give you two a month.

Aaron's forehead creases, his jaw ticks, and his brows furrow. He knew this was a stupid ass idea.

No, but for real, you need to cut that poor girl loose, Smoke. Face it, people like you and me, we aren't the relationship type. Yeah, you got a job and your own crib, and that looks real good on paper, but what else you do you have to offer a woman? Your fine face, sexy ass body, and huge dick are all that we're after, the rest of the stuff is just perks. Good luck. Call me when this doesn't work out.

Aaron sits quietly as Reynisha's words sink in. He's pissed. Pissed that he agreed to do this. Pissed that he's having such a hard time getting Kara to let her guard down. Pissed at the day he's had. Mostly he's pissed because Reynisha has a point. His dick is what keeps the ladies coming back, his dick is all that Kara wants right now, and as much as Aaron wants to do right by her, he has to face facts. He's never been in a real relationship before. This is new territory for him, and her fear of him fucking up is getting in his head and making his own fear of failing her even worse. Maybe he should just put an end to this. Focus on WELCO and his freelance jobs, and she can focus on school.

"Everything okay?" Kara asks.

Without saying a word, Aaron puts his phone away and retreats to his room. He lies on his bed, looking at the ceiling. Kara stands by the bed awkwardly as if she's not sure whether to lie next to him or not.

"Aaron..."

"If you don't mind, I'd like to be alone."

"What happened?"

"Kara, I'm asking you to please... Leave. Me. Alone."

He turns his head and looks at her. Tears stream down her face, and as sorry as he is that he's caused them, he just can't deal with this shit right now. Kara reluctantly leaves the room, and a few seconds later, Aaron hears the front door close.

Two weeks go by, and Aaron hasn't spoken to or seen Kara. He's gone back and forth on whether he wants to continue their relationship. He's in the garage sanding off a birdhouse he built for a client while he runs the pros and cons of being with Kara through his mind--an exercise that has become a daily occurrence--when suddenly his phone rings. It's Tone. Aaron considers not answering it, but he hasn't seen his boy in a minute, and talking to him will offer a distraction from all the shit he has going on with Kara.

"What's up, man?" Aaron answers.

"Smoke! Yo, man, ain't seen you in forever. Nigga, where you been hiding?"

"I could ask you the same thing. Last I heard from you, you was hooking up with some Puerto Rican chick. How's that going?"

"I don't stay with Valeria no more, but we still fuck occasionally."

"Where are you now?"

"Back at my mom's."

Aaron stifles a sigh. He knows what this means. It's only going to be a matter of time before Tone pisses his mom off and needs to stay with Aaron again. If it comes to that, he'll help his boy out, but there will be some ground rules, and not just because of Kara. Although from the way things are going, she might not even be an issue anymore.

"Listen, Valeria is the reason why I'm calling. She's throwing a party for a friend and told me to invite some of my friends, so…"

"Since I'm your only friend, you're inviting me?"

Tone sucks his teeth. "Nigga, I got other friends."

"Name one."

After a pause, Tone says, "Man, fuck all that. You coming to this party, or what?"

It sounds better than staying home and overthinking his relationship or whatever the fuck he and Kara are.

"Sure. Send me the address."

An hour later, Aaron parks a few blocks away from a house on Arbor Vitae. He enters the house. The door is wide open, with folks milling about. When he enters the house, Aaron spots Tone in the kitchen.

"What's up, man," Aaron greets him with a half handshake, half hug.

"What's up. Glad you could make it."

Tone hands Aaron a red solo cup. Aaron takes it and can smell the red liquid before it gets to his lips. He takes a sip and coughs a little after swallowing.

"Goddamn, nigga, what's in this?"

"It's a little concoction I made."

"Tone, did you just give me moonshine?"

"Naw. I do know how to make that shit, though."

"Of course, you do, with your country ass family."

Tone and Aaron chuckle. Soon Aaron's chuckles turn into laughter. The alcohol is already hitting him hard.

"You always was a lightweight."

"Fuck you."

"It's good, though, right. Here, have some more."

Tone pours more into Aaron's cup. It's in a pitcher and looks like Kool-Aid, but it don't taste like it. Aaron takes another swig as he looks around. The house is a one-story family home. The party extends from the living room into the backyard, where someone is grilling. The kitchen is where the makeshift bar has been erected, so a large crowd of folks are hanging out in here, too. Aaron notices pictures of Latino family hanging on the living room walls and in the oak curio cabinets. Whoever made those cabinets did a shoddy job. Aaron could make better ones in his sleep.

"Nigga, what the fuck are you staring at?" Tone asks.

Aaron turns his attention back to Tone and notices him looking at him like he has three heads.

"The curio cabinets. I build better ones."

"I'll make sure to tell my parents." A soft female voice says.

Aaron turns around and sees a fine ass Latina chick looking back at him. She has long dark hair, a cute button nose, ruby red lips, and soft brown eyes. She offers him a warm, friendly smile, but Aaron's not naïve. Her eyes betray her. He knows what she wants, and his friendship ain't it. Her knockout body is reminiscent of Salma Hayek from the movie "From Dusk til Dawn." Aaron helps himself to a long look while he takes her in.

Another Latina girl, who is also fine as shit, comes up next to Tone and pulls his face to hers by grabbing the collar of his shirt. They make out right there in front of everyone. Tone grabs her ass and squeezes. They clearly don't care that they aren't alone. Doesn't seem to matter since everyone in the room is shitfaced. Speaking of which, Aaron grabs the pitcher and attempts to pour himself some more, but he can't stop swaying. The pretty girl carefully takes the pitcher from Aaron and pours him a refill.

"Thank you," he says.

Aaron still maintains his usual charm even when drunk, and he can see the pretty girl take notice.

"What's your name?" he asks.

"Luisa. What's yours?"

He almost says Aaron, but that's what Kara calls him.

Stop thinking about her. He sips his drink.

Aaron doesn't know what he was thinking, trying to

be someone's boyfriend. Reynisha's right. This. This is what he's good at. Seducing women and giving them what they both want.

"I'm Smoke," he replies.

"How did you get that name?"

"That's a long story."

"I have time," she giggles.

Without uttering another word, Luisa takes Aaron by the hand and leads him away. He looks at Tone, who gives him a proud papa look and goes back to focusing on Valeria. Luisa takes Aaron into an empty bedroom. She sits on the bed, then taps an empty spot for him to sit, and he joins her. She stares at him, and he stares back. She leans in, and so does he, and soon they're kissing.

Aaron lays back holding onto her so she's on top of him. He gives her ass a squeeze, and she gives him the green light to keep going.

"More," she moans into his ear.

Aaron slides his hands under her skirt and takes off her panties. She grabs his dick through his jeans.

"Your dick feels impressive," she purrs.

"It is. You want to see it?"

"Yes."

Aaron pulls his dick out, and she bites her lip. It's sexy, but not nearly as sexy as when Kara does it. He grins at her to mask his pain. Reynisha's words slap him in the face. *Your fine face, sexy ass body, and huge dick are all that we're after.* Aaron closes his eyes and pushes the words out of his head. That was all Kara was after. Why did he think she would want more? Because she did, didn't she? Whenever they were together, it felt right. They felt perfect together. He couldn't have been the only one to feel that.

Luisa slides down Aaron's body until she's facing his dick. She licks him nice and slow before taking his dick in her mouth. It feels good, but he's having trouble enjoying it. His brain is on autopilot. Her moans are clear, but they sound far away. He feels far away. Why did he come here? This isn't what he should be doing. He needs to see her. They need to clear the air. He should be with...

"Kara," he says softly.

Luisa takes his dick out of her mouth. Aaron looks down at her bewildered face and is ashamed.

"I'm so sorry. I need to go." He puts his dick back into his pants.

"Did I do something?"

"No. I need to tell her...I need to..."

Aaron gets up and slowly backs away. He heads to the door when he turns and looks at Luisa. She looks confused and hurt.

"I am very sorry. I should not have used you to fix me. Three months ago, I was a different person. Three months ago, I would have gladly fucked you into next week."

"So, why aren't you?"

"Because three months ago, I wasn't in love, and now I am. I'm sorry. Goodbye, Luisa."

"Bye, Smoke."

Aaron exits out the back, so he won't run into Tone. He looks at his truck, knowing he can't drive it in his condition.

"Fuck."

He can't call Niecey because she doesn't drive, and Aunt Sheila's out because she's out of town with her new boyfriend. His mom is not an option. It's times like this when he wishes his Uncle Duke was still alive. He'd get him out of this. Aaron pulls his phone out and calls Kara.

"Hi, Aaron." She sounds like she's been crying, and it hits him like a punch in the gut.

"Hi, Kara. I need you to come get me."

"Where are you? I hear music."

"Tone invited me to a party, and I came to get my mind off you. I drank too much, and I can't drive."

"I see."

Aaron expects her to tell him to go to hell.

"Text me the address. I'll be right over."

Praise God. Aaron doesn't know how he's going to fix things between them, but he's not going to rest until they're fixed. Kara's worth it.

Seven

Kara spots Aaron waiting for her at a nearby coffee shop. He insisted that she pick him up there. He didn't want to have to deal with Tone after ditching the party so abruptly. There was something in the way he spoke that told her something was off. Kara enters the coffee shop and sits across from him in a booth.

"Aaron, what's wrong?"

He looks at her like he can't form the words.

"I hooked up with another woman tonight. We didn't exactly have sex, but we came very close. I'm so sorry," he speaks so softly, yet she hears every word.

Kara closes her eyes. She hopes that she'll wake up and this nightmare will be over. When she opens them, she sees Aaron. Pain, guilt, and sadness hang over him like a dark cloud.

He continues, "I let Reynisha's words get to me. Between what she said and your fear of getting hurt and my own fears that I'm not cut out for a relationship, I let all of it overwhelm me, and I foolishly decided that going back to being unattached would be easier."

"Do you still feel that way?"

Fresh tears spring into her eyes. She brought this on herself. She's been worrying herself silly these past two weeks, not knowing where she and Aaron stood, and it's all her fault. The tears she shed for Aaron were different than the ones for Bryan. With Bryan, her tears came from being manipulated and heartbroken. Her tears for Aaron came from the huge mistake she made that may have driven him away.

"No," he finally says.

"Are you sure?"

"I'm sure."

A waitress comes by and refills his coffee. Aaron takes a sip. His guilt-ridden state stood out to such an extent that Kara's just now noticing his glassy, red eyes. He's clearly still under the influence but looks to be sobering up.

"Can I get you anything, sweetie?" the waitress asks Kara.

"Get whatever you want," Aaron offers.

"No, thank you. I'm fine."

Kara's much too upset to eat. She wants to apologize to Aaron for making him talk to that girl. But mostly, she wants to apologize for not being completely honest with him about her issues.

Aaron grips his coffee mug tightly. "I guess this makes me as bad as ole boy."

Kara shakes her head. "No. Bryan played me and Denise to boost his own ego. And he didn't confess—he got found out. You're nothing like him. I'm sorry that I made you pay for his mistake, and I'm sorry I haven't been upfront with you."

"About what?"

"My parents."

"What about them?"

"Two years ago, my father up and left me and my mom. He left us for some woman he met at work. She was the sandwich lady who came by his office during lunchtime to offer her wares. Apparently, she offered him something else because he got her pregnant and left us shortly after. My mother..."

Tears fall down her cheeks as she remembers the day.

"She's getting better, but she was a wreck. I had to take care of her. I was eighteen, and I had to quickly become an adult right at the beginning of my senior year. That's why I missed out on college the first time around, and it's why I hate my father."

Aaron moves from across the table to sit next to Kara, and he wipes the tears from her face.

"I am so sorry, baby. No wonder you're so scared. I will make this up to you, Kara. I promise."

"You don't have to…"

"Yes, I do."

"Aaron, I'm the one who fucked up. I got scared about how deeply I feel for you, and I brought my issues and baggage into this. I wasn't honest with you."

"I wasn't honest with you either. I'm obviously scared, too, Kara, and I should have told you that. I'm also stressed out from work…"

"What's happening with you at work?"

"See—" he says. Kara sees the concern etched on his face. He speaks as if his thoughts are racing. "We're making things more complicated than they need to be. If you had known about my fear and my stress, would you have had me contact Reynisha?"

"No."

"And if I knew about your parents, I wouldn't have overwhelmed you with how I feel."

They look at each other like neither is sure what to say next.

"What should we do now?" Kara asks.

"Be honest with each other. I know that this was supposed to be about hooking up and nothing more, at least for you, but these past two months have only confirmed how much I want you. I'm in love with you, Kara."

Kara's heart beats at full speed. She wants to fall into his arms, but she can't; she needs to make sure what she's feeling is real and not just wishful thinking.

"I…um…"

"Shh. It's okay. I don't need you to say it back. I know I'm going to have to earn your love."

Aaron kisses her, and she melts into his arms. She has no idea how he plans to earn her love, but whatever it is, she's decided to stop being scared and let him.

Eight

Over the next few months, things went well for Kara. She's been taking classes and working for two months now. She's even made some new friends and loves all her professors. It helps that Evelyn is doing better as well. This gives Kara a lot less to worry about. Then there's Aaron. He was not kidding about earning her love. He's done everything from grand gestures, like flowers and teddy bears sent to her house, to personal things, like waking up early and showing up at her house to walk Trixie so she can sleep in. He even fixed the table and chairs he had stored in the garage and put them in the dining room. Kara joked about wanting to eat dinner somewhere besides the couch, and he got to work.

Evelyn has met him, and she likes him. Kara has met his Aunt Sheila, and, of course, she still hangs out with Denise. She hasn't met his mom Pauline yet, but she's looking forward to it. The only thing she doesn't know much about is his Uncle Duke. She knows he taught Aaron everything he knows about repairs and building things and the things about Wanda, but not much else. Aaron's tight-lipped about that. She doesn't want to push him too much, so she keeps her mouth shut. He's been going above and beyond for her, and she wants to pay him back.

It's ten after eight when Kara rings Aaron's doorbell. She has fresh individual box braids in her hair. She wanted to look nice for what she has planned for him. They go down a little past her butt, and she's wearing a long trench coat.

She sees his large frame come to the door and gets excited. Aside from school, work, and Aaron, Kara has been working on herself. She's added journaling to her daily meditations, and it's done wonders. She now feels ready to give Aaron the relationship he has wanted and the one she truly deserves.

He opens the door and smiles. They saw each other this morning when he walked Trixie, but he's looking at her like he hasn't seen her in years.

"Hi," she says, biting her lip.

"Hi," he smirks, warning her not to do that again. "I like your braids. When did you get them?"

"Thank you. Went to the salon not long after you left."

Kara enters the house and takes off her trench coat. She has on a black negligee with a matching thong.

Aaron's eyes look like they're going to pop out of his head "Wow."

"Again, thank you."

"What did I do to deserve this?"

Kara approaches Aaron and places her hands on his chest. They gaze into each other's eyes.

"You've been very good. I know things were strange between us. I thought something casual would work, but I found myself falling for you so quickly, and it scared me. I tried to make you prove yourself, and that scared you. I finally think we've made it to a place where we're not scared, and we know who and what we are to each other. I love you, Aaron."

Kara strokes Aaron's face, and he takes her hand, kissing her palm.

"I love you too, Kara."

"I'm here to say I forgive you, and I hope you forgive me."

"Nothing for me to forgive."

"I disagree." They both chuckle, "I'm also here to give you a grand gesture of my own."

She pulls out a chair from the table and makes him have a seat.

Kara smiles and takes Aaron's phone. She pulls up Pandora and selects "Erotic City" by Prince. She crawls over to Aaron seductively and slides her body onto his. As she straddles and dry humps him, she looks him in the eye. The yearning in Kara's eyes makes Aaron's dick jump. He wants her so badly, but he wants her to take her time with him. He wants them both to savor this.

Kara licks his face from his chin to the top of his lip. Turning around, she grinds her ass against his dick. She takes his hand and puts it down into her panties. She's soaking wet, and Aaron can't wait to taste her. She moans as he fingers her.

She removes his hand and places his fingers on his lips. He sucks her wetness off them.

Aaron let out a relieved moan. She loves him, too.

After removing her bra, Kara places his hands on her breasts. Aaron massages them, playing with her nipples, which elicits a giggle from Kara. He loves making her do that. Aaron turns her around to face him, takes Kara's hard nipple into his mouth, and sucks on it. This causes her to place his hands on her ass. His dick is so hard, he might poke a hole in his pants. Aaron takes it out and makes her jerk it. Her breast never leaves his mouth, and his hands still grip her ass. Her moans are like a symphony to him. He lifts her up by her ass and sits her on the couch. He takes her panties off before removing all his clothes and lying down.

"Sit on my face," he orders.

Kara sits on Aaron's face, and he immediately gets to work. She bends down and sucks his dick while "Untitled (How Does it Feel)" by D'Angelo plays. Aaron smacks Kara's ass, and she licks the shaft of his penis. He catches his breath and grunts with pleasure. She has no idea what she's doing to him. Between eating her sweet, wet pussy, and feeling her full lips wrapped around his dick, Aaron is close to losing it. As if she's read his mind, Kara puts his whole dick in her mouth and deep throats him. Aaron moans, then re-buries his face between her legs. She comes up for air and moans loudly. He slides her off him and gets up to bend her over the couch. He grabs a bunch of condoms from his room and tosses them onto the couch.

"How much fucking are we going to do?" Kara asks playfully.

Aaron doesn't respond; he just gives her a wicked grin and a wink. He puts a condom on and pushes his dick inside her, pounding her hard. She smiles, loving every minute. He pulls her up and holds on to her. Kara turns her head so they're looking at each other, and they kiss, Aaron never breaking his rhythm.

"Ohhhh, Aaron. Oh, shit!"

"You like that, baby?"

"Yes."

"Say it."

"I like it."

"You love this dick?"

"Yes, *yes*!"

"Say it."

"I love your dick. Now, say it's mine and only mine."

"It's all yours, baby. Only yours. I promise."

He kisses her, turns Kara over, and spreads her legs open, resting them on his upper body. Grabbing her by her hips, he reenters her. Kara moans and squirms.

"Don't squirm," Aaron commands.

Kara does as she's told, and Aaron sucks on her toes as a reward.

"Uhhhh. Fuck, fuck! Aaron, *shit*! I'm coming!"

Kara gives such a high-pitched squeal Aaron can barely hear it. He pulls out his dick, takes off the condom, and comes on her chest. He gets up and brings back a soapy towel and a dry one. He wipes her down and dries her off before lying on the couch and pulling her on top of him.

"Spend the night," Aaron says.

Kara looks up at him. "Really?"

"Yes. I love you, and I want you to stay with me."

Kara looks at Aaron adoringly. "I love you, too."

Aaron responds by kissing Kara over and over. When he's done devouring her lips, he gently places her head on his chest, grateful to have finally made her his.

Nine

The next morning, they're still on the couch. Aaron has a t-shirt and some sweats on, and Kara's wearing one of his T-shirts and nothing else. He's wearing a headset and playing a multi-player game online.

Kara lies between his legs and sucks his dick. Aaron's hand is behind her head. He gently pushes her head down.

"Chris, watch out for that nigga on your left, man," Aaron says.

He lets out a stifled grunt and tries not to let out a moan. "Shit."

"Smoke, you okay?" Chris asks.

"Yeah, I'm cool," Aaron replies.

Kara looks up at him and giggles. She goes back to business.

Aaron plays for a few seconds longer before he lets out a louder, stifled grunt.

"Smoke...are...are you jacking off while we're playing, man?"

"No. My girl's sucking my dick."

Aaron takes off his headset from all the yelling, whooping, and hollering being done on the other end by the other players.

Kara rolls her eyes. "You really had to tell them, didn't you?"

Aaron smiles down at her. "What? It's your fault, and I couldn't have them thinking I was jacking off."

He puts the headset back on and continues playing while the other guys congratulate him.

"I'm gonna take a quick break, y'all. I'll be right back," Aaron says.

The other guys chuckle and tease him.

Suddenly, the front door opens, and Pauline enters.

"Ma, what are you doing here?"

Kara comes up and dashes out of the room quickly.

Aaron stands, covering his penis with a couch cushion. The other players hear everything and cackle, prompting Aaron to take off his headset and turn off the game.

Pauline looks at him with unsurprising disappointment.

"Do you have your rent money?"

"Yeah." He turns around, drops the cushion, and adjusts himself.

He goes into his room and grabs his wallet. Pauline listens as he and Kara have a quick exchange. He comes out and hands her three hundred dollars cash. Pauline counts it.

"You know that's not necessary, right?"

Pauline ignores him and continues counting. She puts the money away and looks up at Aaron.

"You can tell your little friend she can come out now. I'm leaving."

"Why did you come here anyway? It's not the first of the month."

Pauline points to the finished table and reupholstered chairs.

"Sheila told me about the furniture. I wanted to see for myself. When did you do that?"

Aaron shrugs. "A couple of months ago."

She softens. "It looks good. You did a good job. They look almost like when Duke made them."

"Thank you."

"You getting enough work?"

"I am. I got the WELCO job, so I've been doing repairs at apartments lately."

"Good. Now, if only you'd stop with the fast-ass girls."

"You mean Kara? She ain't fast."

"Oh, so I didn't just walk in on her sucking your dick?"

"That doesn't make her fast, ma. We're dating."

"Dating?"

"Yes."

"Sheila didn't mention that."

"I asked her not to. I was planning on introducing you to Kara myself. And you do realize you don't have to call Aunt Sheila to check up on me. You can always call me yourself."

"Tell her to come out here."

"Why? What are you going to say to her?"

"Nothing. If a young lady is dating my son, I think I should be able to meet her."

"Okay."

Aaron goes and gets Kara. She sheepishly comes out, still wearing nothing but Aaron's tee shirt.

"Hi, Ms. Tompkins," Kara says nervously.

"Hello. Kara, is it?"

"Yes, ma'am. Kara Matthews."

Pauline looks at Aaron. "Well, she has manners. I'll give her that. Too bad her manners didn't come with clothes."

Aaron can see Kara's competitiveness kick in.

"Okay, Miss Kara. Tell me about yourself."

Kara stands confidently. "I was born and raised in LA. I'm twenty. I attend USC. I have a 4.0 GPA, and I come from a good home. I'm an only child, and I love your son. What else would you like to know?"

Pauline looks impressed, and Aaron smiles.

"I guess that's it," Pauline says. She heads out the door, and Aaron walks her out.

Pauline turns to face him. "Cocky little thing, isn't

she?"

"She's an athlete. You know how they are."

"An athlete?"

"She used to run track."

"That explains how quickly she ran," Pauline chuckles, then shrugs, "I'll admit, she does seem nice."

"Thank you. I know how painful that must have been for you."

"Don't get smart with me, Aaron."

Aaron smirks. He always enjoys messing with his mother and getting a rise out of her.

Pauline gives him a kiss on the cheek. "Stay out of trouble."

"Will do."

She gets in her car and drives away.

Later in the week, Aaron is busy in the kitchen making dinner when Tone walks in. Aaron comes out of the kitchen, surprised and ready to curse someone out.

"Tone, whatchu doing here, man?"

"What up, Smoke? Ain't seen you in a minute. Thought I'd stop by and see how my homey is doing," Tone says, and goes straight to the refrigerator and helps himself to a soda. He looks around for something to eat. "Damn, nigga, why you got so many vegetables in here?"

"It's just an onion and a couple of bell peppers."

"Whatever, you got any Hot Pockets?"

Tone searches in the freezer, and Aaron releases an exasperated sigh.

"Tone, why are you really here?"

He closes the freezer door and leans against a counter. "My moms is tripping, again. Talking 'bout she gave me more than enough time to find a job."

"She kicked you out again?"

"Yeah, so I gotta stay here for a minute. Just until Tamika… you remember her?"

"Vaguely."

"Yeah, well, her nigga is getting ready to go to county. He's gonna be in there for a while, and she said I could stay with her."

"Tone, why don't you just get a job and find your own place?"

"Because I've told you, I'm working on my rap career, and I can't let anything distract me from that."

"So, fucking random women isn't a distraction, but a steady paycheck is?"

Tone rolls his eyes. "You're starting to sound like my moms, Smoke."

"Your mom may have a point."

"Man, whatever. I'mma go get my shit out the car."

"No, you're not. I'm about to have some company."

"Oh, shit. Yo, call her up and tell her you got a friend, and see if she wants to bring over one of her friends."

Before Aaron can say anything, there's a knock at the door. Tone opens it, and Kara's eyes widen, clearly dismayed to see him. She looks over at Aaron. He gives her a look and shrugs, letting her know he was not expecting Tone either. Kara comes in, and there is an uncomfortable energy in the room.

It's Tone who breaks the silence. "Shit, Smoke, I thought you came to your senses and got back to hooking up with those fine ass bitches you was with. You still fucking with her?"

"I'm not fucking with anybody. Kara and I have been seeing each other for a minute."

"Luisa told Valeria how you ditched her at the party. She made you sound like a bitch. I can see she wasn't lying."

"Motherfucker, you literally just asked me to let you stay here."

"C'mon, nigga. Stop being sensitive. We talk shit like this all the time."

"You ain't never called me no bitch."

"Fuck it. You actin' like one. Look at this shit."

Tone walks around the house. It looks less like a broke twenty-something's place and more like a mature adult home. Aside from the table and chairs, there are brand-new lamps and a throw rug on the floor. The house also looks cleaner in appearance. Everything is organized and placed neatly.

Tone continues, "We used to sit up in here smoking weed, fucking bitches, and drinking. Now, look! You start fucking with this chick, and I find you in the kitchen, cooking."

"If you don't like it, then get the fuck out of my house!" Aaron barks.

"Are you listening to yourself, nigga? You going out like a chump over some pussy."

Aaron frowns. "You need to leave."

"Your punk ass gonna make me?"

"If I have to."

Tone chuckles and takes a seat on the couch. He turns on the TV, stretching his long legs on top of the coffee table.

"Tone, you not hearing me, man. You need to leave."

"And you're not hearing me, nigga. Make me."

Aaron opens the front door dragging Tone by the collar. Aaron throws him onto the lawn. Tone gets up and stumbles, he looks pissed and stunned that Aaron kicked him out.

"Fuck you, nigga. You picking a bitch over me?"

"I'm not picking no bitch. I'm choosing to spend the evening with my lady, which means you need to go."

Tone gets in Aaron's face. When Aaron doesn't back down, Tone spits in his face. Aaron wipes away the spit and considers walking back into the house, but he doesn't. As if Tone waltzing in the house like he owns the place and calling Kara a bitch weren't enough, Aaron is reminded of all the shit from before, and something in him stirs. He punches Tone in the face. Hard.

Tone gets up and shoves Aaron, and they start fighting. Tone gets a few good swings in, but Aaron overtakes him. Some neighbors are watching from their porches as Aaron grabs Tone by his collar and throws him against his car. Tone gets in his car and drives off, giving Aaron the finger.

"Fuck you, Smoke!" Tone yells.

Aaron goes back inside, where Kara has a bag of frozen veggies ready for him. She gently places it on his eye, and they take a seat on the couch. Kara kisses the side of Aaron's face over and over. He closes his eyes and sighs deeply. Opening them, he pulls Kara closer to him by her waist, and she rests her head on his shoulder.

"Is it weird that I was a bit turned on by that?" Kara asks.

Aaron looks at her and smirks. "A little, yeah."

Kara chuckles and makes a silly face. It works, and Aaron grins. He stops and looks forlorn. He and Tone are done. He should feel relieved, but he feels sad. Aaron doesn't have very many friends, and Tone was the one he knew the longest.

"I'm sorry about your friend," Kara says.

Aaron recovers, not wanting her to feel sorry for him. He clears his throat. "Fuck that nigga."

Kara smiles, trying to lighten the mood. "What were you making?"

"Pasta."

"You want some help?"

"Sure."

They get up and walk to the kitchen, and Aaron stands behind Kara with his arms around her. She looks back at him and smiles. Aaron smiles back pushing all thoughts of Tone and their fight from his mind. This whole encounter does make him wonder what else he'll have to sacrifice to be with Kara.

Ten

It's the end of the fall semester at USC. To celebrate, one of Kara's professors is having a mixer at his home. She and Aaron arrive in his truck. It's a brisk evening, the fall air having a slight chill. Kara has on black jeans and a cream-colored scoop-neck top with long sleeves, and a mid-size black leather purse hanging off her shoulder. Aaron is wearing a dark gray, long sleeve shirt and blue jeans.

The front door has a sign on it, signaling that it's open for guests. Kara opens the door and sees more signs directing them to the den. They enter to find a buffet of hors d'oeuvres and various options of soda, wine, and beer.

Kara's classmates see her and wave, and she smiles and waves back.

Her professor, Dr. Stewart Lyman, approaches her and Aaron. "Hello, Kara."

"Hello, Dr. Lyman. This is my boyfriend, Aaron."

Aaron shakes Dr. Lyman's hands. "Nice to meet you, sir."

"Nice to meet you, too, Aaron. And there's no need to be so formal. You can call me Stewart. You both can."

"Thank you for having us," Kara says.

"My pleasure."

Kara is pulled away by some of her classmates, so Aaron takes a seat in the corner. Dr. Lyman's Maltese comes over and sniffs him, and Aaron smiles at the pup, giving it a pet.

A couple of hours pass, and aside from a few hellos and how do you dos, no one has really spoken to Aaron. Instead, he's spent most of his time with Dr. Lyman's dog. Kara has come up to check on him a couple of times, and he always replies that he's fine.

Dr. Lyman taps his glass to signal a toast. "I just wanted to thank all of you for coming and to propose a toast to surviving your first semester of college. Here's to surviving the rest of the year!"

Everyone holds their glasses up, then applauds.

"It's a bit of a tradition to have an art symposium of sorts at my soirees. Is anyone brave enough to volunteer and show off their talents?"

No one raises their hands. Dr. Lyman looks at Aaron, who's feeding Dr. Lyman's dog some prosciutto.

"Aaron, I know you're not a student, but do you have any artistic gifts you'd like to share?"

Kara interjects, "Dr. Lyman, Aaron works in home repair and renovation, not in the arts."

Aaron stands up. "It's fine. I don't mind."

Kara looks at him and mouths, "What are you doing?"

He smiles and mouths back, "It's fine."

Aaron hasn't done this in a while, but it's like riding a bike. He takes a seat at the grand piano and plays "Rhapsody in Blue" by Gershwin. It was one of his grandmother's favorite songs. At one point, he visited Grandma Lou's as much as he hung around Duke.

When he finishes, he receives thunderous applause. He looks over at Kara, and her mouth is open in shock. Aaron gets up and walks over to her. He playfully closes her mouth and gives her a kiss. Returning to his seat, he continues playing with Dr. Lyman's dog.

"Aaron will be a tough act to follow, but please, I encourage someone else to take the plunge," Dr. Lyman announces.

A few hands go up, and one of Kara's classmates leans over to her and says, "Wow, your boyfriend is amazing."

Kara looks over at Aaron. He plays with Dr. Lyman's dog as if he didn't just blow everyone's mind, especially hers.

Kara replies, "Yeah, he is."

A couple of hours later, they walk to Aaron's truck. Kara looks at Aaron like she's trying to figure out a puzzle. What other talents has he been hiding? She thought it was just stuff with his uncle he hadn't told her. There's obviously more to this man than she expected, and she's not okay with being left in the dark. He looks over at her.

"What?" he asks.

"Seriously? You want to tell me what that was back there?"

"What are you talking about?"

"Aaron, you are so guarded. I had no clue you could play the piano. You tell me all the time how much you love me but never really let me in. I've told you pretty much everything about my parents, Bryan, my track career—"

"Kara, we haven't been together that long. We still have a lot of time to learn stuff about each other. And you know plenty about my life."

"I know *some* stuff about your life. But what happened back there feels like something I should have known."

"Why? How would that ever come up naturally in any of our conversations?"

"I mean, when I told you how I took up track, you could have brought up how you took up piano."

"You took up track because you were a hyperactive kid, and your mom thought sports would help. I learned the piano because my grandmother made me."

"That's another example. I've told you all about my family, and I don't know much about yours aside from your mom, Sheila, and Denise."

"Okay, what do you want to know?"

"What happened to your Uncle Duke?"

Aaron looks at Kara, offended. "I don't want to talk about that."

"Jesus Christ, Aaron."

"*What?*" he says in a hushed, exasperated tone. They're in a white neighborhood, and the last thing they want to do is make a scene.

Kara is still taken aback. She's never seen him this upset with her.

Aaron lets out a deep sigh and calms himself.

"Kara, I'm not that much of a talker. You knew that when you got with me. I redecorated my home for you. I got into a fucking fistfight with one of my closest friends because he disrespected you. I am trying so hard to show you how much I love you to make up for fucking up so badly. You're making me feel like nothing I do is good enough."

"I never said that."

"You don't have to."

"Aaron, I just want you to open up to me more."

Aaron turns and walks to the car. Kara drops the subject, following him. He drives to her house in silence.

"We're not going to your place?"

"No."

Kara looks at him sorrowfully. He glances at her. His

annoyance has been replaced with melancholy. Not sure what else to say, Kara gets out and walks to the house. She looks back and sees Aaron watching her. While she stays with him on most weekends, she tries to stay at home a few days a week for Evelyn's sake. Whenever he drops her off, he always makes sure she gets in safely before driving away.

Kara closes the front door and looks out the living room window. Aaron looks in her direction but not directly at her. After a minute or so, he drives away.

Kara rushes upstairs and knocks on Janae's door.

"Come in," Janae announces.

Kara enters the room to find Janae sitting at her sewing machine altering one of her shirts. Movie posters are framed on the wall and the room is decorated with antique furniture.

"I thought you just altered that?"

"I did, but I came up with an idea I thought would look better. How was Dr. Lyman's shindig?"

"It was fine. How was hanging out with Tony?"

Janae looks up at Kara with playful suspicion. Her fake glasses sit at the tip of her nose like a schoolteacher about to reprimand a student. This time they're gold to match her hoop earrings and blonde wig. She reminds Kara of Mary J. Blige during the "My Life" era.

"It was great. We had an Herb Jeffries marathon at his place. He's amazing, but you already knew that. What *I* want to know is what's wrong with you. Now spill it. What happened?"

Kara stares off like she's lost in thought. "Aaron can play the piano."

"*Okay?* I know there's more to the story than that."

"He can play it beautifully. He was amazing."

Kara takes a seat on the bed and looks up at Janae. "It's just, he's so reluctant to open up to me…"

"Oh my God, not this again."

"Yes, this again. Why does he find it so hard to talk to me, J?"

"Probably because you are kind of forcing it."

"No, I'm not."

"Kara, up until you, the dude's only interaction with girls has been getting pussy and going about his business. This is the first time he's been with someone he cares about, and you're pushing him too hard. You're demanding a lot from someone who has never done this before. I love you, but this needs to be said. Your persistence is part of the reason he went to that party and fucked around with that girl."

"I know, and I apologized for that. What is this? Aren't you supposed to be on my side?"

"I am. I always am, but whose goofy ass idea was it for him to call his former sex buddy in the first place?"

"Mine, and like I said, I apologized."

"Yes, but did you learn anything from it. Kare Bear, an apology without changed behavior don't mean shit. You pushed him a few months ago, and you're pushing him now. Stop. Let the nigga breathe."

Kara pouts like a petulant child. "I hate it when you're right."

"Really? Cause I love it," Janae smiles and goes back to sewing while humming "Stormy Weather."

Kara lays back on the bed and thinks. She didn't see what she was doing as pushing, but it was. Hell, when she didn't want to talk about her dad paying her tuition, Aaron respected that and didn't press her, and here she is doing the opposite.

"I guess asking him about his uncle tonight wasn't the best idea either."

"Yeah, you probably should have laid off the dead relative he clearly doesn't like talking about and asked him what his favorite color was instead."

Kara gets up. "I'm going to go talk to him."

"Girl, sit your ass down. Give that man some time to think. Go in the morning."

Kara reluctantly sits down. She lies on the bed and thinks about what she'll say to Aaron tomorrow when Janae breaks her concentration.

"Now, on to more important things. What did you bring me?"

Kara opens her purse and takes out a medium-sized Ziplock bag. Inside are hors d'oeuvres from the soiree. She hands it to Janae.

The next morning Kara knocks on Aaron's front door hard so he can hear her. It's seven in the morning. Kara stayed up all night thinking of what she's going to say. She can hear Aaron stomp his way to the door cursing.

"Stop pounding on my damn door. And no, I do not want to hear about how Christ can save my soul." He answers it, half asleep and angry.

Oops. Kara didn't realize he'd still be asleep. Usually, when she stays over, he's up by five in the morning, already working out.

Kara takes him all in. He looks delicious in a wave cap, boxers, and a white sleeveless shirt. He sees Kara and immediately widens his eyes and calms down. Aaron wipes his eyes.

"Sorry," Kara says. "I guess I was a bit too eager to talk to you."

"Sorry, baby. I thought you were those religious nuts. Come in."

Kara comes in and walks up to Aaron. She looks up at him earnestly and wraps her arms around his waist.

"I do notice how hard you try to be a good boyfriend. And I do appreciate it. You really are a great boyfriend."

"Thank you. I really do love you, Kara."

"I know you do. I love you, too."

Aaron lifts her up and kisses her. She brushes her tongue against his lips and kisses him back.

"I had a talk with Janae, and she said I should back off a bit and cut you some slack."

"Tell her I said thank you."

"I wasn't trying to be demanding. I just want to

know you better, and sometimes it feels like pulling teeth just to get the bare minimum out of you."

Aaron puts her down and takes her by the hand. He takes a seat on the couch, and she sits on his lap.

"I know. And I'm sorry about that."

She snuggles up to Aaron. His scent draws her in. Soon, she's lying on top of him. She scoots up so they're eye to eye. He smiles and runs his thumb across Kara's bottom lip. Goosebumps. Simply put, that's what Aaron gives her. No matter how quick his touch is, it sends sensations through her body, and Kara shivers.

"You okay, baby?" Aaron asks, the timbre of his voice deep and huskier than normal.

"I'm okay," Kara replies, the intensity in her voice matching his. She kisses his thumb and lets him stick it in her mouth. After tasting his thumb, she's ready to taste more. Aaron takes the hint and cradles Kara's face in his hands, kissing her. Giving her what she wants as they nibble each other's lips.

Kara lets out a breath and kisses Aaron a couple of more times before she speaks.

"Janae told me that I should have started our conversation with something less deep, like your favorite color."

Aaron snickers. "That definitely would have gone over better."

"So, what's your favorite color?"

"Navy blue."

"Your favorite food is Italian."

"Good guess."

"Your favorite movie?"

"*Coming to America*."

"That's a good one. Favorite sport?"

"Basketball."

"Favorite team?"

"What kind of question is that? Lakers, obviously."

"Favorite player?"

"The better question would be, who's my favorite athlete?"

"Okay, who's your favorite athlete?"

"You."

Kara grins from ear to ear. As cheesy as it was, hearing him say that makes her feel special. They kiss some more. Aaron tickles her, and soon her uproarious laugh fills the entire house. Aaron runs his hand up and down her body, and her finger traces over his lips. They look in each other's eyes, neither wanting to look away.

"Goddamn, you're beautiful," Aaron whispers.

"So are you," Kara replies.

Aaron picks her up and throws her over his shoulder. Kara squeals.

"What are you doing, cave man?"

"What you think? Make up sex."

Aaron carries Kara to the bedroom with her giggling all the way.

Eleven

2012

Kara graduated summa cum laude a year ago. She has a bachelor's degree in business and economics, and now has a demanding job working for a catering company as their business associate.

It's 8:50 p.m., and the Abrams bar mitzvah isn't scheduled to end until 11:00 p.m. Kara does another quick sweep of the buffet table to make sure they aren't running low on anything. She comes across the grilled fish and almost throws up. Kara backs away slowly, taking a deep breath. What the hell was that? The smell of fish has never made her nauseous. She loves fish. It's the only way she'll eat tacos, for God's sake. And living in LA with an unlimited supply of taco trucks doesn't make picking fish every time a simple task. Kara carefully makes her way to the bathroom. She splashes some water on her face, and her boss, Nancy, enters.

"You feeling okay, sweetie?" Nancy asks like the concerned mom she is. Nancy doesn't have the best relationship with her daughter, so Kara has basically become a surrogate.

"Yes, I'm just..." Kara runs to the closest stall and vomits.

"Kara, go home. I can handle it from here."

"But we still have two more hours," Kara coughs.

"Sweetie, it's fine. A few of the guests have left already. No way this little shindig goes to eleven."

Kara washes her face, rinses out her mouth, and pats her face dry with a cloth towel. This is by far the fanciest hotel ballroom they've ever catered at. Crazy that it's for a thirteen-year-old kid. Kara remembers the hotel manager telling her that over seventy percent of the clientele who secure the ballroom are brides-to-be. She and Aaron could save their whole paychecks for an entire lifetime and still wouldn't be able to afford this place.

Aaron.

How's he going to react? They've talked about kids, but having one seemed like something in the far distant future.

"Kara." Nancy's voice breaks Kara's train of thought.

"Yes?"

"Go home."

Nancy offers her a warm smile. Kara can't imagine why she and her daughter don't talk. Nancy's a sweetheart and a fucking warrior. She's five foot even, with a mix of blonde and gray hair styled in a feathery bob. She's never without makeup and dresses in business suits. She once told Kara that she purposely wears pastel colors because it throws men off their game. They see her size and her choice of color and think she's a pushover. It's then that she unleashes the beast. Simply put, Nancy's the best.

"Okay. Please email me later, letting me know how everything went."

"Will do, babe. Now leave."

It's 9:30 p.m. when she walks in from work. Aaron is folding laundry in their bedroom. She knows because he's playing "Electric Relaxation" by A Tribe Called Quest. Aaron says it's the perfect song to fold laundry to. She and Aaron have been living together since her junior year at USC. Kara only moved in after having a long talk about it with her mother. Evelyn gave her blessing. She claims that she knew Aaron would win out someday, so she started preparing herself when Kara and Aaron first started dating.

Janae found a friend on campus in the form of a fellow trans Black girl named Sasha. They dated for a bit during Janae's brief break up with Tony but decided to be friends and then roommates. They now share an apartment together in Torrance. Janae's still in school getting her master's degree and works as an assistant at an accounting firm, and Sasha is a burlesque dancer who also waits tables.

When Kara first moved in, she insisted on helping Aaron pay rent and utilities. He told her it wasn't necessary, so they compromised. Kara buys groceries and helps clean the house, and Aaron takes care of everything else.

Things have been going well for Aaron, too. He now works for SMG, Samuels, Mitchell and Garnet, a construction and remodeling company. They have contracts with various residential properties throughout the greater Los Angeles area. That's how he met his new friend, Rod. They go to ball games, play cards and video games, or just hang out together.

Aaron has worked for SMG for two years now. He has a bigger paycheck, a 401K, health benefits, and decent work hours, 6 a.m. to 2 p.m. Kara gets off work at 4:30 p.m. unless she's needed for an event.

He walks out to greet her. "Hey, I thought needed to stay at the bar mitzvah?"

"I did, but I don't feel very good; so, Nancy let me come home early."

"What's wrong?"

"I feel nauseated. I threw up about an hour ago."

"*Damn.* Go lie down. I'll bring you some tea."

Kara goes into the bedroom. She takes off all her clothes and sticks them in the hamper. After going into the bathroom, she wraps her flat ironed hair. She puts on a shower cap and gets in the shower. The warm water feels soothing. Dear God. What if she's pregnant? Financially it's going to be a drain. She and Aaron have a vacation fund they started a few months ago. That's now shot to hell. Kara adds more hot water. She's always wanted to be a mom, but she didn't expect to become one so soon. Kara rubs her belly. She's always pictured what her and Aaron's kids would look like. She sees an adorable little boy that looks like Aaron.

Aaron.

How is he going to respond? He wants kids. He's told her so, but she can tell the idea of fatherhood makes him nervous too. She obviously doesn't think Aaron would abandon her like both their fathers did, but she does worry that he'll put a lot of undue pressure on himself and try to carry that weight alone. He's gotten better, but he's still pretty closed off.

When she gets out, Aaron is putting away the last of the folded laundry. He's laid out her nightgown, and a cup of tea sits on the nightstand for her. She drops her towel and puts on the gown. She's too tired even to put on lotion.

Gingerly, she gets into bed and takes a sip of tea. Aaron lays on the bed next to her. She rests her head on his shoulder. He kisses the top of her head.

"What am I going to tell Nancy? I've only been at this job for six months."

"You don't have to tell her right away. We'll get you a test, one of the super expensive name-brand ones," he chuckles.

Kara gives him a gentle smile. "You don't sound scared."

"Oh, I'm terrified, but you don't need to worry about that right now."

They both let out a chuckle. This relaxes Kara a bit more. She takes Aaron's hand and squeezes it.

"Promise me you won't try to carry this all by yourself. Promise me that you will let me in when you start to feel overwhelmed and scared."

"I promise I'll try, but I don't want you worrying about me. Especially in your condition. I don't want to cause you any stress."

Kara lifts her head and looks up at him. He is so amazing. No matter what, he always puts her needs first.

"Aaron. I need you. I need you in one piece and I need you to stop sacrificing yourself for me and let me protect you sometimes, too."

"Okay. I will try. I promise."

The way his dark brown eyes penetrate hers makes her melt. Aaron takes her face in his hands and kisses her.

"Well, I guess I better get used to being woken up at 3:00 a.m. because you have a craving."

"If it helps, I'll probably just be sending you out for ice cream. Nothing outlandish."

"That does help."

Kara lets out a sigh. Life really is incredible. All this week, she's been feeling woozy. She thought it was her job. Being the first point of contact for a grieving family or a company throwing a fundraiser comes with a lot of pressure. If the initial meeting goes well, they're hired. If not, then the job goes to another catering company. The pressure to always perform, especially as a Black woman, has left Kara feeling unbelievably stressed lately. She was sure that was why she was off her game. And now, hours later, she and Aaron are joking about her possible cravings, and she may have a little life growing inside of her. She's happy, excited, and scared. The worry is etched on her face. She can tell by the way Aaron's looking at her.

"What's wrong, baby?"

"We're not even married, Aaron. And whose insurance will the baby be on?"

"Kara, we're not even hundred percent sure you're pregnant yet. You've been stressed lately. Truth be told, you've been stressed since you started this job. That could be why you're throwing up and why you're late."

"But what if I am pregnant?"

Kara hears how small and lost her voice sounds. Times like these are when she needs Aaron's calming presence the most. He can tell and comes to her rescue, snuggling her closer.

"If you are, we'll be fine. I make enough money to keep us afloat. And you'll get paid maternity leave."

"I'm not really worried about money. How would we be as parents?"

Aaron thinks it over. "We'd be loving parents who try their best to provide a great life for their kid."

"I guess. But you must admit, we didn't have the best role models. Both our fathers are cowards who left us, and your mom isn't exactly the warm and fuzzy type."

"That's true, but neither of us are our fathers, so you

don't even need to worry about that. And as for my mom, yes, she can be a bit harsh, but she loves hard and fiercely. That's something we can aspire to."

Kara finishes her tea. God, she loves this man. He always knows exactly what to say.

"How's your stomach?" Aaron asks.

"A little better," Kara smiles. "Janae's going to be so excited."

Aaron chuckles, "Yeah, Auntie Janae. She's going to love that. And despite what you think of her, so will my mom."

"You think she'll be excited even with me as the mom?"

"For a grandbaby? Hell yeah, she'll be thrilled. And it's not that she doesn't like you, Kara. That's just how she is. Hell, I'm her son, and sometimes she acts like she doesn't even like me."

Aaron slides his hand underneath her night gown and rubs her belly. The sensation of his strong, callous hands massaging her feels so good.

She closes her eyes and releases a moan, "Mmmmm."

Kara opens her eyes when she realizes something. She shoots Aaron a silly, accusatory look. "You realize this is all on you, right?"

Aaron looks at her quizzically. "Excuse me?"

"This probably happened from that time you were working out. Remember? You were lifting weights without a shirt on."

"I remember minding my own business doing bench

presses when you came out to the garage, pulled down my shorts, and straddled me."

"Exactly. You know what seeing you all sweaty does to me."

Aaron laughs. "Whatever."

Kara suddenly feels like she's going to faint or puke. Shit! It's puke. It's definitely puke. She rushes to the bathroom.

He hears her vomiting and asks, "You want me to get you some ginger ale and crackers?"

Kara catches her breath. "I'm okay," she says as she vomits some more.

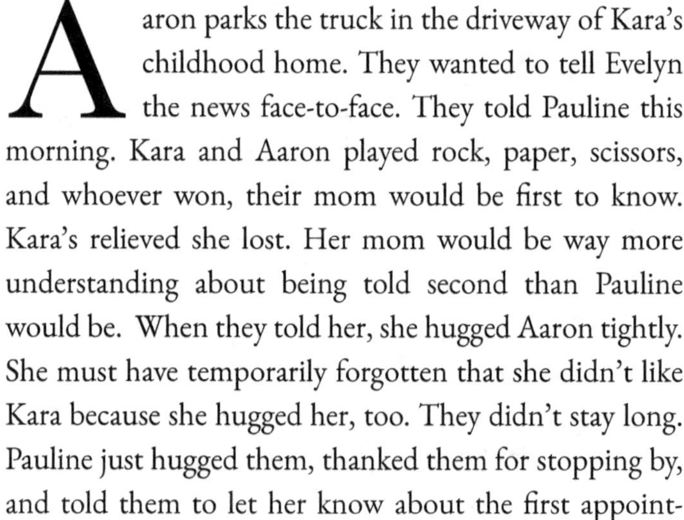

Aaron parks the truck in the driveway of Kara's childhood home. They wanted to tell Evelyn the news face-to-face. They told Pauline this morning. Kara and Aaron played rock, paper, scissors, and whoever won, their mom would be first to know. Kara's relieved she lost. Her mom would be way more understanding about being told second than Pauline would be. When they told her, she hugged Aaron tightly. She must have temporarily forgotten that she didn't like Kara because she hugged her, too. They didn't stay long. Pauline just hugged them, thanked them for stopping by, and told them to let her know about the first appointment. It was like she was congratulating a co-worker.

"Your mom seemed happy, but..."

"But what?" Aaron asks.

"She seemed like she couldn't wait to get us out of there."

"Kara, baby, it's Saturday. She does her food shopping, and I told you with her and Aunt Sheila, it's a blood sport. They know exactly when each store is bringing out a specific item. They synchronize their watches for Christ's sake. Yeah, she was kicking us out, but it wasn't personal."

"I just think that hearing about your first grandchild would beat out being the first in line when they bring out the orange juice at Ralphs."

"Please don't let this bother you," Aaron requests.

"Okay. I won't."

Aaron takes her hand and kisses it. He hops out the car, then quickly jogs over to her side and opens the door for her. He offers her his hand. She takes it and giggles at his unnecessary but sweet chivalry.

"You didn't need to do that, you know," Kara teases.

"I know, but I will soon. You're going to need help getting out of the car and getting out of chairs before you know it."

"That won't be for another six months."

Aaron has a playful look of guilt on his face.

"I'm sorry, baby, but I overheard Aunt Sheila telling Nieccy that the babies in our family grow at an alarming rate in the womb. I've seen pictures of my mom at four months along. Everyone kept thinking she was about to deliver."

Oh, holy hell. Seriously? Unable to think of a coherent sentence, Kara says... "Yikes!"

"Yeah, sorry," he shrugs

They make their way to the front door. Trixie can be heard barking from the backyard. That's weird. During the day, her mom usually lets Trixie in the house. She takes naps on her doggie bed. Kara uses her key and opens the door.

"Mom? I would have called, but me and Aaron have something exciting to tell you," she calls out.

Kara instinctively turns toward the living room. Evelyn's head pops up like a piece of toast. Her hair is askew, and her blouse is unbuttoned. Right as Kara's about to ask her what's going on, a man pops up. He hops off the couch and grabs his clothes. He's currently without pants, and his shirt's unbuttoned. Kara stands there speechless with her mouth agape. She looks at Aaron, and he's trying not to laugh. Kara nudges him in the ribs. He quiets down, but the grin hasn't left his face.

"Umm...honey. I wanted to introduce you to Richard in a much less embarrassing way," Evelyn giggles. She looks like a teenager being caught by her parents. Kara can't help but find this whole scenario silly, and she laughs.

"Oh my God. We came here to tell you I'm pregnant, and you're here making out like a girl in the back of her boyfriend's car."

"Looks like they were about to do a little more than

make out, baby," Aaron mutters to Kara, and she nudges him again.

When Kara looks at her mother's face, Evelyn has tears in her eyes. She rushes through buttoning her blouse and runs over to give Kara a hug.

"My baby is having a baby," Evelyn says.

"Yeah, I am." Kara hugs her mom tightly.

Evelyn kisses Kara all over her face like she did when Kara was little. Evelyn hugs Aaron. He hugs her back tightly and lifts her off her feet.

"Aahhh! Boy, put me down," Evelyn squeals.

Aaron chuckles at her. He adores Evelyn and she loves him, too. She always brags about how her son-in-law can fix anything. It's even resulted in some more free-lance repair jobs for Aaron.

Her mom's visitor stands by the couch smiling at their happy family when he finally says something.

"Congratulations Kara and Aaron. I've heard so much about you. Evelyn won't stop bragging about you both. I'm Richard, by the way."

"Hello," Kara replies. Richard has heard about them? Then why is this the first Kara has heard about him?

"Hey, Rick," Aaron answers.

"Okay. I know you're probably confused, but Richard and I met about a year ago. Well, we re-met. Wait, let me start over..."

Evelyn's flustered, so Kara offers her an olive branch.

"Mom, it's okay. Calm down. You and dad have been

divorced for seven years. I didn't expect you to become celibate."

Evelyn looks calmer and lets out a relieved breath.

"Oh, good. I thought you'd be a little concerned."

"Mom, I swear to you. I'm fine."

"Great!" Evelyn takes Kara's hand and leads her over to Richard.

"Richard is my boyfriend. We first met years ago when I got you your car. He owns the car dealership. As a matter of fact, he's the one who sold it to me."

"Really?" Kara smiles, "Well, I guess I owe you a thank you. I love my car."

"You're more than welcome. If you ever need any repairs, my mechanic will do it and won't charge you. I'll cover it."

"Thank you, but that's not necessary. I have him for that."

Kara points at Aaron. She's still astonished that she managed to find a man who can fix basically everything.

"Yeah," Aaron agrees. "That's all she keeps me around for. Fixing things and knocking her up."

Kara and Evelyn look at Aaron like he's lost his damn mind.

"Aaron!" Evelyn berates.

"What? I was trying to lighten the mood. Kara's obviously still surprised, and Rick's embarrassed as hell."

Kara and Evelyn continue to look at him like he's a child who has been told to get a switch.

"Okay, I'm going to the kitchen to get something to drink. Anybody want anything?" Aaron backs away.

"I will have a lemonade." Kara squints her eyes at him.

Aaron mockingly squints back at her. "Coming right up."

Evelyn giggles and takes Richard's hand. They all have a seat. Crazy that they've been standing the whole time. Everyone is so off-kilter, no one thought to sit down. Aaron's right, Kara is surprised. She and Evelyn are close, so she's still wondering why her mom kept this from her.

Aaron comes back out with a platter of lemonade of everyone. They each take a sip.

"So, you sold mom my car?" Kara asks, trying to get them back on track.

"Yes, yes. We started following each other on social media, and as luck would have it, we ran into each other at the supermarket a year ago, and not long after, we started seeing each other."

"And when did you tell your kids you were seeing somebody?" Kara asks.

There's a slight bite in her tone, but she can't help it. Now that the initial shock is gone, she feels weirdly betrayed. Kara couldn't be happier that her mom is seeing someone, but when was she planning on telling her?

Evelyn clears her throat and gives Kara her signature "mom" look, a mixture of compassion and sternness.

"I don't have kids. My ex-wife and I broke up a year ago, and we never had children."

"A year ago? Were you seeing my mom while you were still married?"

"You don't have to answer that," Evelyn says sharply. Her sharpness is directed at Kara. "Kara, may I have a word?"

"Sure, mom."

They go upstairs to Kara's old room.

"What was that?" Evelyn closes the door.

"Mom, are you serious? You started seeing him when he was married? How is that any different than what dad did to you?"

"Kara, this is supposed to be a happy occasion, and you are ruining it."

"I am not."

"Yes, you are. This is why I didn't want to say anything to you. I knew the minute you found out when Richard and I got close, you'd be upset."

Evelyn calms down. Kara sits on her bed and holds her face in her hands. Maybe she's tripping this hard because of the hormones or something. And she is hungry. Aaron's always teasing her about how grouchy she gets when she needs food. Whatever it is, she is ruining what is supposed to be a great day. She and Aaron are going to be parents and her mom has found someone that seems like a good man after all these years.

"I'm sorry," Kara whispers.

Evelyn sits next to Kara and kisses her on top of her head.

"He was going through a rough patch in his marriage when we got reacquainted. Shortly after we became friends, he filed for a divorce. I was there for him, and as the divorce proceeded, we became more. We didn't start being serious until after he filed."

"You don't have to explain yourself to me. I was out of line."

"You were. But you were also shocked, and you're pregnant."

Kara leans her head on her mom's shoulders, and Evelyn holds her.

"I'm guessing you all told Pauline first." Evelyn looks playfully affronted.

"Yes, sorry."

"That's okay because I will be hosting the baby shower."

Twelve

Four months later, Aaron pulls into a parking lot. He looks over at Kara's fully pregnant stomach.

"How are you feeling?"

"A little better. Last night was rough."

"Yeah." Aaron kisses her forehead.

Last night will forever go down as the "Great Puke Fest of 2012." Kara could not keep anything down. Aaron took her to urgent care, and after a two-hour wait where Kara vomited four more times, they were told it was normal and to go home. Kara had to calm him down because one of the male nurses pissed him off. He kept acting like Aaron being concerned for Kara and his unborn child was an inconvenience. When they got home, Aaron got to work brewing tea and rubbing Kara's feet. He helped her up and took her to the bathroom each time she felt sick. Thankfully, she stopped being nauseous sometime after 3 a.m. Aaron had already requested the day off due to Kara's OBGYN appointment. Altogether they probably only got four hours of sleep, if that.

They sit in the waiting room of the doctor's office. It's dimly lit with generic artwork that includes flowers and stock photos of families in various states of play. One is of a nice white family playing football on the beach.

Where do they get these pictures? Aaron thinks.

It seems every doctor's office he has been in since he was a kid has this same type of art. They must all get a discount or something.

After a while, a nurse opens the door that leads to the exam room.

"Kara Matthews."

Kara and Aaron get up and head inside. They sit in an exam room whose decor is like the waiting room but with a more sterile feel. Aaron sits in a nearby chair and watches Kara. She has nothing on from the waist down and is covered by a hospital gown. She looks up at the ceiling and takes a deep breath. He can tell she's anxious. He gets up and takes her hand. She looks over at him, and he smiles, leaning down to kiss her lips.

"Don't worry, baby."

Kara strokes his face with her open hand. "I love you so much, Aaron."

It never gets old. No matter how many times this beautiful creature beside him says "I love you," his heart always skips a beat.

"I love you more, baby."

"Agree to disagree," she argues with a big, sweet grin on her face.

Kara's face has gotten fuller, along with her breast, ass, and belly. Her skin glows, and she looks radiant. It's like staring at a work of art.

"You excited to find out what we're having?" Aaron asks, kissing her knuckles.

"I'm excited, but I don't care what we have as long as it's healthy."

"Bullshit. That's what everybody says."

As he and Kara laugh, Aaron thinks about how much he's hoping for a girl. When he told Niecey and Janae, they teased him saying he was going to be even more of a push-over for a baby girl than he already was with Kara. He'll never admit this to any of them, but they're right.

The doctor knocks on the door.

"Come in," Kara calls out.

Dr. Patal peaks inside with a smile before entering.

"Hey you two."

"Hi, Dr. Patal," they reply in unison.

"You guys ready to find out what you're having?"

They both nod anxiously. But before the main event, Aaron wants to make sure Kara doesn't go through last night again.

"Before we get started, I wanted to ask if there's a way Kara can get a prescription for Zofran? I was reading up on it, and between her morning sickness and having to swallow the prenatal vitamins, her nausea has gotten much worse."

The doctor nods and smiles at him. Dr. Patal is wonderful. Aaron and Kara couldn't ask for a better doctor. Especially after they foolishly went down a rabbit hole of horror stories online featuring the worst birthing experiences. Almost all of them were due to a doctor's negligence. When they met Dr. Patal, she assured them that she had delivered hundreds of babies and hasn't received a single complaint. Her office was filled with pictures of smiling babies, toddlers, children, and teens throughout the years. Most parents keep in touch with her. She has even delivered all eight children for one couple.

"Yes, I was made aware of your urgent care visit by the nurse. Nice job doing your research, Aaron. And sure, we can get Kara a script for Zofran. That's no problem."

"Good," Kara smiles.

Aaron's relieved, this is the most relaxed he's seen her all day.

Dr. Patal sets up the ultrasound and squirts gel on Kara's belly before putting the probe on her stomach. Aaron leans in to get a closer look as he holds her hand. Dr. Patal points out the heartbeat, the baby's nose, mouth and eyes, and a penis. Aaron and Kara look at each other and kiss. They turn back and look at their son, a feeling of warmth coursing through him. He knows she can feel it, too, when she squeezes his hand.

A couple of hours later, Kara and Aaron sit at a café and have lunch. She has a bowl of minestrone soup, and he is eating a BLT and fries.

"Grab some fries. You should eat more than that." Aaron pushes his plate towards Kara.

"I'm fine. I'm honestly a little scared to eat."

"Take the Zofran."

"I did, but what if it doesn't work?"

"Baby, cancer patients use it for chemo. It'll work."

Kara takes a few fries. "What do you think we should name him?"

Aaron chews a fry and gives it some thought. "I don't know. Maybe something of African origin."

"Shaka Zulu? Hannibal?"

"A warrior and a conqueror. Why not?" Aaron smiles. "I don't know. Do you have any ideas?"

"I was thinking AJ."

"AJ?"

"Yeah, as in Aaron Maurice Tompkins, Jr."

Aaron gives Kara a warm smile. Of course, she would suggest something sweet like that. "Maybe."

"You don't like it?"

"No, it's fine. If you really want to name him that."

"I do. I'm really blessed to have great a man like you as his father."

"Are you trying to make my dick hard?"

"Is it working?"

"Yes."

They're back home. Kara lies naked on her side with Aaron naked behind her. Her leg is lifted so he's able to enter her. One of his hands is on her breast while the other holds on to her belly.

"Oh, God. Don't stop!" Kara cries.

"Don't worry, baby, I won't," Aaron whispers.

Kara moans and grabs the hand that's holding her belly. The baby moves, and Aaron stops.

"Holy shit! Did you feel that?" he asks.

"Of course, I did fool. I'm the one carrying him."

"Why you always go to talk shit?" Aaron tickles Kara sides.

"Aaron, stop!" she giggles.

"You weren't saying that a few seconds ago."

"And yet you stopped."

"He moved! It threw me off. We have fucked plenty of times since you got pregnant, and he's never moved before."

Kara laughing her ass off at how ridiculous her child's father is. She laughs so hard she lets out a loud fart.

"Goddamn, baby! C'mon," Aaron laughs leaping out of the bed.

"I'm sorry. You know I'm gassy. You fucked me at your own risk."

Aaron laughs so hard, he crumples onto the floor. Kara leans down from the bed and laughs at him.

"Come back to bed," Kara whines.

"Alright. Don't fart again."

"I make no promises."

Aaron climbs back onto the bed. He lowers himself so he's facing her belly. He kisses it over and over. He feels the baby move again, and Kara rubs the top of Aaron's head.

"Hey, little man. I'm your daddy. And the amazing woman carrying you is your mom. It's going to be about five more months before we meet you, and we both can't wait. Do me a favor though. Stop making your momma fart 'cause it's killing me."

Kara bops Aaron on the top of his head. He takes her in his arms and kisses her on the lips.

"Aaron?" Kara says sweetly.

"Yes, baby. What do you need?"

He kisses her down her neck and sucks on it. She giggles and wraps her arms around his shoulders. She leans in and whispers in his ear...

"Can you go to Burger Barn and get me some cheesy fries, a root beer float, and a patty melt?"

Aaron leans back and looks at her. Really? Now? He lets out a hearty chuckle.

"You just let one rip, and now you want me to get you not one, not two, but three things with dairy in them? Dairy, Kara. You know the shit that already made you gassy even before you were pregnant. Have I got that right?"

"Yes, please. I love you."

Kara gives him her patented sugary sweet smile. The

one he can't say no to. Admittedly, he can't really say no to her no matter what expression she has on her face.

"Well, since I won't be getting any, might as well get myself a cheeseburger and a strawberry shake."

"Ohh!" Kara eyes light up.

Aaron gets dressed then grabs his wallet and keys.

"Let me guess, you want me to replace the root beer float with a shake?"

"No, ask them if they can put strawberry ice cream in the float."

Aaron looks at her horrified. What kind of nonsense is this?

"Kara, that's nasty."

"No, it isn't."

"Nope. No, I am not buckling on this. That is nasty. Vanilla or chocolate go with root beer, not strawberry."

"Don't be so narrow minded."

"I'm not being...you know, what? I'm not doing this with you. I'm going to get us some food and get you your nasty ass float."

Aaron heads to the door.

"Thank you, Aaron."

"You're welcome, baby."

"Oh, and Aaron?"

"Yes."

Aaron looks at her suspiciously, expecting her to add to her order. Instead, she lets out a small toot.

"You thought that was going to be louder, didn't you?" Aaron shakes his head.

Kara bursts out laughing. "Yeah, I did."

"Why did I agree to procreate with you?"

"Because you *looovvve* me," Kara teases.

Aaron walks over to her and cups her face in his hands. He kisses her again and again and again.

"Damn right I do."

Kara treats him to a kittenish smile before tonguing him down.

"Mmmm. You think your food can wait?" Aaron rubs his nose against Kara's.

She wraps her arms around him and licks his ear. "Okay. But make it a quickie."

"Done."

Thirteen

Monday morning, Aaron arrives at work and sees his friend, Rod.

"Rod, what up, dude?"

"What up, my nigga? Did you find out what you're having?"

Aaron beams with pride. He's having a son!

"A boy. Kara wants to name him after me."

Rod playfully punches Aaron on the shoulder.

"Nice. Congratulations, man."

"Thank you."

They enter the conference room for a weekly meeting. There's a platter of bagels, orange juice, and coffee on a table in the back of the room. Aaron and Rod make their plates, pour themselves some juice and take a seat. Some of their co-workers come in and greet them. Aaron is well-liked and gets a lot of pleasant hellos from folks.

Everyone gets situated with plates of breakfast and cups of coffee.

Their supervisor, Terrence, walks in and greets everyone. "How was everyone's weekend?"

"Smoke found out he's having a boy," Rod announces, and everyone applauds.

"Congratulations, Smoke."

"Thank you."

"I have more good news for you. For all of you. We won the bid on the remodel. We'll be working on the house in Manhattan Beach starting next week. This job will be at least four months."

Everyone cheers. More work means more overtime, which equals more money.

"Smoke, I'll need you to work some longer hours, but I will try to make sure they don't interfere with Kara's due date."

"Thanks, Ter. I appreciate that."

Terrance nods at Aaron in acknowledgement and proceeds with the meeting.

Over the next couple of months, family and friends rotate taking Kara to the doctor. She can drive, but it's easier not to. The further along she gets in this pregnancy, the more her body turns on her. Some days it's her back pain, and others severe acid reflux. And when that happens, driving is out of the question. Today is one of those days.

She sits and waits in the living room for Aaron to come get her. She rubs her stomach and takes deep breaths as she tries to get comfortable on the couch. Her phone buzzes. She reads the text from Aaron.

Sorry, baby. I can't take you. I got hung up at work. But my mom is on her way.

Kara looks at her phone in disbelief. He must be joking. Over the past two months, Pauline hasn't taken her to the doctor once. And Kara knows Aaron has asked her.

She texts Aaron back. There has to be someone else. Anyone else.

What about my mom? Or Janae or Sheila or Denise? Hell, even Richard.

She waits for Aaron's reply. While Kara is still in the process of getting to know him, Richard has been warm, funny, and kind. He's even shown more excitement over the baby than Pauline has.

Kara, my mom doesn't hate you, and she's happy to do it. Besides, everyone else is busy or at work. It'll be fine.

Pauline pulls up. She gets out of the car and walks up to the door, and lets herself in.

"Ready?" she asks Kara.

Kara nods. Pauline heads back to the car as Kara pushes herself up from the couch and waddles to the car. They drive to the doctor's office in silence. When it looks like Kara is going to say something, Pauline turns on the radio.

Not speaking. Got it. Kara fights like hell not to roll her eyes.

Kara sits at the table and waits for Aaron to come home. He comes in looking exhausted, and for a second, Kara reconsiders saying anything, but she quickly changes her mind when she reminds herself Aaron will always be too tired to talk with this new project going on, so it's now or never.

"We need to talk," she says matter-of-factly.

Aaron sighs. He's clearly not in the mood for a discussion, but he takes a seat at the table across from her anyway.

"What's wrong?" he asks.

"You need to talk to your mom," Kara demands.

"Why? What happened?"

"It's what didn't happen, Aaron. Look, you can chalk this up to hormones and say that I'm just being overly sensitive, but I am tired of her attitude."

Kara is emotional but keeps her composure.

"She comes over and walks in the house—I'm not

even going to bring up the fact that she never bothers to knock and just waltzes right in here…"

"You just did," Aaron smirks.

His attempt to add some levity to the conversation fails. Big time. Kara isn't in the mood for him to make jokes. This whole Pauline situation is stressing her out. He needs to understand that.

"Whatever. She comes in, asks if I'm ready and walks back to the car. I'm six months pregnant; it takes me a minute to get up. She could have at least stood by just in case I needed help. And when we're in the car, she says nothing, absolutely nothing to me. She didn't talk to me at all. Then when we're at the doctor's office, I asked her if she wanted to come back with me to see the ultrasound and hear the baby's heartbeat. She says, 'No, I'm fine,' and goes back to reading a magazine." Kara sighs, "Aaron, you said she would be thrilled about this baby, but I don't see it. And if that's the case, why should we even involve her at all?"

"So, you want me to cut my mother out of our child's life before he's even been born?"

"No, I want you to talk to her about her fucked-up attitude towards me."

Aaron rolls his eyes. "Okay, fine. I'll talk to her."

"Don't do that, Aaron."

"Don't do what? I said I'd take care of it."

Kara gets up from the table. This is bullshit. She has every right to be pissed, and he's treating her like she's a child having a tantrum.

"Forget it. Forget I even said anything."

She walks to their bedroom.

Aaron follows. "Kara, why are you mad? I told you that I would talk to my mom."

"Because you're only doing it to shut me up, not because you care about how her behavior makes me feel."

"Jesus Christ! I just got home from a twelve-hour shift. I don't need this shit right now."

Kara has tears in her eyes. "Fine."

She goes out to the living room and grabs her purse before she heads out to her car. She ignores her back pain. The last thing she wants is to be anywhere around that man right now.

Aaron walks after her. "Where are you going?"

"I'm going to stay with Janae and Sasha for a couple of days."

"Kara, what the fuck? You can't just leave because we're having a disagreement."

Without saying a word, Kara gets in her car and drives off. The last thing she hears as she drives away is Aaron shouting, *"Kara!"*

The next morning, Aaron knocks on the door of a pale-yellow, one-story house in South L.A. Aunt Sheila answers the door. It's always amazed Aaron how strong the genes are in his family. Sheila and his mom could be twins even though

Pauline is three years older. Sheila is the definition of the *cool* aunt. She gave Aaron his first sip of beer and even took him to his first titty bar to cheer him up after his mom kicked him out. She had always been a fixture in his life, but she stepped up more after Duke died.

"Hi, Baby Boy," she says with a hug and a smile.

"Hi, Auntie," Aaron hugs her back. "Is Ma here?"

"Not yet. She just texted that she's on her way. Come on in."

Aaron walks into the house. Denise comes out of her room.

"Hey, Smoke."

"Hey, Niecey."

"What's wrong? You look like you haven't slept in weeks."

"It was just one night. I've been working on this property in Manhattan Beach, so that's been taking a lot out of me."

"I'll make some coffee." Sheila goes to the kitchen and calls out to Aaron. "Pauline told us about the new remodel your job is doing. Looks like they're working you hard."

Denise jumps in, "They must be for him not to be sleeping well."

Aaron sighs and looks forlorn. "The exhaustion is from the job. The lack of sleep is from Kara."

"You need to leave that poor woman alone. She's pregnant," Denise teases.

"Niecey, what the fuck are you talking about?" Aaron says, confused.

"Women are not sex machines, Smoke, and she's carrying a whole ass human inside of her."

"That's not why I haven't gotten any sleep, fool." Aaron rolls his eyes.

"Watch the name-calling. Then what happened?" Denise sucks her teeth. "What did you do?"

"What makes you think I did something?"

"Nigga, because I know you."

Sheila comes back in and hands him a cup of coffee.

"Niecey, leave him alone." Sheila addresses Aaron, "What's going on with Kara?"

Aaron sips the coffee and takes a seat. "She thinks Ma doesn't like her. And she asked me to talk to her about it, but I was dismissive. I was tired. I had just gotten home, and the first thing she does is come at me with this stuff about her and ma. Well, she didn't like my response so last night she stormed out and went to stay at Janae's."

"Told you he messed up," Denise giggles.

Both Sheila and Aaron shoot her a dirty look. Sheila's is playful. Aaron's is not.

"Don't you have more important shit you can be doing right now?" Aaron snaps.

"What's more important than bugging you?" Denise laughs. He smiles and flips her off. He can never stay mad at Niecey for too long. It's always been that way.

"That's enough, you two."

Sheila puts her hand on Aaron's shoulder.

"You came here to talk to your momma, didn't you?"

Aaron nods his head.

"I hate to break this to you, Baby Boy, but Kara's right. She's not your momma's favorite person."

Aaron shakes his head in exasperation. "But why? That doesn't make sense."

Can Kara be a bit stubborn and controlling? Yes, but that affects him more than his mom. Whenever Kara's around her, she's polite and Pauline is…Pauline. He's told Kara that his mom is just the way she is. But that obviously isn't working anymore, and he needs to step up and fix this. The last thing he wants is Kara saying Pauline can't be around their child. That will cause all kinds of hell.

"Not sure. All I know is whenever Kara comes up, Pauline usually calls her stuck up or something. You need to ask her what her problem is."

Denise looks down at her phone and smiles. "Guillermo's out getting some food; y'all want something?"

"Where's he at?" Sheila asks.

"He's in line at the breakfast pop-up near Grand Central Market."

Aaron's pleased that Denise has settled down, and Guillermo's cool. He didn't mean to, but he overheard Denise, Janae, and Kara during one of their girl talks. Aaron usually works out or busies himself building something when they come over, and he's home. On his way to meet up with Rod, he heard Denise talking about all the guys she hooked up with in college. She stacked up as many numbers as Aaron did back in the day. His over-protectiveness told him to warn her, but his good sense won out. Denise is her own woman and can do what she wants. She's also smart. Case in point, she met Guillermo her senior year, and the two have been inseparable ever since.

"Tell him to get me the bacon, egg, and cheese."

"Okay. You want something, Smoke?"

"Naw, I'm good."

Aaron spies Denise giving her mother a look. Sheila smiles back at her. The women in this family stay plotting against him. He doesn't know why he even said no. Niecey's going to make Guillermo get something for him. Guaranteed. Denise's phone rings.

"Hey, baby. Yeah, so my mom wants bacon, egg and cheese..." Denise heads to her old room.

"I want my bacon extra crispy!" Aunt Sheila calls out.

"Momma, I don't know if they do that!"

"Ask him anyway."

Sheila sits next to Aaron and gives him a side hug. "Life was simpler when it was just bitches and Tone, wasn't it?"

Aaron laughs. "It was, but it was also empty. Kara and my son are my world. I love them more than anything. I just wish that were enough."

Aaron lays his head on her shoulder. Sheila takes his hand and squeezes it.

"It may not seem like it right now, but it is enough,

Baby Boy. Your love for your family is what brought you here today."

Aaron kisses Sheila on the cheek. "Thank you."

Pauline comes in and stops short when she sees Aaron.

"What are you doing here?"

Aaron lets out a deep sigh and stands. "We need to talk."

Pauline puts her purse down and gives Sheila a hug and a kiss. "What about?"

"Kara."

Pauline turns to Aaron and looks confused. "Why do we need to talk about her?"

"Ma, why do you dislike Kara so much?"

Pauline looks at Aaron in disbelief. "Excuse me? Did I not take her to the doctor's office yesterday after you asked me? And at the last minute, too, I might add. You're lucky my supervisor is an idiot and didn't notice I was gone."

"And I appreciate that, but according to Kara, you refused to talk to her on the ride there, and when she asked you to come back for the ultrasound and listen to your grandson's heartbeat, you refused." Aaron looks over at Sheila. "And according to Auntie, you talk shit about her."

Pauline looks at her sister in disbelief.

Sheila shrugs. "What? You do talk about that girl."

Pauline takes a seat.

Aaron kneels in front of her. "Ma, I need peace in my

home. I'm stressed out from work and anxious about becoming a father. Please be nice to Kara. She's very pregnant, very uncomfortable, and very sensitive right now. I love her, and I need you to do better."

Pauline rolls her eyes, "Fine."

"Seriously, Ma."

"Okay. I said fine."

Aaron stands. He knows it's not much, but that's the best he's going to get out of Pauline. Guillermo walks in and kisses Pauline and Sheila each on the cheek.

He hands everyone a sandwich, including Aaron, who he gives two.

"I told Niecey I was good, man. You didn't need to get me this."

"Smoke, you're about to go have a talk with a pregnant woman. As a man who is one of seven kids, trust me, you shouldn't go empty-handed."

Aaron smiles. Man's got a point!

"Thanks."

He gives Guillermo a half hug, half handshake, and heads to the door.

"Alright, y'all, I'm out."

Pauline follows him out. "You really are in love, aren't you?" she asks, placing her hand on her hip.

Aaron turns and faces her. He offers her a warm smile. Aaron can understand how this all may seem to her. His maturity when it came to pursuing a relationship with Kara even threw him for a loop. He can only imagine how all of this looks from her point of view.

"Ma, I've been with her for five years. It's safe to say that I am."

"Don't get smart with me, boy," she says. The usual sharpness in her voice is gone. She sounds soft, almost kind.

Aaron kisses Pauline on the forehead. She gives him an understanding nod, then turns and walks back inside the house.

Aaron gets in his car, ready to get his woman back.

Forty minutes later, he knocks on the door of Janae's apartment.

Sasha opens the door, and Aaron smiles at her. Sasha's a sweet, bubbly ball of energy. Light-skinned with auburn hair currently hiding underneath a dark, wavy wig. Sasha has freckles peppered around her nose and cheeks. She's plus sized like Janae, and she always has on girlie outfits. She currently has on a light pink sweater with the words "cutie pie" written in glitter across it. She's paired that with white cotton shorts and hot pink opened-toe sandals.

"Hey, Smoke," she beams.

"Hey, Sash. Is Kara here?"

"Yeah. Come on in." Sasha notices the sandwiches. "You went to that pop up joint downtown?"

"Guillermo did. And how did you even know about that?"

"Everybody's been talking about it on Twitter." She points to her laptop. "Kara was still pretty upset earlier. You should probably let me go with you."

"Good idea."

Sasha knocks on Janae's bedroom door.

"Come in," Janae calls.

Sasha opens the door. Janae is rubbing Kara's foot. Janae and Kara look up and see Aaron. Kara looks at him with a mix of sadness and anger. He hands Kara both sandwiches. She takes one and hands the other to Janae.

Janae gets up. "C'mon, Sash, let's give them some privacy. I'll share this with you."

As Janae walks by Aaron, she gives him a reassuring pat on the back.

"Do not screw this up, Smoke," Janae mutters. She looks Aaron square in the eyes.

"Yes ma'am." Aaron smiles at her and Sasha as they leave. He takes a seat on Janae's bed and takes Kara's foot. He massages it while Kara eats her sandwich.

"I spoke to my mother." Aaron runs his knuckles along the arch of her foot.

"Did she hang up on you?"

"No, I spoke to her in person."

"You braved talking to her on food shopping day?"

"That's how much I love you."

This earns him a smile. Praise Jesus.

"What did she say?" Kara takes another bite of her sandwich.

"I told her she couldn't treat you like she has been, and she agreed to be nice to you."

"Thank you."

"You're welcome."

Aaron places her foot on the bed and takes the other one, massaging it.

Kara scoots closer to him. "I didn't want to cause you anymore stress, but you do get why I had to say something, right?"

"Yeah, I do. But you can't storm out whenever we disagree on something. You can't say you want me to be more open, then when I am and you don't like what I say, you leave. I can live with you being mad at me, but I can't live without you."

Kara scoots so close that they're now face-to-face. She rubs her nose against his. "I'm sorry."

He kisses her forehead, nose, and lips. "I'm sorry, too. Please come home."

"Okay."

Fourteen

Kara comes out of the bedroom after a nap and sees Aaron putting the finishing touches on the baby's crib right outside the garage. She's perfected a scooting technique to get her out of bed. She still needs help getting up from the couch, though. He uses a paint sprayer to cover the crib in white. Kara heads to the kitchen, grabs a bottle of water, and takes a sip when her *other* water breaks. Um, what the hell? This kid isn't due for another two weeks. Impatient little munchkin. She frowns at her belly while carefully walking around the fluid.

She waddles over to Aaron. He has headphones and a protective mask on. She taps his shoulder. He takes off his headphones and turns to her.

"Aaron, my water broke!"

Aaron stands, his eyes wide. "*When?*"

"Just now."

"Are you having contractions?"

"I haven't yet."

"Alright. Let's head out."

He grabs his car keys and takes her hand. As they drive to the hospital, she sends one text after another.

"Who you texting?"

"My mom, Janae, and Denise. You should let your mom know."

"I can, but the grapevine with the ladies in my family works fast, you know that. Denise will tell Sheila, and Sheila will tell my mom."

Aaron looks over at Kara.

"Are you sure you don't want to call your dad?"

She takes back her earlier "What the hell?" because... what the hell?

"Where is this coming from?" Kara looks at Aaron.

"I don't know. I was just thinking," Aaron sighs, "Look baby, you not talking to him because he split with your mom seems cruel after all this time. It's been seven years since he left, and five years since you spoke to him. And don't think I haven't noticed him calling your phone. Don't you think you should let this go? Your mom is happy. Rick's a great guy..."

"You're right. He is a great guy, so why would our son need a cheating asshole for a grandfather when he has Richard?" Kara snaps.

She can't believe Aaron would bring that son of a bitch up at a time like this.

"Baby?" Aaron says calmly.

"What?"

"Kara please don't be upset. I just...I don't know why I brought it up, except to say that. There's a piece missing, baby. I see your anger, but I also see your pain. I don't like seeing the woman I love in pain."

"Then you shouldn't have knocked me up because I'm about to be in a lot of pain."

"Kara," Aaron looks at her warmly but he's clearly not in the mood for jokes.

"I know, and I get it. I'll think about it later."

"That's all I ask."

Aaron takes her hand and kisses it.

They enter the hospital and head towards the elevators. The maternity ward is on the fourth floor. While in the elevator, Kara gets a phone call. It's Janae.

"Hey, girl. How are you?"

"I'm good. No contractions yet."

"Okay. I'm on my way. I had to call the office and tell them I wasn't coming, but I should be there in ten minutes."

"Okay."

Kara and Aaron get off the elevator and head to the nurses' station.

"Hello," Aaron says.

The nurse looks up and sees them. She gives them a warm smile.

"Hello. Are we ready to bring a little one into the world?"

"It looks that way. Her water broke about twenty

minutes ago. She hasn't had a contraction yet, though." Aaron carries Kara's overnight bag on his shoulder while he holds her hand.

The nurse looks at a nervous Kara. This is really happening. She's going to meet her son. Tears form in her eyes. Aaron wipes them away and smiles at her.

"Okay. Let's get you situated, momma."

Kara lies in the hospital bed. She has an IV in her arm and a catheter connected to her nether region. And holy shit, was that painful. She makes a mental note for the next kid to get the epidural before the catheter. Now that she has the epidural, she's feeling a lot better.

Aaron sits beside her and strokes her face.

"I still don't get why I had to leave the room."

"Because they stuck a large needle in my spine. As tough as you are, Smoke, even you would have fainted."

Aaron looks like he's not buying it. "Please, there's no way I would have fainted."

"Yeah, okay."

They hear Janae at the nurses' station. "Kara Matthews. Where's her room? I'm her sister."

"Go get her." Kara points to the door.

Aaron opens the hospital room door and calls out. "Janae! Get your loud ass in here."

Janae rushes into the room all aflutter. She playfully hits Aaron. "Shut up, Smoke."

She walks over to Kara and gives her a kiss on the cheek. Today's fake glasses are tortoise shell to compliment her charcoal gray business suit. Complete with a honey blonde pixie cut wig and high heel pumps.

"Girl. Oh my God! You guys—the traffic was insane! Who would have thought coming from Downtown Torrance to Del Amo would take so long? There was an accident, and it backed up everything. And on top of that, I had to leave early at the last minute. I told you about that on the phone."

Kara nods and chuckles at Janae's flair for the dramatic.

Janae continues, "Anyway, I told my boss your due date and asked him for a couple of days off, and he agreed. Then I'm at my desk, and I get your text, so I run to my boss and tell him. And he's like, 'I thought she wasn't due for two weeks,' and I'm like, dude, I don't know. Babies just come when they feel like, I guess. So, he's like, 'okay, but you gotta do some overtime.' And you know I'm salaried, so I don't get extra cash for that shit. I'm like nigga, what? Anyway, I guess I'm doing overtime, but I get to see my nephew be born."

Janae takes a breath and sits, stretching her legs out as if she's just run a marathon.

Aaron smirks. Kara knows that smirk; he's getting ready to say something to get on Janae's nerves.

"Are you good? Can we get you anything? Some water, maybe? I know, Kara, get out of the bed so Janae can lay down."

Janae playfully shoves Aaron's shoulder. Him and

Janae should have their own show. They're an endless supply of entertainment for Kara.

"Shut up, Smoke. If you weren't becoming a father, I swear I'd kick your ass."

Kara rolls her eyes at the two of them.

Aaron smiles. "No, you wouldn't. You are always so dramatic."

"I could have sworn I told your Black ass to shut up. Twice," Janae replies. She turns to Kara. "Did I or did I not tell this trifling fool to shut up twice?"

"You did," Kara giggles.

"Oh, it's like that. Y'all just going to gang on a nigga?"

"Yeah," Janae says.

"Always," Kara adds.

"Alright. I see you," Aaron says, giving them both a playful stink eye. Janae and Kara laugh at him.

A monitor next to Kara's bed beeps. Janae leans over to look at it. "What's that?"

"It monitors the baby's heart rate," Aaron replies.

"I still can't believe y'all are about to be parents."

"I know right? It's crazy," Aaron says.

"A little person is going to be calling us mommy and daddy. I can't wait, but I'm also super scared." Kara's voice is jittery.

"Girl, please. You had Momma Evie as a role model. You're going to be an amazing mom." Janae squeezes Kara's hand.

Evelyn comes into the room. "Why, thank you,

Janae darling." She runs up to Kara and hugs her, giving her a kiss. She does the same to Aaron and Janae.

"How are you feeling, sweetheart?" Evelyn strokes Kara's forehead.

"I'm...oh..."

"You okay, baby?" Aaron asks.

"I think I just had a contraction. That wasn't so bad."

A nurse comes in and checks on Kara. "You're four centimeters dilated. We're going to give you some Pitocin to induce labor, which means you're going to start feeling those contractions."

"Okay. No problem."

Two hours later, Kara regrets saying, *No problem.*

"I want to push," she cries, tears forming in her eyes.

"Janae, go get the doctor," Aaron orders.

Janae runs out of the room in search of Kara's doctor. She comes back with two nurses. One Korean and the other a Nordic looking blonde.

"We'll get the doctor if she's fully dilated," the blonde one says.

"Okay, so check and see how dilated she is," Aaron says.

The other nurse jumps in, "She was checked two hours ago, and we don't want to risk an infection. We'll check again in an hour."

"An hour?" Evelyn says, "She's ready now. Just check her."

"Ma'am, calm down. We're not going to risk an infection. We'll check back later."

The nurses leave. Are those bitches on a coffee break? What the fuck?

"No. Where are they going?" Kara asks. Tears are now streaming down her face.

"Fuck this. I'll deliver the baby," Aaron says.

"Smoke, are you fucking crazy?" Janae asks.

"What? These motherfuckers aren't listening, and Kara's in pain. It's cool. I've seen this on TV a million times."

Evelyn rolls her eyes at Aaron. "Oh, my God. Janae, go try and find a doctor. I'll deal with this."

"Okay, baby, push," Aaron says.

Kara looks at him like he's crazy.

"C'mon, Kara, let's do this. You push, he'll slide right out, and I'll catch him like a football."

Kara laughs. That really helped. She's lucky to have a man who knows how to talk her down.

Evelyn realizes what Aaron's trying to do and laughs too. Janae comes back with Kara's doctor and the two nurses from before.

"Hey there, Ms. Kara. I hear you're ready to push," Dr. Patal says. "Okay, let's take a look."

The doctor looks under Kara's blanket. "Oh, wow. I can see the top of the head." Dr. Patal turns to the nurses. "When we're done here, you two can explain why you didn't check her dilation when she requested it." The nurses blush and glance at each other.

Their humiliation doesn't last long as the doctor gets in position and orders Kara to push. She does.

After twenty minutes, the baby is born. A few seconds pass, and no noise is heard. Kara looks at Aaron with fear. He tries to hide his emotions and comforts her by squeezing and kissing her hand. The baby cries, and everyone collectively breathes a sigh of relief. That was the longest two seconds of Kara's life. The idea that they couldn't bring their baby home after everything they had been through would have destroyed her.

The doctor holds him up. "Here's your son." She turns to Aaron, who has tears in his eyes. "Papa, would you like to cut the cord?"

Aaron wipes his eyes. "Yeah." He cuts the cord.

The nurses get the baby cleaned up and hand him to Kara. She holds him against her breast, and he suckles. He's the most beautiful baby she's ever seen. Now that he's here, she never wants to let him go. Evelyn and Janae approach. Evelyn kisses Kara and cries. She kisses AJ on top of his head. Janae hugs Kara carefully then hugs Aaron. AJ is surrounded by his parents, grandmother, and auntie. He is—and always will be—surrounded by love.

Fifteen

Three days later, Aaron and Kara bring AJ home. When they open the door, Pauline, Sheila, Denise, Janae, Evelyn, Richard, and Rod are there. Evelyn, Richard, and Pauline organized a welcome home party for AJ. The dining area is full of decorations, including a banner that says, "Welcome Home AJ," and lots of balloons. The table is filled with everything from a fruit and veggie platter to chicken wings, potato salad—made by Sheila—greens, and Richard's special jambalaya. It fills the house with the smell of home cooking.

While folks busy themselves making their plates, Pauline swiftly takes AJ away. "Give me my grandbaby."

Sheila and Denise gather around her and ooh and aah at AJ.

Rod gives Aaron a hug. "How you doin', man?"

"I'm tired. But not nearly as tired as her." Aaron

points to Kara.

"Smart. Always make sure to acknowledge what your woman just went through." Richard playfully slaps Aaron on the back.

"Yeah, I am not crazy," Aaron smiles.

Kara sits on the couch with Evelyn. She holds Kara as she lays her head on her shoulder. Aaron brings them both a plate of food, and they each thank him with a kiss, Evelyn on his cheek and Kara on his lips.

Everyone takes turns holding the baby. AJ spits up on Richard, causing everyone to laugh.

"Whoa, I just got this shirt," Richard smiles. Kara catches his eye, and he shoots her a smile. It's different from the one he had seconds ago. That one conveyed laughter and joy. This smile communicates warmth and unconditional love. Kara has grown to really love Richard.

Kara smiles back at Richard, then mouths the words, "I love you," to him. He mouths them back and gives AJ a kiss on the forehead.

Evelyn takes ahold of AJ. He gazes into his grandmother's eyes. Richard scoots closer to Evelyn, his arm tenderly wrapped around her waist as he watches grandmother and grandson bond. "Hello, my sweetheart. I'm Grandma Evie, and this is your Grandpa Rick."

"Little man knows who I am. Go on, tell her. Say, 'I know who he is. I just threw up on him.'" Evelyn gives Richard a kiss on the cheek. He returns with a kiss on the lips that lasts quite a while.

"Okay, that's enough, you two. Not in front of the baby," Janae says.

"You stay out of grown folks' business, young lady," Evelyn smirks. She turns to address Kara, "This reminds me so much of when you were a baby, Kara. Enjoy this because it goes by so fast."

"Indeed, it does," Sheila adds.

"Okay now, Evie. It's been five minutes. It's my turn to hold the little dumpling," Pauline says.

"Five *more* minutes," Evelyn playfully pleads.

"Nope. Should have thought about that before you started making out with your man," Pauline teases.

"Don't hate," Evelyn retorts.

"Honey, nobody's hating. I don't have time for any man."

"You know, Pauline, I'm sorry to hear you say that because I got a cousin who's single," Richard replies.

"What he look like? And what does he do?" Pauline asks.

"Changed your tune real quick, didn't you?" Sheila says.

"Shut up," Pauline responds. "Go on, Rick."

"Well, his name is Fletcher, and he works in finance."

"Sounds kind of nerdy. That is not Pauline's type," Sheila says.

"Excuse you, I can be very open-minded," Pauline says, feigning offense.

"Ha!" Aaron laughs. This results in Pauline throwing a grape at her son.

"Seriously though, send me a picture of him, Rick. And, Evie, hand over the munchkin."

Evelyn hands AJ to Pauline. "That's okay." Evelyn looks down at AJ with a sweet smile. "I'm going to be your favorite grandma anyway."

Pauline laughs. "Chile, please, I'm going to spoil this boy so much he's gonna be like 'Evie, who?'"

A chorus of laughter fills the room. Pauline even shares a sweet moment with Kara and smiles at her. Kara smiles back. It's everything she's ever wanted, the people she loves all in one space doting on her little one. Her mind goes to her dad. She knows Aaron has a point but she's just not willing to let him in. At least not yet.

The day wears on. Evelyn and Richard wash dishes while Pauline rocks AJ to sleep. Kara sleeps on Aaron's shoulder as they sit on the couch. Denise and Sheila went to the grocery store and are currently filling up Aaron and Kara's pantry and fridge.

Aaron watches Rod and Janae as they talk about the latest Batman video game. They both are so animated and lively that Pauline has to shush them to make sure they don't wake up AJ. Rod compliments Janae on her hair—worn in cornrows with laid edges—and wire-rimmed fake glasses. They exchange numbers and make plans to hang out. Aaron has never seen his boy this enthusiastic around anyone. He cannot wait to tell Kara about this.

Later that night, Kara awakens to a sharp pain in her abdomen. It hurts so bad she falls out of bed. AJ stirs and coos. Kara cries. Aaron awakens and checks on the baby. He sees AJ sleeping and looks on the floor to find Kara curled up in pain. Aaron hops out of bed and carries her back to the bed. She grabs him and cries into his bare chest.

"Baby, what's wrong?"

"Uuutteruss."

"Okay. Yeah, you pumped a lot today. That must be why this is happening."

Aaron gets out of bed and picks her up again. He carries her into the bathroom and sets her on the closed toilet seat and turns the shower on.

He goes back to the bedroom and picks up AJ's "Rock With Me" crib with AJ still asleep in it. AJ wiggles and makes a little noise.

"Shhh, buddy. It's okay," Aaron whispers.

Aaron places the "Rock With Me" next to the tub, then goes and gets a bottle for AJ from the fridge. After grabbing the bottle warmer from the room, he returns to the bathroom and sets everything up. "Water warm enough?" he asks.

Kara is already in the shower. "It's perfect."

"Good." Aaron takes off his pajama bottoms and joins her. They keep the shower door cracked so they can still see AJ.

She leans against Aaron's strong body. They look over at AJ. He's still asleep.

"Smart move grabbing his bottle," Kara says.

"Yeah. I don't know how long we're going to be in here or when he'll wake up. I figured I'd be prepared."

Aaron holds Kara, being careful not to grip her too tightly. "Is this helping? You feeling better?"

"Yes." Kara turns around and kisses Aaron on the lips. "My mom wants to know when we're getting married." Kara realizes what she just said. "Sorry to drop that on you. It slipped out."

Aaron chuckles. "It's fine. And it's a fair question. Auntie Sheila and Denise have been asking me too. I say we get through AJ's first year before we start planning something like a wedding."

"Aaron?"

"Yes, my love."

"You're a good man. You always take care of me and tell me what I need to hear, even when I reject it. You are a good man, and I love you."

Aaron holds Kara close. His lips brush against her ear. It sends shivers down Kara's spine. "Thank you. I love you so much, baby," Aaron whispers, his voice dripping with love, and his dick hard as a rock.

"Down, boy. You have six weeks before I'm able to handle sex. Maybe more."

"A woman's body is an extraordinary thing, but it sure does take a long time to heal from stuff."

"Gee, Aaron we're so sorry." Kara rolls her eyes.

"It's okay. Don't worry your pretty little heads about it," Aaron replies, ruffling Kara's hair.

Kara flicks his nipple. "Hey!" Aaron laughs.

AJ whimpers. They look down and check on him. He awakens and cries.

"See, look what you did," Aaron says. He gets out of the shower and picks up AJ. "It's okay. It's okay, buddy. Momma woke you up, didn't she?"

"No, I didn't. Give him here. He wants some of mommy's milk."

"You sure? I can give him the bottle. Your cramps just started to go away."

"It's fine."

Kara gets out of the shower. Aaron hands her AJ. He roots around in search of Kara's nipple. He finds it in seconds and latches.

"He's hungry as hell isn't he? He gets that shit from you."

"You are so stupid," Kara laughs.

Aaron chuckles, then strokes the top of AJ's head and kisses it.

"Aaron?"

"Yes."

"Thank you for giving me such a beautiful baby."

Aaron looks into Kara's eyes. "Thank *you* for giving me such a beautiful baby."

Sixteen

2014

AJ runs around the backyard of his Grandma Evelyn's house while she and Richard chase him. Aaron and Kara sit at a nearby table, sipping lemonade and watching them all have fun. Trixie lies near their feet, receiving pets from the two of them. She's had a rough night, so any rest the poor pup can get, the better.

AJ runs up to his parents.

"Momma, Daddy. Pep Pig, Pep Pig!"

Aaron checks his watch. Damn, he's right!

"Yep, it's almost time for *Peppa Pig*."

Kara shakes her head. "Unbelievable, he can't even tell time, but he always knows when his shows are about to start."

AJ is only two and has developed quite a little personality. Not only can he tell when all his shows are about to start, they recently discovered that he knows exactly what time to sneak into the kitchen for cookies. Part of the reason they're visiting Evelyn today was to return Trixie. They were dog-sitting while she and Richard went to Napa. Everything was going well until this morning when Aaron and Kara collectively had a heart attack when AJ wasn't in his room. They found him asleep on the couch next to Trixie, both covered in cookie crumbs. As Aaron gave him his bath this morning, AJ confessed...kind of.

"Have you been sneaking cookies when me and mommy are asleep?"

"Love you, daddy. Pee boo"

"No, we're not playing peek-a-boo."

"Love you, daddy."

"Yes, I heard you little man. I love you, too."

That kid was so fucking cute; it killed him. And it almost worked until Aaron reminded himself that Trixie got diarrhea from the cookies.

Aaron asked him again in his stern daddy voice.

"AJ, did you and Trixie eat all the cookies?"

AJ nodded with a sad guilt-ridden look on his cute little face. The boy is too smart for his own good. Sneaky, cute, and smart. It's crazy that these are the traits given to tiny humans who actively try to put themselves in danger.

AJ jumps up and down again. "Pep Pig. Pep Pig."

Aaron picks AJ up. "Alright, buddy, alright. We're gonna head home so you can watch your show."

Evelyn gathers up AJ's toys and puts them in his small bookbag. "That's a good idea. I do not want to be witness to a tantrum."

"Yeah, that last one he had over some chicken nuggets was quite the display," Richard agrees.

They all share a laugh at the memory. Enough distance made the whole thing funny. Not at the time, though. Aaron has learned that meltdowns are his least favorite thing about fatherhood.

Aaron and Kara each give Evelyn and Richard a hug. Evelyn picks up AJ. She and Richard smother him with kisses. Kara carries him to their new car, a white Toyota Sienna minivan. Aaron is following behind her when Evelyn taps him on the shoulder. He turns around, coming face-to-face with her and Richard. They have on their concerned parent faces. Having not been a parent and finding himself a step-parent and step-grandparent, left Richard with only one choice in these situations. Always agree with Evie. Those Matthews women sure know how to reign in their men.

Evelyn smiles, but there's severity in her tone. "You've built a nice life for yourself, my Kara, and my precious grandbaby. You're a good man, Aaron."

"Thank you, Evie."

But...Aaron knows there's a 'but' coming.

"Now, when are you going to make an honest woman out of my daughter?"

Aaron sighs. Here she goes. When it comes to this topic, Evie has the subtlety of a jack hammer.

"We've talked about it, but there never seems to be a right time. If we eloped, you and my mom would kill us, so we'll need to have a wedding. And we just don't have the time to plan it. Her job is super demanding, and I just got assigned to a new property."

Aaron looks back at Kara and AJ. She's playing peek-a-boo with him.

"And then there's AJ. As adorable as he is, he's also a handful, and you both know that."

Aaron takes Evelyn's hand. "I want to spend the rest of my life with your daughter, and I plan to, but this is just going to have to work for now."

Evelyn looks at Aaron, unconvinced. "That's bullshit, sweetheart, and you know it. Life is always going to get in the way. If you sit around waiting for it not to be, you'll be waiting forever."

She goes back into the house. Richard gives Aaron a warm smile and shrugs shoulders.

"You knew this was coming. She's been on y'all for a minute. You couldn't come up with something better than that?"

Now it's Aaron's turn to shrug. "It's the truth."

"Young blood, just because something is true, doesn't mean it's not bullshit."

Richard gives Aaron a friendly slap on the shoulder before following his woman. Aaron heads to the car with a lot on his mind.

Aaron, AJ, and Kara sit in the living room and watch *Peppa Pig*. AJ sits on Kara's lap. Aaron looks over at her as she and AJ cuddle. If someone had told him when he was eighteen that by the time he was close to thirty, he'd be a family man with an amazing woman and a beautiful baby boy, he would have thought they were crazy. The men in his family don't tend to fare well. He has no idea where his father is. Duke's life was one tragedy after another, and even his grandfather worked himself to death and died when he was only fifty-two. None of them probably ever experienced true happiness. Aaron stares at his true happiness. He knows what he needs to do.

"We should get married," Aaron announces.

Kara looks at him in shock. "What?"

"We should get married."

"Where is this coming from?"

"As we were leaving, your mom and I talked..."

"Oh, Lord, Aaron. You don't even need to finish."

"No, baby, listen. She made a good point. Life is always going to get in the way, and we've been together close to seven years. We should get married."

"Aaron, we kind of already are."

"Yeah, but not really. Let's do it."

Kara smiles at him. "You're serious?"

"I am."

"Okay."

"Okay?"

"Yes. Okay. Let's do it."

Aaron holds Kara's face in his hands as he gently pulls her closer to him. They kiss. Aaron hopes that he's communicating all his thoughts in this kiss.

I love you. Thank you for loving me, too.

When they break apart, Kara finds her way back to Earth. She blinks a few times. "Wow, what did I do to deserve that?" she asks.

"Everything," Aaron replies.

~

Kara and Janae look at wedding dresses online. "What do you think of that one?"

Janae takes a closer look. "It's too plain. You need something more unique. Something that shows off your figure, too."

"I've meant to tell you when you got here, those lip and cheek fillers look amazing on you." Kara takes Janae's face in her hands and admires her new look.

"Thank you, Doll. It was one of the last things Tony's sorry ass did for me."

"I'm sorry things didn't work out with you two."

"Me too. It all started to go south when I told him I wanted top surgery. It's like he knew that once I started the next phase of my transition that he wouldn't be able to hide me at home anymore, so he flat-out refused. He even tried to twist it by telling me I should be happy with how I look." Janae rolls her eyes and continues scrolling through wedding dress photos.

Janae hides it well, but Kara knows her sister. She can tell she's hurt. Kara wants to punch Tony in the dick. How dare he try to control Janae's body? And that whole not taking her out in public thing always rubbed Kara the wrong way. Her, Kara, and Aaron go out all the goddamn time. They've never been ashamed to be seen with her. Why the fuck would her boyfriend? But Janae seemed happy, so Kara didn't say anything.

Janae's journey has been one that Kara has always admired, and she's been there every step of the way. From the time Janae started wearing her acrylics to wearing makeup, lashes, and wigs, Kara was right there watching her friend make the brave decision to finally be herself. Kara is one of a small group of people who knows Janae's dead name. Hell, she helped Janae pick her current name. So, hearing that this asshole—who had no problem spending shitloads of money on jewelry, purses, and clothes—refused to help her into this next phase of her life...yeah, fuck that guy.

"You know Rod is..."

"Not an option, Kare Bear. He has a girlfriend. Besides, Rod and I are just friends."

"Please, he is not serious about that Tammi girl, and he does not light up with her the way he does around you."

"Dear God. You and Smoke sound like broken records with that."

"We just think you two would be great together."

Denise comes in with her one-year-old daughter, Lark aka Birdie.

"Thank God. Saved by the bell," Janae says.

Birdie runs over to Janae and gets picked up and tickled. Denise is holding a baker's box.

"What are y'all talking about?"

"How Rod and Janae should be together."

Denise nods placing the box on the table. "He is fine. Way finer than Tony."

Janae shakes her head and laughs. "Okay, I'll admit, he is finer, now can we stop talking about this?"

"Okay Ms. Sensitive," Denise teases. "Kara, there's another box in the car."

"I'll go get it," Kara says.

Minutes later, the ladies sit at the table and eat cake samples. Birdie has cake smeared all over her face. Kara wipes her face off as the ladies laugh at her cuteness.

"Oh, Niecey. Let me show you this dress Janae and I were looking at. I like it, but she thinks it's too plain." Kara goes over to the coffee table and picks up her laptop.

"Shii—oot," Kara almost curses in front of Birdie.

"Nice save," Denise replies.

"Thanks. My laptop needs to be charged and, of course, I can't find my charger. AJ probably took it again."

"Why would he take your charger?" Denise asks.

"Because that little ragamuffin likes to pretend it's a snake when he plays 'Safari Treasure Hunt' with Aaron."

"What is 'Safari Treasure Hunt'?" Janae asks, thoroughly delighted.

"It's a game Aaron made up last week where they pretend to look for lost treasure."

"Every time you tell me about some adorable dad thing that Smoke does, it tickles me to no end," Denise giggles.

Kara smiles, she knows Denise may give Aaron a hard time, but she adores him and AJ and loves their father/son relationship.

"I'll go get Aaron's." Kara goes to the bedroom and brings out Aaron's laptop.

"It's a trip," Denise says. "I never thought I'd see the day where Smoke would let a chick touch his stuff, let alone use any of it."

Kara nods. While Aaron has always been open about sharing his stuff with Kara, he still holds some things close to the chest. And Kara knows it's not because he doesn't trust her. She learned some stuff from Niecey. They talked not long after Kara and Aaron's fight the night of her professor's party. Denise told her that Duke's death impacted the family deeply and that they all still have trouble talking about it.

Kara brings out Aaron's laptop and opens it. She enters his password. There are some old files on the desktop.

One stands out to Janae. "What's that file?"

"I don't know. Old photos maybe."

"Let's look," Janae says.

"No, I'm not going to violate his privacy."

"Violate his privacy? Jesus Christ, Kare Bear, they're just pictures."

"Seriously," Denise chimes in. "What's the big deal? If he's okay with you using his shit, he's not going to care."

That is a good point. Allowing peer pressure to win out, Kara clicks on the file. There are some pictures of Aaron with his friends from back in the day.

"Oh, I remember these. This was when Smoke, Tone, and 'em were trying to be rappers."

"What?" Kara and Janae shout at the same time.

Denise laughs. "He didn't tell you about that?"

"No! I knew Tone was trying to be a rapper. Aaron never mentioned that he was, too." Kara says excitedly. She can't wait to tease him about this. The ideas are already flowing.

"Probably because they sucked." Denise laughs. "There might even be a video of them trying to freestyle."

Janae snatches the laptop and bows her head. "Dear lord, it's your child, Janae. Please let there be a video."

Kara and Denise laugh. Janae's eyes are closed and she holds a hand up to Jesus.

She finds one where Aaron, Tone, and two other guys are having a cipher.

"Thank you, Jesus! I'll be at church Sunday morning."

"No, you won't; you and I are having brunch.

Remember? Niecey can't go because she and Guillermo are taking Birdie to the children's museum," Kara reminds Janae.

"Oh, right." Janae looks up at the ceiling. "I'll make it up to you in some other way, lord."

Kara grabs them three beers and Birdie a juice box. They settle in and watch all ten rapping videos laughing their asses off. Kara takes the laptop from Janae and emails all of them to herself.

Kara points out another video. "What's this one?" Janae clicks on it.

It's Aaron having a threesome with two girls. Denise immediately covers Birdie's eyes and turns her head away. Kara and Janae's eyes grow big, and their mouths are agape. Kara shuts the lid of the laptop. A hush comes over the room.

Kara's in shock. She's not terribly surprised that Aaron at that age would make sex tapes. She's surprised that the Aaron she knows and fell in love with would keep them.

"Should we finish the cake samples?" Kara breaks the uncomfortable silence.

"Uh, yeah. Cake. Let's have more cake," Denise replies.

～

A couple of hours later, Aaron walks in to find Kara at the table with his laptop. He knows he's in trouble and takes a seat across from her.

"What did I do?" he asks.

A smile teases his lips. He knows when he's in trouble to turn on the charm. Most times, it usually works, and he's hoping it will now.

"Where's AJ?" she asks, her voice even.

"My mom insisted that he stay with her tonight. She claims she doesn't see him enough."

"She sees him every week... Nope, you know what? Your annoying ass momma ain't what's important right now."

"Okay, so what is important?"

Kara turns Aaron's laptop, so it faces him. She has the video cued up and presses the space bar. Aaron sees himself fucking Reynisha.

"Oh, oh, shit!" Aaron closes the lid on the laptop. He looks up at Kara. The look on her face tells him if she had a pot of grits, he'd be wearing them right now. "Umm. How many of those did you...?"

"All of them, Aaron. I watched all of them." Kara slides the laptop away. "I think the better question is, why did you keep them?"

"Honestly, Kara, I forgot about them."

"You made thirty plus sex tapes, some with more than one girl, and you forgot about them?"

"As hard as that is to believe, yeah, I did. I haven't watched them in years. Out of sight, out of mind. I have tons of files I don't look at on here."

Kara considers what he's said. "Are you going to delete them?"

"Yeah, sure. I'll do that right now." Aaron opens the laptop back up and deletes every sex video.

Aaron shows Kara all the videos are gone. She closes the lid and looks calmer. Thank God.

"I saved you some cake from the samples Denise brought over. They're in a Tupperware dish on the kitchen counter." She points.

"Thanks." Aaron gets up and helps himself to a piece of cake. He rejoins Kara at the table and takes a bite. "This is good."

"Which one is it?"

"Uh, the marble one with buttercream frosting."

"That's the one we all liked too. Birdie had two pieces."

Aaron chuckles. "I bet she was bouncing off the walls."

Aaron is grateful Denise had a baby a little after AJ was born. He has a built-in best friend. Denise has joked that AJ and Birdie's relationship will be just like hers and Aaron's. The thought makes him smile more.

"She was on a bit of a sugar high, but it resulted in a long nap."

Kara touches Aaron's hand. He looks at her and sees the hurt and discomfort on her face. She would often wear the same expression early in their relationship before they were official. He knows she was scared, given what she had just gone through with that asshole, Bryan. Not to mention the shit with her parents. Hearing all the girls Aaron had been with couldn't have been easy, and now seeing them just brought all of that back. Shit! He rubs his hand over hers and gives it a reassuring squeeze.

"So, is that it?" she asks.

"Is what it, baby?"

"Is that all you were hiding? You're not secretly Batman or something, are you?"

"No, and I wasn't hiding anything. It's kind of hard to hide something when you forget it exists. And if I were Batman, that would make me Bruce Wayne. And if I were Bruce Wayne, we'd be living in a mansion."

"Okay."

Aaron kisses Kara's hand, then goes back to eating his cake. Kara stares at him. He can feel she has something more to say. He looks up at her and smiles.

"Go ahead," he says.

"Go ahead, what?"

"You clearly have another question, so go ahead and ask."

Kara leans in, "How come you never made one with me?"

Aaron smiles wider. "Are you jealous that I didn't make one with you?"

"I wouldn't say jealous, but I'm a little offended."

Aaron laughs. Always the competitor. "You were so

caught up with school that I didn't think you'd be interested. I figured if I asked, you'd say no. I thought you'd be paranoid Evie would find it."

Kara gives an understanding nod. "That would be a genuine concern. How about now?"

Aaron looks at her with hooded eyes. His dick stirs in his pants. When it comes to satisfying Kara's sweet pussy, his dick stays ready.

"Right now?"

"Sure."

He gets up and goes over to her, cake in hand, and leads her into their bedroom.

"You're bringing the cake?"

"Yeah, Imma use it."

A naked Kara lies on the bed while a naked Aaron sets up his camera. He takes the cake he placed on the nightstand, walks over to her, and smears it on her. He lies next to her and licks every bit of cake from her belly to her breasts. He offers her his cake covered fingers, and she methodically licks each one clean. They kiss, passionately and aggressively. Kara tastes good no matter what, but Aaron commends himself on using the cake. It made tasting her even better. Aaron climbs on top of Kara. He teases her, pushing his dick in and out of her. Every time he enters her, he can feel her pussy throb. It's enough to make him come right then, but he relaxes. Aaron wants —no needs her to enjoy this. He wants her to forget what she saw and focus solely on her pleasure.

He increases his speed. He goes fast and hard for a

few thrusts before he switches to the lotus position and holds her by her ass. Aaron adjusts her in his arms before he continues his stride. Her arms and legs are wrapped around him, clutching onto his body.

"Uhhh. Oh, God. Aaron. Fuck!"

He goes faster. His fingers dig into her ass as he tries to hold on. The sweet scent coming off Kara's sweaty skin isn't making this any easier.

"You like how I fuck this pussy?"

"Shit! Yes. Aaron." Kara cries. Her voice becomes so high-pitched that when she says his name, he can barely hear it.

"You want me to slow down?" Aaron asks.

"No," she moans.

Kara lets go of him and bends down taking his dick in her mouth. She sucks it like it's giving her oxygen. Aaron cradles Kara's head in his hands as he guides her back and forth.

"Ohhh, shit. Baby, goddamn."

Kara slides his dick out of her mouth. "You want me to stop?"

He catches his breath. "No."

"You want me to slow down?"

Aaron looks down at her and growls, "No. Now quit stopping and put that dick back in your mouth."

She deep throats him.

"Baby, I'm gonna come."

Kara takes him out of her mouth. She licks and sucks on his balls while jerking him off. Kara looks up at

Aaron. He stares down at her with dominion and worship. They belong to each other. Kara responds by lying back down on the bed, opening her legs, and offering him what's his. He gets on top of her and gives her what's hers. His strokes are deep and intense. Time feels slower. Before he knows it, he pulls out and comes on her stomach.

They lie in bed with the video playing, both still naked. She jerks Aaron off while he fingers her. They go back and forth between watching the video and kissing. She climbs on top of him, and he pauses the video.

"You want to make another one?"

Kara licks his lips. He licks hers back, then kisses her.

"Yes," she says longingly.

Aaron loves to hear the need in Kara's voice. It drives him crazy. He grabs her ass, then smacks it. "I'll bring the camera back out."

As Aaron sets the camera back up, Kara smirks. "You know, the videos with the girls aren't the only ones I saw."

"What do you mean?"

"Janae, Denise, and I saw the videos of Tone, some other dude, and *you* trying to be rappers. And can I just tell you that I don't appreciate you leaving out such vital information," Kara laughs.

Aaron avoids eye contact. He lets out a defeated sigh. "You sent the videos to yourself, didn't you?"

"Of course, I did!" Kara laughs at his naïve question.

Aaron playfully rolls his eyes. "Great. Now I need to find something equally humiliating to use against you."

"Good luck," Kara sings

Aaron shakes his head. "Honestly, those are more embarrassing than the sex tapes."

Kara laughs even harder. Her face changes color as she tries to catch her breath.

"Please don't tell AJ about them," Aaron pleads.

She takes a few breaths before responding, "I don't know. I was thinking they could be used as a teaching tool for him. If he ever comes to us with some crazy pipe dream for a career, we can always show him yours. That'll scare him straight."

The thought of AJ seeing those clips simultaneously amuses and horrifies Aaron.

"I guess. Jesus, I don't know what the fuck we were thinking."

"You were young and dumb. You all thought money, pussy, and cars were the most important things in life."

"Yeah. That sounds about right. Thank God my mom kicked me out or else I wouldn't have gotten my act together." Aaron gets back into bed. "Enough talking."

He grabs Kara and pulls her on top of him.

She squeals and giggles. The sound makes Aaron's heart soar.

Seventeen

Kara admires herself in the mermaid embroidered lace wedding gown. This is it! This is the one. Denise and Janae try on light peach, spaghetti strap, chiffon bridesmaid gowns with ruffles. Janae even managed to find a pair of glasses that matched the gown.

Evelyn takes pictures on her phone as they admire themselves in the mirror while Sheila enjoys a complimentary glass of champagne provided by the boutique owners.

Kara turns toward Sheila. "Is Pauline coming?"

"I think so."

"You told her three o'clock, right?"

"Yes. I even sent her a reminder this morning."

Kara wonders what could be taking her so long. She missed the bridal shower brunch hosted by Nancy at her house and now she's missing dress shopping. Pauline has been nicer to Kara, in her own way, but Kara can't help but feel like she's still doing most of the heavy lifting.

An hour later, and with Pauline still nowhere in sight, the ladies leave the store with their respective dresses.

Kara is in the bedroom, trying on her dress again and looking at herself in the mirror. She still can't believe she found the perfect dress. And she's so grateful to her mother who paid for it. She hears Aaron enter with AJ in tow. She hurries to take off the dress and greet her family.

"Kara!" Aaron calls out. He sounds annoyed. Kara wonders what possibly could have happened taking AJ to the playground. For the most part, Aaron usually just gets hit on by numerous single moms.

"I'm in the bedroom, but don't come in."

"Why?"

"I'm taking off my wedding dress. I wanted to try it on again."

"But you've already tried it on."

"Yeah, but I liked the way it looks, so I wanted to try it on again."

"Fine. Whatever. Did you invite my mother to the dress fitting?"

Kara puts the dress back on its hanger and slips it back into the garment bag. She quickly puts on some sweat shorts and a USC tee shirt.

This isn't going to be a pleasant conversation, so the

first thing she does when she walks out is give Aaron a kiss. He still looks pissed. Crap.

AJ is on the floor playing with his crayons. He is having them talk and battle each other. Kara smiles at him and gives him kisses, and he giggles. She goes and wraps her arms around Aaron's mid-section. He softens a bit but is still very perturbed.

"You know you fucked up. That's why you're hugging and kissing on me." Aaron looks at her with a disapproving expression.

"Aaron, don't curse in front of AJ."

"Don't change the subject. Why didn't you invite my mother?"

"I did."

"No, Kara, you told Aunt Sheila to invite her."

"I'm sorry, but I forgot. I've been so busy. I need to work overtime to make up for the days I'm going to miss because of the wedding and honeymoon. And we can't afford a wedding planner, so I've been looking at venues, meeting with the reverend, and finally finding my dress..."

"With Janae, Denise, Sheila, and your mom's help. How do you think it made my mom feel to be left out of all that? I'm her only child, and this is going to be her only time to participate in something like this." Aaron takes Kara's face in his hands. "Baby, I asked my mom to be nicer to you and she has been, but you need to meet her halfway."

Kara feels like shit and looks away. Angry Aaron she can handle, but disappointed Aaron? That fucking stings. And he's right. She hasn't been making much of an effort to make Pauline feel included. Kara told herself that the wedding was her and Aaron's day, and they shouldn't have anything or anyone around that would cause any stress. But that was just selfish. She's been enjoying this whole journey, even the stressful parts. Pauline deserves to be part of it. That can't happen unless Kara tells Aaron how she really feels.

She lets out a heavy sigh. "Aaron, the truth is your mom still makes me a little uncomfortable. I'm sorry. I know she's trying, but whenever I drop off AJ, her friendliness feels forced. Even when she hugs me, it feels like she's doing it to make sure I don't say anything to you."

Aaron crosses his arms. "How do you know she doesn't feel the same way about you?"

Ouch. Kara hadn't thought of that. She always saw herself as being kind and polite with Pauline. What if she thinks Kara is just putting on an act? Maybe they both are walking on eggshells to avoid any conflict or get Aaron involved again.

"I guess I don't know. I try hard to be nice and I know she doesn't do warm and fuzzy, but it's hard trying to become close to someone who doesn't seem interested."

"Alright, we're having this out."

"What do you mean?"

"I'm inviting her over to dinner, and we're going to talk about this once and for all."

"Once fa ahh!" AJ shouts.

"That's right, little man," Aaron smiles. AJ giggles and claps his hands. Kara and Aaron clap for him. Kara's claps are genuine, but she can't believe even her own baby is against her.

"Okay," she replies. She can tell Aaron can hear the reservation in her voice.

"Baby, don't worry. This will work," Aaron says confidently.

"If you say so." Kara begins to mentally prepare herself for battle.

They sit at the table and eat a meal of pork chops, scalloped potatoes, and mixed veggies. AJ has chicken fingers and tater tots. He smooshes his tater tots and giggles. He then eats the mashed tots. Kara's grateful she has him to focus on. His presence adds levity to an otherwise awkward evening. She cuts a piece of pork chop and eats it, slowly swallowing. It's a shame this is so uncomfortable because Aaron put his foot in this meal. His cooking has gotten so much better over the years. Pauline wipes her mouth then takes a sip of the sparkling water Kara poured for her. She makes a face that shows she's not a fan. Jesus Christ, this is going to be a long ass night. Aaron looks at Kara, then his mother. He releases an annoyed sigh, unable to take this anymore. Kara wishes that he'd call this whole thing off and they can watch "House of Cards" or something.

"Look, I suggested we do this to get everything out in the open between you two, and now no one's talking," Aaron announces.

So much for a quiet evening of Netflix.

"What's there to get out? Your fiancée obviously doesn't want me around," Pauline says.

"That's not true," Kara argues.

Here we go! Round one, and Pauline's already coming out swinging below the belt. Kara does kind of deserve it, but did she have to go in right away?

"Then why haven't I been invited to a single wedding activity with you and the girls?"

"Because you make me uncomfortable."

"How? I have been nothing but friendly to you since Aaron and I talked."

"That's just it. You're being nice to me because your son asked you to, and that was fine before. After all, I'm the one who asked him to talk to you, but it's been two years. I thought by now you would be nice to me because you liked me."

Kara sees the relationship Aaron has with Evie, and even Denise and Guillermo's mother, Teresa, are close. Kara can't help but feel a little jealous. Yes, she has Evie, but it would be nice if her future mother-in-law showed her some inclination that she mattered to her. Kara doesn't want to deal with a lot of tension whenever she's around Pauline. Honestly, her coldness was easier to deal with than her fake friendliness.

Pauline looks down for a bit. When she looks back up at Kara, she smiles warmly and has tears in her eyes. The sincerity throws Kara off. Pauline's crying. The idea of hurting Kara made her cry.

"I have been taking my frustration and anger out on you, Kara, and I know it's not fair. I'm so sorry, but I can't help it."

"Why are you frustrated?" Aaron asks.

Pauline looks at him with heartache in her eyes.

"I see the man you have become, the man I always knew you were capable of being, and it fills me with pride and sadness. I'm sad, frustrated, and angry that this change came from you being with Kara. I wish some of it had been because of me."

Kara looks at Aaron. He is speechless. They both are. Pauline is jealous of her?

Kara chimes in, "Pauline, that's not at all true. Aaron and I were just talking about how if you hadn't made the tough decision to kick him out, he wouldn't have been forced to grow up and get a more realistic career path." Kara takes her hand. "Yes, I have had an influence on Aaron, too, but it's not comparable to yours. It's just different."

"She's right, ma. Look, I had a lot of issues I was forced to face when I was younger. I had to sort my life out after you kicked me out. I'm not going to lie. It hurt.

It made me avoid real relationships with women. I figured if my own mother could abandon me then…"

Aaron's voice trembles. This must be so hard for him. He's not used to being vulnerable. He clears his throat and wipes his eyes, and just like that, he's back to being Aaron again. Kara wishes he'd stop forcing himself to push down his feelings. But one step at a time. Clearing the air with Pauline is more important.

He kneels in front of Pauline and continues, "I now understand that when you saw me going down a path like Duke's, you did what you thought was best. But I need you to know that even when I was getting in trouble, I was always listening, always taking in everything you taught me. How could you possibly think you've had no impact on my life?"

Tears stream down Pauline's face. "It doesn't happen frequently, but there are times when I think about how much Louella failed Duke, and I didn't want that to be the case with you and me. I wanted to make sure I helped make you a better man, too."

"Of course, you did." Aaron stands up and pulls his mother to him, holding her tightly.

Pauline looks over at Kara, who is holding AJ. "Kara, come here."

Kara walks over. Tears flow from her eyes. This certainly wasn't how she expected this evening to turn out, but she couldn't be happier. Aaron takes AJ from her and backs away. Pauline pulls Kara into a hug.

"I'm so…" Pauline starts.

"I know. I'm sorry, too. From now on you'll be involved in everything, I swear. I didn't mean to hurt you, Pauline. I'm so sorry."

"Story!" AJ pipes up.

Kara and Pauline separate and smile at AJ. Aaron kisses his cheek and laughs. Leave it to the munchkin to break up an emotional moment. And there he goes again, knowing when it's time to do something without knowing the actual time.

"That's right. It's story time." Kara wipes her eyes.

Kara goes to the small bookcase that Aaron built. AJ's is a smaller version of the bookcase in their bedroom. It sits behind the dining room table, up against the wall, and is filled with all kinds of children's books. They needed a place for all the story books Janae kept buying AJ. It even has a little sign above it that says, "AJ's Library."

Kara picks out the "The Brave Little Toaster." She shows AJ the book and he squeals in delight. That sound will always be her favorite. Second only to his laughter. The family heads over to the couch. AJ sits on Aaron's lap while Kara and Pauline sit on either side of him. Kara opens the book and is about to read when she offers the book to Pauline. Pauline smiles and takes it.

"Peanut, grandma's going to read to you tonight, okay?" Kara says.

"Okay, momma," AJ replies snuggling in Aaron's lap.

Pauline brushes her hand along AJ's cheek and gives it a little pinch. She looks up at Aaron.

"You remember when I used to read this to you?"

"Yes. It's one of the few books J didn't get him. I bought it...because of you."

Pauline leans over and kisses Aaron's face. She opens the book and begins to read.

Eighteen

It's the day of the wedding, and all the ladies are in the middle of getting their hair done. Music from Kara's phone blasts the room from the nearby speaker. She's switching it up, playing R&B from the seventies and eighties. "Time Will Reveal" by DeBarge fills the room. Janae sings along.

"J, baby, please stop. You're beautiful, a math genius, and fly as shit, but you can't have everything, and your Black ass cannot sing," Denise says as she curls Birdie's hair.

Everyone laughs. Janae stops laughing long enough to give Denise a sarcastic frown and flip her off. Denise replies by blowing her a kiss. Janae chuckles. Along with the glasses that match her dress, Janae has on a long, straight dark brown ponytail extension. Kara's hair will be in a bun, while all the bridesmaids have ponytails.

Kara chuckles, then takes a sip of her mimosa courtesy of Nancy, who sent over bagels and cocktails to the bridal suite. Unfortunately, Nancy can't be at the wedding. She's catering one in Marina Del Rey. As disappointed as Kara was about that, it didn't compare to how freaked out she was when Regina, her stylist, told her she couldn't do her hair the night before. Regina's son had a fever, and while Kara hoped he would get better, Regina ended up taking him to the emergency room. He's doing well, but he has the flu. Kara doesn't know what she was thinking about getting married during flu season. She factored in every possible bad outcome except for her hair not getting done.

As luck would have it, Richard's sister owns and operates a hair salon on La Brea. She shut down her shop, and her and all her employees are currently at work getting everyone glammed up. Richard's paying for it. He's the best stepdad ever. A twinge of guilt hits Kara. She wonders if her own dad knows about today. Some of his relatives are coming, so he must know. Kara is sure they have their opinions about Stephen not being here. Over the years, a few have shared their thoughts on him and Kara being estranged with Evelyn, but no one has ever said anything to her. Evelyn has obviously moved past all that and has told Kara to contact her father when she's ready. Kara knows she should be over it as well, but she's not. Her dad was Superman to her, and he failed. What's to stop him from failing again? Evelyn is seated next to her; she looks over and takes Kara's hand.

"You nervous, sweetheart?"

"A little. I shouldn't be though. Aaron and I have been together for so long. Why am I scared?"

"Because this is a huge step. The ceremony is a show of commitment. It takes a lot to go through it."

"How nervous were you when you married...*him*?"

"Very. We were eighteen, and even though Stephen and I had known each other for years, it still was nerve-wracking. That's to be expected. Just concentrate on what you and Aaron have, everything else will fall into place."

"But you and...him were once so in sync and...what if me and Aaron...?" Kara's voice shakes. The very idea of losing Aaron terrifies her.

Evelyn stops Shelly from doing her hair and turns to face Kara. She gently asks the stylist doing Kara's hair to give them some space. Evelyn looks her daughter in the eyes with a loving and serious expression.

"That will never happen. You and Aaron are forever. I know it."

"Damn right," Pauline chimes in. She gets up from her chair and walks up behind Kara gently touching her shoulders while looking at her in the mirror.

"My son is crazy about you. You must know that by now."

"I do."

"Then you also must know that he ain't going nowhere, and I know you aren't either."

Pauline hugs Kara from behind, and Kara clutches on to her. "And I'm sure he's just as nervous as you are."

Aaron and Rod are at the barbershop with AJ. Aaron is a nervous wreck but is currently too distracted by his crying child. AJ is getting a haircut, and it's not going well. Kara was the one to take him to his first haircut. Ever since then, he's insisted that she be there. Aaron, of course, goes too, but AJ is adamant that his mom be there. Always.

"Ahhh! No, no. I want Momma," AJ cries.

"Buddy, it's okay. Mommy's getting ready for the big day today," Aaron tells him.

AJ continues to cry. Even louder. He and Kara agreed to not see each other before the ceremony but fuck it. These are desperate times. Aaron calls Kara on Skype while Rod distracts AJ with "Baby First" YouTube videos on Aaron's iPad. Aaron's grateful he remembered to bring it.

She answers with rollers in her hair. "Aaron, what happened to the agreement?' she smiles.

Goddamn, she looks good. Sans makeup and with her hair all rolled up, he's still entranced. He can only imagine how gorgeous she'll look when she's done getting ready.

"Why are you looking at me like that?" Kara giggles.

"Next time I see you, I'm putting another baby in you," Aaron smolders.

Kara blushes. "Aaron, your mom can hear you."

"I stand by what I said."

"Good lord." Pauline can be heard off camera.

Kara laughs. "Is this why you called? To tell me you're going to get me pregnant?

"No, your son was having a complete meltdown. He's fine now that Rod is playing with him but as soon as the barber starts trying to cut his hair…"

Aaron turns the phone to the barber and nods for him to start. He tries to cut AJ's hair again, and even "Baby First" ain't helping. The boy is screaming bloody murder. AJ's tries to push the barber away and hop out the chair. When he successfully gets out the chair, he falls on the floor, cries, and runs away. Rod, Aaron and the barber chase him.

"Aaron," Kara calls out.

Aaron gets back on the call. Rod gets AJ, but he's trying to squirm out of his arms.

"He was crying for you. I thought seeing you would help."

"Okay. Let me talk to him."

Aaron turns the phone so AJ can see his mom.

"AJ. AJ, it's mommy. Please don't cry, my little munchkin."

AJ sees Kara on the phone and reaches out to her. "Momma!"

"It's okay, baby. It's just a haircut. You can do this. I know my munchkin wants to look as nice as his daddy and Uncle Rod, doesn't he?"

AJ has a sweet pout on his face. "Yes."

"Okay, then you're going to have to get a haircut

without me. Can you be my brave little man and do it for mommy?"

"Okay."

"Good boy."

"I want chicken nuggies." AJ looks up at Aaron with his big brown eyes.

Aaron smiles. "Fine, we'll stop at McDonald's and get you a Happy Meal."

AJ smiles. "Yay!"

The little con artist sits still and gets his hair cut. This whole time all he had to do was bribe him. Why the hell didn't Aaron think of that?

Afterward, Aaron, AJ, and Rod arrive at the venue, the Appleby Center. It was named after some rich white lady, Bernice Appleby. She gave money to the city of Carson and has a library named after her right next to city hall. Apparently, Nancy knows the family and got Evelyn and Pauline—who insisted on paying for it—a nice discount. Going half on the wedding and signing over ownership of the house to him and Kara was Pauline's wedding present.

Aaron and Rod head to the groom's dressing room, tuxedos in hand. Aaron shines AJ's shoes while he munches on his chicken nuggets.

Rod hangs up his tux.

"Hey yo, Smoke, why didn't you want a bachelor party, man? The one I threw for my brother was insane. We could have gone to Vegas. It would have been drinks, fine dining, and strippers the whole weekend."

Aaron doesn't look up. "I didn't want to risk it."

"Risk what?"

Aaron lets out a sigh. He's not annoyed by Rod's question, he embarrassed by his past behavior. "When Kara and I first got together, I kind of cheated. I don't need that type of temptation around me."

"You think you would have done something?"

"No. Absolutely not. I haven't since that one time. But why chance it?"

"I feel you."

"How are things with you and Tammi?"

"Okay, I guess."

"You guess? Nigga, you been with her for how long?"

"We been together for a minute."

Aaron stops shining AJ's shoes and looks up at his boy. "Rod, you my cat, right?"

"Right."

"So, I know that you know that I can tell when you bullshitting. You been with Tammi for a couple of years now, man. If you ain't serious about her, you need to cut her loose. Cause at this point, you just wasting her time and yours."

"When did you know Kara was the one?"

"May 13th, 2007. The day I met her."

"See, that's what I want. To meet someone and just vibe immediately."

"You already have."

Rod looks away, deep in thought. "What does it mean though? Like am I gay now?"

"Why would you be gay? Janae's a woman. And even if you were, who fucking cares. If you find somebody and it works, and you're happy, that's all that matters."

Rod smiles. He looks a lot calmer. "When did your Black ass get so insightful?"

"Nigga, I've always been wise. You ain't been paying attention."

Aaron finishes up with AJ's shoes. "Alright, little man, you done eating? Ready to get dressed?"

"Yes, Daddy." Aaron helps AJ get dressed.

Minutes later, Aaron, AJ, and Rod look at themselves in the mirror. Aaron holds AJ up.

"What'chu think, buddy?" Aaron asks. AJ gives a thumbs up and giggles. Aaron kisses him on the cheek before handing him to Rod. "Can you take AJ to my mother and ask Kara to come here?"

"Sure."

"All the ladies should be in the bridal suite."

Rod narrows his eyes. "You're not getting cold feet, are you? Not after all that shit you just said."

Aaron shakes his head. "Naw, nothing like that. I just want to see her."

"You really trying to test your guy's luck, huh?"

"Fuck it. We already saw each other."

"Not dressed you haven't, suppose she's already in her wedding gown."

Aaron thinks it over. "Rod, there are God knows how many women in that suite right now. Do you honestly think they'll be dressed and ready on time?"

"Imma tell Kara you said that."

"Imma tell Janae you're in love with her.'

"Aight, nigga damn. I was just kidding."

The ladies are getting the final touches of their makeup done. Kara still has on a t-shirt and shorts. Her hair and makeup are done, and she feels stunning. Her hair is in a slick back bun, and her makeup has a natural and fresh look that makes her skin glow. There's a knock on the door. Janae answers. It's Rod with AJ in tow. Rod puts AJ down, and he runs to Kara. She lifts him up and kisses his face.

"Look at you with your big boy haircut. You looking sharp, my little munchkin."

AJ giggles and hugs her. Kara notices Janae and Rod talking to each other and grabs Denise so she can come see.

"What? Why did you pull me over here?" Denise asks. Birdie follows her.

Kara nods over at Rod and Janae. Her and Denise watch them like they're watching their favorite soap opera.

AJ sees his cousin and climbs out of Kara's arms. He takes Birdie by the hand and they walk over to Pauline, Evelyn, and Sheila. The three women cuddle the little ones. Kara watches the three grandmothers and thinks about when her and Aaron will be grandparents. Denise nudges her and she turns her attention back to the two lovebirds.

Kara returns her attention to the sweet flirting already in progress. She snickers. Rod looks like he's forgotten why he's there.

"Hi, Rod," Janae says, sounding like a love-struck teenager.

"Hey, Janae," he says, sounding equally as foolish.

They talk about an upcoming "Lord of the Rings" marathon they're having next weekend at his place.

Janae looks over at Kara and Denise. Their goofy asses give her a thumbs up, grinning from ear-to-ear. Janae rolls her eyes and blushes. Rod chuckles.

Denise blurts out. "You two should kiss."

Kara laughs so hard she almost falls over. She looks up and sees the murderous look of embarrassment Janae has and laughs even more.

Janae shouts, "Kare Bear, your fiancée wants to see your trifling ass."

"Did he say why?" Kara asks a last bit of laughter escaping.

"He doesn't have cold feet. He just wants to see you," Rod answers.

"Okay." Kara tells herself that Pauline is right, and Aaron is probably just nervous too.

Aaron is pacing and going over his vows when there's a knock at the door.

"Come in," Aaron says.

Kara enters. Aaron sees her and smiles. She looks beautiful. An irresistible need to touch her overtakes him. He goes up to Kara and kisses her. She kisses him back.

"Wow." She smiles.

"I know. It's going to be a while before we're alone again. I just wanted a few moments with you," he says.

Aaron turns on the stereo in the room to 2000s R&B. "The Only One for Me" by Brian McKnight plays. He and Kara share a slow dance as they stare into each other's eyes. He mouths the words, "I love you." She mouths, "I love you, too." They kiss deeply. Pretty soon, Kara is taking off Aaron's pants, and he's taking off her shorts and t-shirt.

The ceremony begins. Aaron stands at the front of the altar and eagerly waits for Kara's entrance. Birdie walks down the aisle with Sheila. She is sprinkling rose petals.

"Granny, I did it."

"Yes, you did, baby. You're doing so good. Gimme some sugar."

Sheila picks Birdie up and kisses her. They take their

seats. Aaron smiles at her and waves at Birdie. She waves back and leans against Sheila. Next up is AJ as the ring bearer. He drops the pillow holding the rings and runs down the aisle to Aaron before wrapping his arms around Aaron's legs. Everyone laughs. Pauline picks up the pillow and the rings and runs them up to AJ. He realizes what he's done and cries.

"I messed up," AJ weeps.

"It's okay, sweetie," Pauline replies.

"Yeah, buddy, it's okay. Everyone thought it was cute," Aaron assures him.

"Come on, baby; come sit with grandma." Pauline reaches out for AJ.

"I wanna stay with daddy."

"It's okay, ma. I'll hold on to him."

Pauline sits back down while Aaron holds AJ in his arms.

The ceremony continues. Janae and Rod walk down the aisle, arms linked. Rod looks at Janae and gives her a sweet smile. Janae smiles back shyly. Aaron smiles even wider. He really hopes Rod gets over his fear and gets with Janae. They're perfect for each other.

Denise walks down next with Guillermo. Finally, Kara walks down the aisle with Evelyn on one side and Richard on the other. She holds her bouquet in one hand and Evelyn's hand with the other. Aaron sees her and is awestruck. Her gown is...he can't find the words. She somehow managed to look even better than when he last saw her, and that was only an hour ago. When she reaches him, Aaron puts AJ down. The little one stands in between his parents. Evelyn and Richard sit next to Pauline, each one beaming with pride. The preacher addresses family members and guests.

"Aaron and Kara have written their own vows, which they will deliver now. Who wants to go first?"

"I'll go," Kara replies.

Kara looks at Aaron, her eyes filled with love. AJ holds each of his parents' hands and looks up at them.

"Aaron, when I first met you, you reminded me of a king. I saw past your tough exterior and saw a warm, kind, and loving man, and that scared the hell out of me."

Janae, Evelyn and Denise laugh and glance at one another. They know more than anyone what it took to get Kara and Aaron to where they are now.

Kara continues, "I saw you that you were more than just fine—even though you are..."

Aaron smiles. "Thanks, so are you."

Kara giggles then becomes serious. Tears form in her eyes. Aaron forces himself not to cry, but it's hard with the way Kara's looking at him. Like she couldn't be more grateful to have him. "You're my protector, my king, my everything. I couldn't fathom loving someone as much as I love you."

The tears run down Kara's face like a river, and Aaron wipes them away.

"I love you so much, and the past seven years have been the best part of my life."

Aaron tries to talk but is too choked up. He gives up not trying to cry. AJ squeezes his hand.

"It's okay, Daddy."

Aaron smiles down at him, then composes himself. He needs to get these words out. Looking back up at Kara, he lets out a shaky breath. He's overwhelmed by how much he loves her.

"Baby... you know about my past with women—"

"We all do," Pauline interjects.

Really? Now? Laughter can be heard throughout the crowd. It's his own fault, he should've known better than to set his mother up like that.

Aaron responds with playful snark, "Thanks, Ma," he continues, "Anyway, I still can't really explain it, but you captivated me like no other. I had to be near you. I had to make you mine. You said that I reminded you of a benevolent king. Someone who commanded power but who was kind. I remember the first time you told me that, thinking how no woman has ever seen me that way. I never even looked at myself that way. Thank you, Kara for seeing me, for loving me, and for being mine. I love you so much, baby."

Kara pulls Aaron to her and crashes her lips into his. The venue erupts in thunderous applause. Aaron and Kara hold each other with little AJ smooshed in between them, smiling

∼

The wedding party poses for the photographer. Aaron and Kara stand back and watch the bridesmaids and groomsmen pose as they wait their turn. Kara leans her back against Aaron while his arms are draped around her. The photographer asked the wedding party to pose as if they were in love and gaze into each other's eyes. That's an easy ask for Guillermo and Denise. Those two will be walking down the aisle in no time. Aaron watches Rod and Janae. At first, they both look a little gun shy, but the minute they start gazing at one another, it's over. Aaron instinctively looks in Tammi's direction. She came as Rod's plus-one. She's standing by the bar, downing a shot of liquor, staring daggers at Janae. Aaron and Kara decided on an open bar. He hopes they don't regret that decision.

Once the wedding party is done taking pictures, Aaron and Kara go up to take theirs. As Janae walks past Aaron, he takes her hand and grins

"Tammi doesn't look too happy about how chummy you are with Rod. If she starts something, you let me know."

"Smoke, I can handle myself."

"I have no doubt, but you're my sister, so if she starts something, you let me know."

Janae smiles. Aaron kisses her on the cheek.

An hour later, the reception is in full swing. AJ dances with Denise and Birdie. Janae and Sasha go around taking pictures of friends and family. Pauline and

Sheila drink champagne and laugh uproariously. Evelyn chats with Richard, and Rod stops by the table with Terrance and some of the other co-workers. Tammi appears to have left. Thank God.

Aaron and Kara dance slowly as Toni Braxton serenades them. They're floating on air with huge grins on their faces.

Kara pulls him down so her mouth brushes against his ear. "I think you got me pregnant earlier."

Aaron smirks. "I told you I was going to. Besides, AJ and Birdie could use a little partner in crime."

Kara giggles as Aaron squeezes her sides. Their dancing becomes even slower. Time goes by even slower. Soon, they're the only ones in the room, swaying in each other's arms and staring into each other's eyes. Nothing could disrupt this moment; nothing can pull them away from each other. And nothing ever will.

Nineteen

2017

A small, chubby cheeked little angel with four pigtails evenly parted on her small head, runs around the house. She has on a *Sesame Street* t-shirt and a Pull-Up.

"Amaya!" Aaron appears to have his eyes covered with his hands but can clearly see the little one as she runs around.

Amaya giggles and hides behind the couch. Aaron uncovers his eyes and pretends to look for her.

"Amaya, where are you?"

The little brown cherub giggles more loudly. Aaron tries to stifle his laughter. He tries not to give himself away but it's hard not to laugh. AJ and Birdie used to do this, too. Hell, all kids do. How do these silly little people think no one can hear them? Or see them? Amaya's little feet are sticking out behind the couch. When she wiggles them, Aaron almost loses it, again.

"Where did she go?" he says to himself. "She's just too good at hiding."

Amaya is still laughing when the door opens, and five-year-old AJ comes in wearing his soccer gear. He's followed by Pauline. He stomps into the living room, looking upset.

"How did the game go?" Aaron asks.

"We lost," AJ replies as he heads to his room.

"It's just a game, AJ. You gotta learn to let that shit go, man," Aaron calls out. He takes this shit way too seriously for a kid. Aaron has seen AJ get just as annoyed with the referee's calls as the parents. Thankfully, he's never tried to throw anything at anyone, unlike the adults.

"There's no point. I tried giving him a pep talk in the car, and he wasn't hearing it," Pauline says.

"He's competitive as hell. He got it from Kara. I just give him his space and wait for him to calm down."

"Daddy! Look for me," Amaya cries out from behind the couch.

Pauline and Aaron crack up. Aaron mouths, "oops," and Pauline laughs harder.

"I'm sorry, baby girl. Let's have a time-out. Come on out and say hi to Grandma Paulie."

Amaya runs out from behind the couch and hugs Pauline's legs.

"Granny Paulie!"

"Hey, Sweet Pea." Pauline picks her up and kisses all over her sweet little face.

Pauline holds Amaya as she addresses Aaron, "I don't mind picking up the kids, just please, next time, give me a little more notice. My new supervisor isn't as gullible as my old one."

"I know, and I'm sorry. Kara was supposed to get him, and I would have, but I didn't want to take Amaya out for at least another day."

Pauline looks at Amaya, who has a silly grin on her face. "She is looking better."

"Yeah, she's out of the woods. I just wanted to be careful. Keep her home an extra day to be safe."

"How did this happen anyway?"

"I took her to the playground like usual. Next thing we know, all these kids, including her, are puking for two days straight. Patient zero had a fever, but his parents brought him to the park anyway."

Pauline looks appalled. "Stupid-ass parents."

"I know. I found out these are the same people who caused the great hand, foot, and mouth outbreak last year."

"Seriously?"

"Yep."

"You should have gone to their house and punched them in the face. Let them find out why you're called Smoke."

Aaron laughs. God knows he wanted to. Him and

Kara ended up catching that shit, and when they say it hurts more when adults have it, they weren't lying.

"They're white. I would have been arrested or killed."

Pauline puts Amaya down, who promptly grabs ahold of Aaron's leg and hangs on. Pauline goes into the kitchen and opens the fridge. There are bottles of water and cans of flavored sparkling water.

She turns to Aaron. "I swear to God, Kara kills me with this stuff. I come over and every time, this is all y'all have to drink. There's never anything with flavor in this house. My grandbabies are going to be the only Black children in the world that don't know what Kool-Aid tastes like."

Aaron smiles. "Follow me."

He swoops Amaya up and puts her on his shoulders. Pauline follows him to the garage. His workshop and gym have been upgraded, and there's a refrigerator in the corner. He opens it and hands Pauline a mango flavored Snapple.

"That's what I'm talking about." Pauline takes a sip. "How did you manage to sneak this?"

"I told Kara that the garage is my man cave, and I am allowed to have anything I want in my fridge."

"Mmmm-hmmm… she doesn't know, does she?"

"No, she does not, and you bet not tell her!"

Pauline laughs and playfully hits Aaron on the shoulder. He grabs a Snapple fruit punch, and they head back into the living room. He sits Amaya on his lap and gives her a sip of his juice. Pauline sits next to him.

"How long is this gonna keep going, Aaron? The late nights, early mornings, constant emails and phone calls. I feel like it's been ages since I've seen Kara."

"It's going to last until she's made a manager."

Pauline rolls her eyes. "Who knows how long that will take? She's been there over five years."

Aaron has made this exact point to Kara more times than he can count. She needs to move on and work at a place that won't mistreat her.

"I know. I keep telling her she needs to leave. But she thinks that with all the time she put into the company, she should stay. She feels like she owes it to Nancy."

"I only met Nancy a couple of times, but I think even she would agree that the way things are going, Kara is better off somewhere else."

"You're preaching to the choir, Ma. I told her Nancy's daughter and son-in-law are not Nancy. They are not going to look out for her like she did. And those bastards don't have a fucking clue about how to run a business. Everything falls on Kara's shoulders."

Amaya chimes in, "Daddy, you said no-no words."

"I know, baby. Daddy's sorry." Aaron kisses Amaya's little hand.

"I still don't understand why Nancy retired so quickly," Pauline says.

Aaron sighs. "Kara didn't want this going around for Nancy's sake, but she was diagnosed with dementia."

"Oh, my God!" Pauline holds her hand over her mouth in shock.

"Yeah, I know. Before the dementia set in, Nancy promised Kara a manager position. Next thing you know, she gets sick and this daughter who Kara's only heard about in passing swoops in and takes over."

Pauline shakes her head. "She needs to get another job."

"Thank you. Talk to your daughter-in-law, please. Cause she is not listening to me."

Aaron is at the end of his rope. Kara keeps reassuring him that this will all work out for the best. Her need to take care of another parental figure is clouding her judgment, and he doesn't know what else he can say to make her see that.

Later that night, Aaron tucks Amaya in and gives her a kiss. She giggles, her cute little chubby cheeks lifting and looking even more pinchable. Unable to resist, Aaron does just that.

"Goodnight, baby girl."

"Night, Daddy. Momma home?"

"No, not yet, baby."

"She's never here. Are me and AJ bad?"

Aaron's heart breaks. He may not have the words right now, but he's going to say something to Kara tonight. He cannot have his children thinking that they did something to cause all of this.

"No, sweetheart. Mommy just has to work a lot."

Amaya looks sad. "Okay."

Aaron kisses her on her forehead. "It's okay, My-My, mommy will be home more once she gets a better job."

Aaron goes to AJ's room. He lies in his bed halfway asleep. Aaron kisses him on his cheek. AJ opens his eyes and smiles at his dad. Aaron's happy to see his son has calmed down.

"Hi, Daddy."

"Hey, little man."

"Sorry I got mad today."

"It's okay, buddy, but you can't let your losses go to your heart, and you can't let your wins go to your head."

"What does that mean?"

"It means you shouldn't let losing get to you, and you shouldn't let winning make you think you're better than others."

AJ thinks about what his father said. "I guess that makes sense."

Aaron smiles and hugs AJ. He tucks him in, and AJ drifts to sleep.

Kara walks in at 11 p.m. Aaron is sitting at the table with two glasses of scotch. She takes a seat, and he slides her the drink. She takes a sip. Kara looks exhausted, but he has to say something. He's reminded of the time she was pregnant with AJ and insisted they talk about his mom when he came home dead tired from work. Aaron shakes his head at the role reversal.

"You can't keep this up," Aaron says.

"I don't want to have this fight with you, again, Aaron."

"I'm not fighting. I'm telling you that this isn't work-ing. I miss you. Amaya and AJ miss you. AJ stopped asking if you were going to be at his games, and Amaya asked me tonight if she and AJ did something bad. She thinks that's why you're gone all the time."

"Seriously? You're using the kids to make me feel like shit?"

"I'm not using the kids for anything. I'm telling you what happened."

"You don't think I feel guilty leaving in the morning and not knowing what time I'll be home? Aaron, I'm doing this for us. Once I'm a manager..."

Aaron's frustration boils over. "Jesus Christ, Kara. They. Are. Not. Going. To. Make. You. A. Manager."

Aaron knows his words sting. He sees the look of devastation on her face and immediately regrets his anger. He takes a breath to calm down and speaks to her softly.

"Has Gretchen given you any indication that she's going to uphold Nancy's promise to you? Cause if she did and then took it back, you can't take them to court. You have a verbal agreement made by a woman who now has dementia."

Aaron takes Kara's hand. "Baby, you need to find a new job. I love you and I'm sorry, but I can't stand by and watch while your intelligence, drive, and hard work are being taken advantage of."

Kara still looks defeated and sad. "You don't believe in me?"

"No Kara, it's the exact opposite. What I don't believe is that these people deserve you as an employee."

Aaron desperately needs her to understand this

dynamic isn't working, but he'd let his frustration get the better of him and now she's questioning his devotion. He must make it up to her. He needs to make this up to her. Aaron brings her hand to his lips and kisses it. He gets up and brings his face close to hers and kisses her. Taking her by the hand, he leads her to their bedroom. He lays her down on their bed and continues to kiss her. He knows she's exhausted and stressed. Talking about this can wait for another time, now he needs her to relax and let him take care of her.

"I'm sorry. I didn't mean to upset you, and you know, maybe I'm wrong. But something needs to give. They can't keep stringing you along."

Aaron can feel the tension in Kara's shoulders ease. She kisses him back.

"I know, and I know I sound like I'm making excuses for Gretchen and Jonathan, but they're new to this, and as soon as they get the hang of it, I'll get back to having normal work hours. They have told me this. And they know about Nancy's promise to me, and they have told me they plan to uphold it."

Aaron doesn't buy that bullshit for a second, but he doesn't want to start another fight. He just kisses Kara some more. Soon he's removing their clothes.

"I feel like we haven't done this in ages," Aaron says. His voice filled with anticipation. It's been torture not having Kara in his arms all this time and jerking off in the shower isn't cutting it.

Aaron lays on top of Kara. She wraps her arms

around him. She thrusts her hips forward, letting her wet pussy rub against his dick. That's Kara's not-so-subtle way of telling him she's ready. He loves it when she does that. Aaron teases her opening, then pushes himself inside her. Kara catches her breath and lets out a gasp. He fully intends to give his wife everything she's been missing, thanks to that fucking job.

That's right. Lay back and enjoy, baby, Aaron thinks.

His thrusts become more urgent, as do Kara's cries. Aaron pushes himself deeper, ensuring that he hits that spot. This causes Kara to dig her nails into his back.

"Maybe it's because it's been so long since we've done this, but this is amazing," Aaron says.

Kara giggles. God, he has missed her laughter so much. Even a small giggle is enough to make his dick throb inside of her. Her pussy responds with some throbs of her own. They kiss deeply. Aaron kisses her lips, chin, cheeks, and neck. He's sucking on her neck when Kara's phone rings.

"Ignore it," Aaron says.

It stops. Moments later, it's ringing again. Kara looks at her phone. Aaron turns her face toward him and kisses her. Her phone keeps ringing, and Kara breaks away from the kiss. Aaron narrows his eyes, frowning.

"I'm sorry," Kara says.

She answers the phone. "This is Kara... Hi, Gretchen... Yes. Okay, I'll send you a link for a Zoom meeting, and I'll go through it with you, again." Kara gets out of bed and puts on a robe, heading to the living room.

She looks back at Aaron. Her eyes are apologetic, but the look on his face tells her he's not interested. He turns his back to her. How many times has he been in this position? *Fuck!* He was just here less than two hours ago. Waiting for Kara to come back to him while she helps that lazy bitch and her piece of shit husband. It's not lost on Aaron—and it can't be lost on Kara—that these two horribly unqualified white people are basically making her do their jobs as well as hers. Her problem is that she thinks it's going to pay off, but based on how they're treating her, Aaron thinks Kara's hanging on to a pipe dream. He picks up his phone to see the time. It's 12:30 a.m. What the fuck could they need her to do this late? Aaron puts his phone down and rolls over. He closes his eyes but knows that sleep won't come.

The next morning, Aaron gets a large cooler ready with ice, orange slices, and water bottles for AJ's soccer practice. Toast pops out of the toaster. He heads to the kitchen to put the finishing touches on the kids' breakfast, eggs, bacon, and toast. Kara comes out of the bedroom. She looks even more exhausted than when she first came home. Aaron puts the plates of breakfast on the table.

"Kids. Breakfast is ready," Aaron calls out.

Kara goes to the kitchen and pours herself a cup of coffee. She takes a seat at the table.

"You weren't in bed when I got back to our room," Kara says.

"I slept on AJ's floor."

"Aaron, I..."

"Nope, whatever it is, I don't want to hear it. It was after midnight. We were having sex, and you jumped right out of my arms to go running to them. There's no explaining that, Kara."

Aaron busies himself by making sure the kids' backpacks have everything they need. He has to drop Amaya off at daycare, then he has to drop AJ at off school before he heads to work. He has way too many things to juggle and remember, and frankly, he doesn't feel like talking about this anymore. He and Kara can get into this later.

"Jesus Christ, is it too much to ask you for a little support?" Kara snaps.

Oh, hell no! They're getting into this now. Aaron can't believe his ears.

"*Support?* Woman, what the fuck do you think I've been doing? What do you think I *am* doing? Making every meal for our kids, getting AJ to school and practice, getting Amaya to daycare. Begging my mom, your mom, Denise, Richard, Rod, or Janae to pick up the kids because, once again, you can't. Cleaning the house every week and working full time myself. How can you even fucking say that shit to me?"

Kara's near tears. "You could be more patient. I'm stressed enough as it is. I don't need to come home and be made to feel like I'm a terrible wife and mother."

"I never said you were terrible. But you are absent. Hell, even when you're here, you seem like you don't want to be."

"That is not fair."

"Neither is how you've been treating me and our kids like we're a burden or an afterthought."

"I am trying."

"Well, I don't know what to tell you, Kara, cause you're failing."

"Fuck you, Aaron!" Kara shouts.

"Fuck me?" Aaron yells.

Aaron sees the look of alarm on Kara's face. He turns around and sees AJ and Amaya. Shit! AJ holds his little sister's hand as she weeps.

Tears stream down AJ's face. "Stop fighting. Amaya and I won't bother you anymore, and I'll quit soccer. Just stop fighting."

Kara and Aaron rush over to them and give them hugs and kisses. The kids wiggle away from Kara in favor of hugging their father. Aaron notices the heartbroken look on Kara's face. He wanted her to realize their babies are hurting, but not like this. Before he can say anything to her, she rushes to the bedroom and closes the door. Aaron hugs his children as he hears his wife weeping in the next room. Fuck!

Twenty

Kara enters her cubicle and sits behind her desk. She picks up a picture of her, Aaron, Amaya, and AJ from last year when they went to the county fair. It seems like ages ago. They were happy, complete. Now everything is a fractured mess. Gretchen comes into the office, and Kara gets up and heads in her direction.

"Gretchen..."

Gretchen turns around. "Hey, Kara. Thanks again for your help. We needed to get those figures to the CPA. I forget his name..."

"Miguel."

"Right, Miguel. Anyway, he needed those figures this morning and I just plain forgot. With everything we have going on for the Baxter sweet-sixteen, my head has been all over the place. Thanks again."

Gretchen giggles and heads into her office without a care in the world. Must be nice.

Kara follows closely behind her. "You're welcome. Gretchen, can we talk?"

"Sure. Have a seat."

Kara closes her office door. Even though she knows they're alone, Kara would rather be safe than sorry. Gretchen's husband, Jonathan, has the tendency to steamroll her out of every decision. He's even more clueless than she is. Kara sits down and thinks. She's silent for a beat. This may be her last day working here. She's fully prepared to give Gretchen an ultimatum. Either make her a manager or she walks.

"Something has come up within my family, and I'm going to need more time at home, so, I'm inquiring about the manager position."

Gretchen quickly looks away from Kara, as if she wants to avoid this subject.

"Umm..." Gretchen sighs. "There's no easy way to say this, Kara. The agreement you had with my mother is no longer valid."

"I'm... I'm sorry?" Kara stumbles on her words.

Aaron was right. She yelled at him, cursed at him. She did it with her children within ear shot, and he was right all along.

"Jonathan and I have been talking, and we decided to do kind of a rebrand of the company. We'll stay on as owners, and we'll have you stay but with a different title and a two percent raise. You'd be our business associate."

Kara wants to knock this bitch's teeth out. "That's my position now."

"Is it? Oh, well, in that case, we'll have to come up with a new title. We can talk it over with our new manager. You'll be reporting to her. You'll love her; she's an old college friend of mine. Her name is Charlotte Kim."

Kara is fuming but knows how to hide it well. Of course, this was Johnathan's idea. Ever since he and Gretchen took over, he's been threatened by Kara and her closeness to Nancy. It was Kara who visited her at the convalescent home, and it was Kara who has kept everything afloat.

"So not only are you going against the agreement your mother made with me and that you said you would uphold, but you're giving the job I was promised to someone else?"

Gretchen shifts uncomfortably in her seat. "I'm sorry, Kara. But you're just too valuable to us in your current position to promote you. I hope you understand."

Kara takes some deep breaths. "My kids barely see me, and..." She fights back tears. "My husband and I are constantly fighting. And all this time, I told myself that once I got promoted, I would finally be able to fix everything."

Gretchen clearly doesn't know what to say. She looks terrified of what Kara might do next.

Kara dabs her eyes and looks up at Gretchen. "I'm

going to take a personal day."

Gretchen looks relieved. "Good idea. As a matter of fact, take tomorrow off, too. You'll come back on Monday refreshed and ready to get back to work. And honestly, Kara, I think you'll realize that this is the right decision."

She goes back to her desk, picks up her purse and leaves. She plans to hit up Trader Joe's and get some ice cream and a few bottles of "Two Buck Chuck."

Kara is sitting on the couch, guzzling a glass of wine when the front door opens. It's Aaron. He's surprised to see her. It's obvious she's been crying. There's a thick tension in the air. When the kids rejected her, Aaron didn't even come in to check on her. That hurt. While Kara does feel terrible for the burden her absence has put on Aaron's shoulder, she's still pretty upset with him. Even so, she owes him an apology for everything.

"What are you doing home?" he asks.

"I took a personal day. Why are you home?"

"I threw some oxtails in the Crock-Pot for dinner. I need to adjust the temperature, then I'm heading back to work."

Aaron stands staring at her as if he hopes she'll want to talk. She needs to do this. She stands up and approaches him. Aaron's calm, but he's still pissed. She can tell.

"I'm sorry for everything, Aaron. I am. Especially how I spoke to you."

Aaron facial expression doesn't change. He simply

goes into the kitchen and lowers the temperature on the Crock-Pot. He comes back into the living room and takes a seat on the couch.

"What happened?" he asks. His voice is even.

Kara sits beside him. "You were right. They never wanted to give me a promotion. They did, however, offer me a bullshit raise and a bullshit non-promotion with the same title and a bullshit new boss. Some chick who went to college with Gretchen. I looked her up, and she is about as qualified as they are. Go ahead and say it."

"Say what?"

"I told you so."

"Is that what you think this was about? Me one upping you?"

"No, I...look...I'm trying to say you were right and I should have listened to you, and I'm sorry."

"Well, I'm sorry, baby, but I don't forgive you."

Kara can't believe her ears. Shit! She fucked this up so badly. What if this can't be fixed? Fresh warm tears fall so quickly, her vision is slightly blurred. Her heart is thumping in her chest. Blood rushes to her ears. She feels light-headed.

"Aaron, please. I love you."

"I love you, too, Kara. I love you more than anything in this world except AJ and Amaya. But I have been telling you for months that those people were going to fuck you over and you refused to listen. They finally tell you themselves, and suddenly I'm right? It's going to take more than just an 'I'm sorry' to fix this, my love."

"But, I…"

"No, baby. You need to listen. Kara, for the past few months I have needed you. I was drowning and you left me to fend for myself. And I think finally figured out why. All this overextending yourself, trying to keep the catering business afloat, this is about your dad. You're doing this to ease your conscience about Stephen. You saw a lot of yourself in Gretchen. She stopped talking to her mother just like you stopped talking to your father. Nancy's a wonderful person, so in your mind, Gretchen had to be the bad guy. If that's the case, then what does that say about you? To his family, Stephen is the amazing dad, and you're the ungrateful daughter from his first marriage. That's why you worked overtime to take care of Nancy, so you could keep telling yourself that you're nothing like her daughter."

Kara stares at Aaron with a pained expression on her face. Kara's not stupid, she knew the promotion wasn't likely to happen, but something kept making her hold on. She told herself it was because she owed it to Nancy, and to some extent that was true, but Nancy would have wanted what was best for her and working for Gretchen and Johnathan wasn't it.

Aaron continues, "Your dad didn't abandon you. I know you like to tell yourself that. But it just isn't true. That man has been trying like hell to get you to talk to him for ten years. You feel guilty for shutting him out, so you're using this mess with Nancy and them to distract yourself from that."

Kara closes her eyes. She's gone back and forth about contacting her dad. Her mother is in a much better place, and she knows it's not healthy to hang out to her anger but it's so hard for her to let go.

"You need to rectify all this shit with your dad, Kara. Or it's only going to make things worse. You need to forgive him and move on."

Aaron heads for the door. Say something! Don't let him leave, not like this. By the time he gets home, the kids will be with him, and she won't be able to talk to him. Kara gets up and grabs his arm.

"Aaron, please don't leave."

Aaron turns around. His expression is softer, but he's obviously done talking. He simply kisses her on the forehead.

"I told you when we got married that I wanted to be near you. I still do. That hasn't changed. I'm just tired from carrying this load by myself."

Aaron walks out the door, and Kara weeps.

aron hears Kara weeping, and he wants more than anything to turn around and tell her that he loves her, he forgives her and he's sorry to

have hurt her, but he can't. He needs her to understand that this is bigger than an apology. Kara needs to take the steps to make this right. Until then, it will just be something else she'll use to ease her guilt. Something else will nearly break them apart, and Aaron is damn sure his family will not go through this again.

Twenty-One

It's been three hours since Aaron left. Kara has forced herself to drink three cups of coffee, take a shower, and eat a sandwich in lieu of ice cream. She sits at the dining room table with her laptop and sends out her resume to catering companies in the area. She sent Gretchen an email quitting her job and hasn't heard back. Kara taking the day off has no doubt left them busy.

Kara decides that she's also going to email her dad. It'll be hard, but it's necessary. She needs to get that monkey off her back for good. But not today, she's too wound up and emotional.

Janae walks in with a sleeping Amaya. Kara gets up and takes Amaya and lays her down on her bed. She kisses the sleeping child on her forehead and goes back to the living room, closing Amaya's bedroom door. Kara comes out and hugs Janae. Her brown eyes sparkle behind the royal blue-rimmed glasses that match her denim jumper, and of course, she has on blue four-inch stilettos. Her box braids cascade over her shoulder. Seeing Janae makes Kara realize how much she misses her.

"Kare Bear, I haven't seen you in forever."

"I know, girl. Did Aaron tell you everything?"

"Yes, he did, including the talk you had this afternoon and the big fight you had this morning. In front of the babies, Kara. You guys should know better than to act like that in front of my godchildren."

"I know, but I'm trying to fix the mess I made."

"Good." Janae takes a seat on the couch. "So, are you going to quit right away? Or wait until you get a new job?"

"I already quit; I sent Gretchen an email after Aaron went back to work. I can't keep letting my bullshit affect my family. I've been applying for jobs, and I've decided to reach out to my dad."

"Kara, that's amazing."

"Thanks, I just hope I don't regret it."

"You won't. I haven't regretted talking to my mom."

"You mean our mom?"

"No, I mean my mom."

Kara looks at Janae like she's speaking Martian. "Wait, what?"

"I was talking to Momma Evie a while back. It was during one of our monthly movie days. We went to go see 'Claudine' at the New Bev. We talked about how things have been going so well with me. Between the new job and Rod, things have been great, but something felt like it was missing, and as always, that insightful mother of ours figured it out. She found my biological mom on Twitter, and we've been talking. Turns out, my dad passed away five years ago, and she's been feeling a tremendous amount of guilt for never defending me. She tried finding me, but she never knew my current name. And before you say anything, only Momma Evie and Rod knew I had been talking to her. I didn't want to say anything just in case it ended up being a fluke. But she and I have been talking for almost three months."

Kara is speechless. Janae had always vowed never to speak to her either of her parents again. Shit, it was one of the things that she and Kara bonded over. Kara takes a good look at her sister, and smiles. Janae smiles back. She looks calm and centered. Kara couldn't be happier for her.

Janae and Rod started dating not long after Kara and Aaron's wedding. Both took things slow, having ended their respective relationships not long before, but it didn't take long for them to realize what Aaron and Kara knew all along, they were made for each other. Not long after, one of Evelyn's friends from the divorced women's group was looking for a new accountant for her business and contacted Evelyn asking about Janae. This job paid better and offered better insurance. She's been there for a year.

"Hearing you say that makes me hopeful about me and my dad," Kara says.

"He's been trying to reconnect with you for a while. I'm sure it will go great."

"Thanks, J."

"You're welcome, Kare Bear. Where have you been applying to?"

"Shit, everywhere."

"Let's hope you hear something soon."

"From your lips to God's ears."

Kara notices she has a new email. Damn. God must love Janae because he answered that prayer fast.

She reads Janae the email. "Check this out. 'Dear Ms. Tompkins, we received your resume and cover letter and were very impressed by your experience. We would love for you to come in and meet with the owners for an interview. How is Monday at 1 p.m.?'"

Janae gets up and hugs her. "Oh my God! You just started sending out resumes, and now look. What company is it for?"

"Hinton Southern Eats. They're a Black-owned catering company based in LA. Their offices are in Ladera Heights."

"That sounds great, sweetie," Janae beams.

"You staying for dinner?"

"Hell, yes! Those oxtails smell good. You think it would be okay if we snuck a taste?"

"I don't see why it wouldn't."

"I wanna taste," Amaya says, rubbing her eyes. She notices Kara and wakes right up.

"Mommy!" She runs up to Kara with a huge smile on her face. Kara swoops her up and hugs her tightly.

"Oh, my sweet little sugar plum." Kara smothers her in kisses.

Amaya smiles and snuggles up to her mother. Kara holds on to her baby for dear life. She can never be away from her children for that long everyday ever again.

Janae brings them a plate, and they all eat from it.

A couple of hours later, Kara, Janae, and Amaya chill on the couch and watch PBS Kids. "There's no way I'd live on Birdwell Island," Janae says.

"Why not?" Kara asks.

"Are you kidding? As big as Clifford's ass is, think about how big his shit must be."

"Aunnie J, you said no-no word," Amaya says.

"You hush up, sweet baby," Janae replies, tickling Amaya. "Besides," she continues, "what happens when Clifford gets fleas? Emily Elizabeth is just a kid. There's no way she's cleaning all that poop and getting rid of those fleas by herself. It becomes a whole town effort. There's just no way."

Kara gives it some thought. "Good point. I think I'd live in Elwood City."

"I don't know; that seems too expensive."

"Yeah, if you live in Muffy's neighborhood. But Arthur and Buster's neighborhood seems reasonable."

"For you and Smoke, maybe."

"Okay, where would you live?"

"Do you even have to ask? Sesame Street. I'd get me a

job at Hooper's and rent an apartment in the building Bert and Ernie live in."

"Another upside to Sesame Street is that there's plenty of humans to interact with, so you wouldn't be stuck talking to Muppets all day."

"True." Janae smiles.

Aaron and AJ come home. Janae reaches out for a hug from AJ. He runs over and gives his Auntie Janae a big hug.

"Daddy!" Amaya runs up to Aaron. He picks her up and gives her lots of hugs and kisses. After he puts her down and she runs up to hug AJ, soon they're having a hugging competition to see who can hug the other hardest. Amaya wins.

"Hi," Kara says softly.

She's nervous not knowing where Aaron's head is. Yes, he said he'll always want her near him, but who knows how he feels now. What if he's still upset with her?

"Hi," Aaron replies, not giving anything away.

Janae interjects, "Kids, who wants to go to Target with Auntie J? We'll go down the toy aisle, and you each can get one thing."

"Yay!" AJ shouts.

"Toys," Amaya squeals.

Janae takes each child by the hand. She turns to Kara who mouths, "thank you." Janae winks at her and leaves with the kids.

"I'm guessing that obvious bribe was a way to get us

alone so we can talk," Aaron says as he takes a seat next to Kara.

"Yeah, it was."

Unable to figure out how to start, Kara tries humor, "Before you came home, Janae and I were discussing prime real estate on children's shows."

Aaron looks confused. "Okay."

"Do you think we could afford to live in Elwood City?"

It's obvious Aaron's not sure where this is going—Kara's not even sure where she's going with this—but he plays along.

"Maybe, if we lived in Arthur's neighborhood, but not Muffy's."

"That's what I said."

Aaron smiles, and Kara counts it as a win.

"I am sorry, Aaron. I promise I'll do better by you and the kids. I mean it."

"That's all I've been asking for, baby." Aaron brushes his hand along her cheek.

Kara's let out a breath she'd been holding since Aaron came home. Knowing that he's still hers and that they will get through this... holy hell, is she relieved. Aaron pulls her to him and kisses her deeply. Kara rests her head on his shoulder.

"I'm not going to do it today, but I decided to reach out to my dad."

"Okay. Let me know what you need from me."

"I will." Kara smiles at Aaron. She's bursting to tell

him the other news "I sent Gretchen an email quitting my job, and I already have a job interview lined up on Monday."

"Baby, that's great!"

Aaron looks so happy and excited for her. They haven't been this relaxed around each other in so long. He pulls her onto his lap.

"Tell me more about the job," he responds.

"It's a Black-owned company, based in Ladera Heights, and they're looking for a manager."

"That's what's up. It's a good thing I made a special dinner for us. We can celebrate."

"Me, Janae, and Amaya did help ourselves to some earlier. But we left enough for dinner. Speaking of which, I should text Janae and tell her to bring the kids back."

Kara reaches for her phone when Aaron places his hand on top of hers. Kara looks at him and knows that the kids are going to have pizza with Auntie J for dinner. Aaron scoops her up in his arms, stands up, and carries her into the bedroom.

Minutes later, Kara and Aaron lie in bed naked. She's on top of him. He rubs his hands over her body while she traces her fingers over his. Nothing is going to disrupt them this time. Kara felt awful leaving Aaron that night. His touch, his scent, his dick, his body. It's all that she craves, and the fact that she allowed herself to be denied for a stupid ass spreadsheet instruction makes her determined to make up for it. She kisses Aaron longingly. Like she hasn't tasted him in years.

"I am so sorry, Aaron.

"I know you are, baby, and I forgive you. You don't need to keep apologizing. We're going to be okay."

Kara kisses this wonderful man some more. "I know we are."

Aaron responds with a huge grin on his face. "Damn right. Now tell me how you want me to please you."

"I want three things. For you to suck on my titties. I want you to eat my pussy. God, I'm throbbing just thinking about it..."

"...I know. I can feel you."

"I've missed that. I've missed feeling how my body reacts to yours."

"Me, too. What's the last thing you want me to do?" Aaron smirks.

Kara giggles and kisses him, missing the feel of his lips on hers even after only a couple of seconds. "...and I want you to fuck me like you just got out of prison."

"That I can do."

Kara writhes in pleasure as he gets to work. Fuck! She loves this man. He kisses her down her chest and belly. He licks her inner thighs, then rubs his lips over the lips of her pussy, gently nipping at them. This feels perfect. He feels perfect. Aaron licks her folds and sticks his tongue in and out of her. Kara pushes his head in.

"Suck on my clit, Aaron."

"Whatever you want, baby."

He sucks her clit, then flicks his tongue over it, driving her crazy.

"Shit, shit. I'm about to come."

Aaron dives in deeper and alternates between sucking and licking. Kara comes.

"Fuck, Aaron!" Aaron's eyes meet hers as he brings her to another climax. "Goddamn!" Kara's legs shake.

A wicked grin is spread across his face. "You ready for more, baby?"

Kara nods enthusiastically. He climbs back on top of her and slowly, achingly pushes his dick inside her.

"Fuck, that almost made me come," Aaron exhales. Kara wraps her legs around him and giggles. "Oh shit, Kara! Stop clenching."

Kara teases, biting her lip, "You love it."

Aaron growls, then laughs, "You gone get it now."

True to his word, Aaron fucks the living daylights out of her. When they're done, they lie on the bed, sweaty and smiling in each other's arms.

"That was amazing," Kara says.

"Yes, it was," Aaron replies.

Kara's phone rings. They know who it is. She lets it ring. The voicemail icon pops up. They both look at each other and smile. Kara picks up her phone and puts it on speaker.

"Hello, Kara. It's Gretchen. I got your email, and I'm sorry you feel like *your talents weren't being utilized.* I believe that's how you put it..." Gretchen sighs, "Look, there's a certain protocol that must be adhered to, and quitting out of nowhere is incredibly unprofessional. We expect you in the office on Monday, where we will discuss the matter further. Goodnight."

Bitch, what? Kara looks at Aaron. He looks just as pissed as she is.

"Do what you need to. Put an end to this shit for good," he says.

Kara calls Gretchen back. Aaron smirks at her. He knows this won't end well for Gretchen.

Gretchen picks up after the third ring.

"Hello, Kara, I'm assuming..."

"Let me stop you right there because I don't plan on staying on the phone that long. The only thing unprofessional was how you and your dumbass husband claimed your mother's business and are running it into the ground. And for the record, I *adhered to proper protocol...*" Kara mocks Gretchen's tone. Aaron burst out laughing. Kara shushes him and continues. "We live in the state of California, which is an at-will state. Which means..."

"I know what it means," Gretchen says sharply.

"Then you should know I am no longer an employee, so don't fucking call me anymore." Kara hangs up. That felt amazing. She pulls Aaron on top of her and kisses him.

Twenty-Two

I t's 12:50 p.m. on Monday. Kara waits in the office lobby of Hinton Southern Eats. She goes over her talking points and checks her hair in her compact. She feels confident but is still a little nervous. She incinerated the bridge provided to her by her only employer, but in an interesting twist, this didn't affect Kara's hiring ability. Kara found out from friends who also work in the catering business that word spread about her leaving. Not only that, but Gretchen has been bad-mouthing her to anyone that will listen. Unfortunately for Gretchen, Kara's stellar reputation and closeness to Nancy—who is loved by all—made Gretchen's complaints a moot point.

Kara's only been gone literally a couple of days, and things are already falling apart for Gretchen and Johnathan. Just as Kara suspected, they quickly became overwhelmed without Kara to fix everything, and

Gretchen's little college friend has been no help. Clients have been canceling their service. And because Nancy was always on point, she offered full refunds for dissatisfaction. Up until Gretchen and Johnathan took over, no one had ever requested one. This has to be a record for a business going under so quickly. Kara does feel bad that everything Nancy worked so hard for is going up in smoke.

"Ms. Tompkins?"

Kara looks up and sees a light-skinned Black woman with freckles who looks a couple years older than her.

"We'll see you now," she says.

Kara approaches her and offers her hand.

"Hello, so nice to meet you."

"You as well. Thank you for coming. I'm Michelle Barber-Hinton, co-owner and CEO of Hinton Southern Eats. Welcome to our little operation."

Kara smiles. This place already feels like home.

"Follow me," Michelle says. She follows Michelle and silently prays this is the one.

Kara heads to the grocery store after the interview. She buys steaks, some veggies, pasta, and a few other items. After she comes home and straightens the house, she fixes dinner. She puts on the "Boomerang" soundtrack and prepares the food as Toni Braxton and Babyface serenade her.

After she puts a marinade on the steaks, she sticks them in the fridge and proceeds to chop the bell peppers, onions, and broccoli. Next, she boils the pasta and tosses it into the skillet with the veggies. She puts the pasta aside and cleans up everything behind her.

Kara goes to the backyard and dances her way to the grill, listening to Janet sing about "The Pleasure Principle." She cleans it off and turns it on. She gets the steaks out of the fridge and puts them on the grill. Aaron, AJ, and Amaya come home and find the house clean and dinner ready. Kara places the steaks on the table along with the veggie pasta. Aaron helps the kids take a seat at the table and goes to Kara and kisses her.

He notices the steaks. "Kara, did you touch my grill?"

"It's our grill."

"Naw, baby, it's mine. You see, the grill is a part of the man cave."

"Whatever. Does this mean you don't want a steak?"

"I didn't say all that."

Aaron takes a seat and grabs some food. Kara sits next to Amaya and makes her a plate. She cuts up her meat for her as Aaron does the same for AJ. When she's done, Kara selects her own food. They all happily eat. Kara looks at her family. This is something else she's truly missed.

"Mommy, this is good," AJ says.

"Thank you, baby. The secret is the honey mustard marinade."

"You stole that recipe from me," Aaron says.

"And you stole it from Sheila."

Aaron and Kara exchange amused, flirtatious glances.

"Are you two going to kiss?" AJ asks, looking disgusted.

"Hush," Aaron and Kara say at the same time.

When they're done eating, Aaron clears the table. Kara heads to the kitchen and brings back a cake she got from the bakery. The kids smile widely and clap, bouncing in their chairs in excitement. Kara cuts two small pieces for them and two bigger pieces for her and Aaron.

"Dessert? We only have dessert on special occasions," Aaron says.

"I wanted to celebrate."

"The interview went that well?"

"They offered me the position."

"Congratulations, baby!"

Aaron picks Kara up and twirls her around.

"Ahhh!" Kara screams out a laugh. She catches her breath and continues. "Thank you, but I did tell them that I needed to think it over. I wanted to talk to you first."

Aaron puts her down. "About what?"

"It involves a pay cut."

"How big?"

"About ten grand less than what I was making."

"That's a pretty big cut."

"I know, but I'll finally be a manager, Aaron. I'll have an assistant, and I won't need to go to events unless I choose to. They have an associate and supervisor who will oversee that. And this company has only been around for twelve years. Nancy's has been around for thirty. I have made so many connections from working with Nancy that I can use them to help build this company into something bigger. I even suggested that they purchase Nancy's business from the two morons, that way it will be saved, and Hinton can build up their clientele. They're good people with potential, and I could help."

The fire in Kara's belly is lit up. Her passion for Hinton is evident by the sweet smile Aaron gives her.

"I guess I could take on a few more freelance clients to even us out."

"You could. And I did the math, and you'd only have to take on a few of extra repairs jobs each month."

"Alright, if this is what you want, take it."

Kara gives him a big kiss on the lips.

"Ew!" AJ groans.

"Quiet," Kara and Aaron chastise their son.

Five months later, Kara is in her office going over HSE's calendar of events when her phone buzzes. It's AJ's school. She answers right away.

"This is Kara Tompkins."

"Hello, Ms. Tompkins, it's Ms. Orozco. You and I haven't had the pleasure of meeting. I did meet your husband at the parent/teacher meet and greet at the beginning of the term."

"Of course. Is everything okay?"

"Yes, AJ is fine. We just had a little mishap in class today, and I was hoping you and Mr. Tompkins could come in and speak with me as soon as possible."

"Certainly, I get off work at four. I can be there at 4:30."

"Great. I will give your husband a call."

"That's okay. I'll let Aaron know."

"Great. I'll see you both at 4:30."

Kara sends a text to Aaron.

AJ's teacher called. We need to go see her today at 4:30. I'll have my mom pick the kids up.

Aaron replies.

Did she say what happened?

Kara replies.

All she said was that AJ was okay but there was a mishap.

There's a pause before Aaron responds.

Mishap? What the fuck does that even mean?

Kara chuckles at his response.

*Who knows? I bet you were the same age when you
started getting into trouble at school.*

She smiles in anticipation of whatever smart-ass
comment Aaron is going to make. She isn't disappointed.

*I was younger and it wasn't at school, it was at
church.*

Kara parks the minivan and sees Aaron pull up in his
work truck. She gets out and joins him. They join hands
and walk down the hallway of the school.

"You think he got into a fight?" Kara asks.

"Naw, when you get into a fight, they usually call the
parents right after it happens."

They knock on the classroom door. Ms. Orozco
answers.

"Hello, Mr. Tompkins. And so nice to finally meet
you, Ms. Tompkins."

"Nice to meet you as well, Ms. Orozco." Kara shakes
her hand.

"Please, come in."

There are two adult-sized seats set up in front of Ms.
Orozco's desk. The room looks like your average kinder-
garten classroom. There are small mats laid out in a
circular formation on a large rug with numbers and
letters on it. There are toys, games, and art supplies boxed
up in large storage bins. Drawings by the kids decorate
the whole classroom.

There's another woman in the room, and she looks to be about eight months pregnant. She is sitting next to Ms. Orozco's desk. Kara and Aaron each take a seat in the chairs in front of Ms. Orozco's desk.

"Mr. Tompkins, you remember our class aide, Mrs. Fortney?"

"Yes, of course. Nice seeing you again."

"You, too, Mr. Tompkins."

"And Ms. Tompkins, Mrs. Fortney has been the aide for this class for about three years now. She's going on maternity leave in a week."

"Congratulations."

"Thank you."

"I asked Mrs. Fortney to be present, seeing as how it's her current condition that prompted the incident involving AJ."

Aaron and Kara look confused. What could this woman's pregnancy possibly have to do with AJ?

"Allow me to explain," Ms. Orozco says. "This afternoon, I told the class that Mrs. Fortney would be going away for a few months but that she'd be back next year when they're all in first grade. I told them that they could come back to visit us. This prompted a young lady in our class to ask where Mrs. Fortney was going. I firmly believe that it's the parent's responsibility to have the birds and the bees talk with their kids, so I told her and the class that the stork was bringing Mrs. Fortney a baby."

Kara begins to see where this is going. She and Aaron

have never been the type of parents who bullshit their kids, so when AJ asked where babies came from last year, they sat him down and told him. They also explained what homosexuality meant in addition to discussing the different gender identities with him. As soon as they were done, AJ ran off to play with his Transformers, and that was that. Or so they thought.

Ms. Orozco continues, "AJ then raised his hand, and when I called on him, he told me I was wrong. He proceeded to explain that babies come out of their mommy's vaginas. He then explained how babies are made and he used the two of you as an example of sorts."

"What do you mean?" Aaron asks.

"Well, while I was trying to steer the discussion away from the current subject matter, AJ said he's surprised he doesn't have more siblings because you two do it a lot and that he hears you. He then mentioned how loud Ms. Tompkins screams."

Aaron and Kara are speechless. Kara wants the floor to open and swallow her. This is by far the most humiliating thing that has ever happened to her, and her teacher once yelled at her for peeing on herself in front of some of her school friends during a field trip when she was in second grade. It wasn't her fault; she kept telling her to hold it. And even that wasn't so bad after Evelyn cursed the woman out from here to Fiji. But this... this is way worse. She can only imagine all the parents who will be pissed off knowing that their kids got the sex talk from a fellow five-year-old.

Aaron handles it way better. He almost seems amused. How could he be laughing at this? Kara, meanwhile, avoids eye contact with Ms. Orozco and Mrs. Fortney and clears her throat.

"We are terribly sorry, and we'll have a talk with AJ when we get home."

"Thank you. Obviously, AJ isn't in trouble, but there is a certain decorum that needs to be adhered to in the classroom."

"Of course," Kara stammers.

"Do you have any questions?"

"Should we be expecting angry phone calls from parents?" Aaron asks.

"I doubt it. For the most part, I fielded a lot of them and told them I would be discussing what happened with you. That seemed to satisfy most of them. A few even thought it was funny."

"Okay, well thank you for telling us, and again, we are so sorry. We'll head right home and talk to AJ," Kara says.

Aaron and Kara stand and shake hands with Ms. Orozco and Mrs. Fortney. They exit the classroom. As they walk down the hallway, they hear Ms. Orozco and Mrs. Fortney giggling.

Aaron smirks. "You wanna go fuck in the back of the minivan?" he asks.

He cannot be serious. "Aaron, seriously? After what we just heard?"

"What? AJ ain't here. We'll drive away from the

school and find somewhere nice, quiet, and secluded. C'mon, I'll make you scream. What do you say?"

Goddamn, this sexy ass man. "I mean...yeah...obviously."

Aaron smiles. He takes Kara's hand, and they walk out the door.

Twenty–Three

2020

"Mom! Mom?" AJ yells. He frantically tears his room apart, looking for something.

This boy has lost his damn mind screaming in her house like that.

"Jesus Christ, AJ, what is it?" Kara appears in his doorway, hands on her hips.

"I can't find my lucky socks."

"Did you try your sock drawer?"

"Yes. I can't find them, and I need them for the game today."

Kara can't help but be amused. If there's one thing that all athletes have in common, it's being superstitious. She once didn't clean her track shoes for months because she was convinced it would take the luck away and she would lose her races. Evelyn cleaned them behind Kara's back; it was the first time she was ever that upset with her mom. Kara goes back to her and Aaron's bedroom where she was folding laundry and looks for AJ's socks in the pile of clothes.

"Sorry, baby. They aren't in the laundry. I think maybe your daddy accidentally washed them," Kara calls out

"I hope he didn't."

Kara appears in AJ's doorway surveying his room. "And *I* hope you realize that you're cleaning all of this up when you're done."

AJ is so frenzied looking for his socks that he doesn't even hear her. Kara rolls her eyes and shakes her head. She heads toward the backyard to ask Aaron about AJ's socks. She hopes their son gets over this superstitious phase, though she doubts it will happen. He's just as competitive as she is, according to Aaron. She doesn't think she's nearly as bad. Her phone buzzes. She sees it's Evelyn, and she answers it.

"Hi, sweetie. How are you?" Evelyn says.

"Hi, Mom. I'm fine. Your grandson is losing his mind, though. He can't find his lucky socks."

"He left them here. I put them in your old sock drawer."

"He did?" Kara calls out to AJ. "AJ, you left them at Grandma Evie's house."

AJ runs out of his room and takes the phone from Kara and puts it on speaker phone. "Hi, Grandma. Where are they?"

"Hi, baby. I washed them and put them in your momma's old room."

"You washed them? Aw, man. The luck comes from the smell. I haven't washed them since we won our last game."

"I'm sorry, sugar."

"It's okay, Grandma. I'll pick them up later. I've got to find my lucky underwear. Maybe that will work."

"Those are clean, too!" Kara replies.

"Aw, man," he repeats.

AJ hands the phone back to Kara and heads back to his room. She makes a disgusted face and laughs along with Evelyn. She walks into the living room and looks out at the sliding doors that lead to the backyard and garage. Kara takes a seat at the dining table and watches Aaron. He's doing one-armed push-ups with Amaya sitting on his back, counting. Sweat drips from his brow. Sweet Jesus! He's so unbelievably sexy, but especially when he's playing with the kids or working out. Seeing him do both makes her quiver. Aaron looks better than most self-proclaimed gym rats, and he does it all from the comfort of their home. Kara eyes his shirt. He is completely drenched with sweat. Kara is so focused on Aaron and what she wants to do to him that she doesn't quite make out what her mom says. Though, she does clearly hear one word. Cancer

"Wait, I'm sorry, Mom. Did you say something about cancer? Who has cancer?"

"Yes, I said I went to the doctor after I felt something on my breast. Baby, I have cancer."

Kara is in shock. Tears fall down her cheeks. She almost slides off her chair. Cancer? Her mom cannot have cancer. This is bullshit!

She takes Evie off speaker phone. "That can't be right. You need to get a second opinion."

Aaron looks over at Kara. He's about to shamelessly wink and flirt with her. He enjoys seeing her pant in heat while he works out. His smile drops when he sees the frown lines etched into her face and her tears.

"Baby, I need you to get up. Daddy needs to check on mommy."

"Daddy, why is mommy crying?"

"I don't know, baby. That's what daddy is going to find out."

They both go into the house.

Aaron turns to Amaya. "Sweetie, go to your room while daddy talks to mommy."

"Okay." Amaya heads to her room.

Aaron kneels in front of Kara, and mouths, "What's wrong?"

Kara calms herself and finds her words. "Mom listen to me. We'll find another doctor, we'll..."

Aaron waits to figure out what's going on. The

most he can make out is that Evie has shared some terrible medical news. Kara listens and is full-on weeping now. The tears won't stop. Aaron can't decide whether to hug her or hold her hand. She decides for him by clutching onto his hand as she weeps.

"I'm so sorry, Mom. Do you need anything? We'll come over. We'll come by right away. AJ will understand if we miss his game."

She's talking about missing AJ's game? She hasn't missed a game in years. What the fuck is going on?

"Okay, we'll head over after the game. I love you so much."

Kara hangs up and falls out of the chair into Aaron's arms. He catches her and holds her. She hugs Aaron like her life depends on it and cries into his chest. He holds her tighter, rubbing his hands up and down her back. He kisses her on top of her head.

"Kara, baby, what's the matter? Tell me what's wrong."

"Mom has cancer."

"Oh, shit. Fuck. Poor Evie."

"How are we going to tell the kids? They'll be devastated."

"We'll wait until after AJ's game. Maybe we can all tell them together, you know, with your mom."

"What if she dies, Aaron? My mom is my everything."

"I know, baby. It's just a diagnosis. We can't even

think like that. Plenty of people beat cancer. I'm sure Evie will be one of them."

"Amaya saw me crying. She'll want to know why."

"I'll just tell her that we'll talk about it later."

"Okay."

Kara can't let go of him. Aaron can tell and lets her hold on. "It's okay, baby. It's going to be okay," Aaron whispers in Kara's ear. She relaxes but still clings to him.

They drive to Evelyn's house after the game. AJ and Amaya watch *Craig of the Creek* on the built-in TV in the minivan's back seat. AJ has a small MVP trophy from the victory of the day's game. They pull into Evelyn's driveway.

AJ and Amaya run up to Trixie and play with her. She happily wags her tail and licks both children. They enter the house and find Evelyn lying on the couch listening to Leontyne Price's rendition of "Ave Maria."

She turns the music down and gets up when she sees her family.

"You guys sure got here quickly."

"Grandma!" the kids say in unison.

They both run up and hug her tightly.

She hugs them back, taking a sniff of the top of AJ's head.

"You smell like outside," she beams.

AJ and Amaya giggle. Evie says that after every game.

"I have some chocolate chip, peanut butter, and walnut cookies with the names AJ and Amaya written all over them."

The kids jump up and down, screaming. They hurry to the kitchen.

"Two cookies each. I don't want you ruining your appetite before dinner," Kara calls out.

"Let me get them some lemonade," Evelyn says.

"No, Mom, I'll get it. You have a seat."

Kara pours the kids each a glass of lemonade.

They take their snack out to the backyard. Kara, Aaron, and Evelyn follow them. They all take a seat at a big patio table. Trixie follows them and lies on the grass.

"AJ, let me see that trophy of yours," Evelyn says.

AJ excitedly runs back into the car to get it. He brings it back and shows it off to his grandma.

"MVP. Damn right. You know you got your athletic ability from your momma, right?"

"Yep, that's what daddy is always saying." AJ smiles proudly at Evie.

Evelyn looks at Kara. "I remember your first track meet..." Evelyn's voice starts to crack.

Kara hugs her mom. Evelyn lays her head on Kara's shoulder.

"It's okay, Mom. You'll be fine. When do you start chemo?"

Evelyn wipes her tears. She takes Kara's face in her hands.

"I didn't want to tell you this over the phone, but the cancer has already spread to my liver and lungs."

Kara shakes her head. She must have heard her wrong. It's spread already? How? When? None of this makes sense. Her mom has always been healthy. She and Richard jog a couple times a week. She drinks plenty of water and eats vegetables. How can this be happening?

"I'm sorry, baby, but they're giving me six months."

Kara gets up and runs back into the house, distraught. Aaron follows her. AJ and Amaya are confused. Kara can hear Evelyn attempt to ease the children's discomfort by offering them more cookies.

Kara is sitting on the bed in her old room. Aaron comes in and glances around. It looks exactly like it did from when Kara moved out to live with him. Aaron sits next to her and takes her hand. She rests her head on his shoulder.

"I still can't believe she kept the room like this. She said that whenever she missed me, she'd come in here, and it helped. She said it made her feel like I was on my way home. I was so determined to live my own life and leave her, and now she's going to die. I feel like such a terrible daughter." Kara wipes her tears.

"Kara, you were twenty and spent the past two years looking after Evelyn. Of course, you wanted some freedom. That doesn't make you a bad person."

"I shouldn't have run out. She's probably hurt, and the kids are probably so confused."

"Evelyn's playing with the kids and feeding them

cookies to distract them until we come back. I think their dinner has been officially spoiled."

Kara shrugs. That's the last thing on her mind right now. "Whatever."

Aaron thinks of something. "Be right back."

He runs downstairs and comes back up quickly. He has something wrapped in a napkin in his hand. He sits back down beside her and unwraps the napkin. Cookies. He knows her go-to when she's upset is junk food.

"I managed to snatch three cookies."

Aaron takes one and gives her the remaining two. They eat their cookies in silence.

"Feel a little better?" he asks.

"Yes and no. It's crazy. I miss her already."

"Let's go back down and spend as much time with her as we can."

Kara nods. They head back down to the backyard. AJ and Amaya are hopped up on sugar. They're jumping on a trampoline Evelyn pulled out for them.

"Mom, what were you thinking? That trampoline is heavy. You could have had Aaron get it."

"It's fine. Stop fussing. If it'll make you feel better, he can put it back."

"That's if it ends up going back," Aaron says.

"Where's Richard?" Kara asks.

"He's at work. I haven't told him yet. You were the first. Telling him and Geri is going to be hell."

•   •   •

Kara holds her mom's hand. Evelyn squeezes Kara's.

"I know you won't approve, but I'm going to reach out to your father."

Kara looks at her, stunned. Three years ago, Kara sent an email to that asshole after working up the strength to do so. Aaron even gave her a pep talk. And what happened? Nothing. He never even responded. This only further solidified Kara's opinion that her father is a selfish piece of shit. Why on earth would her mom want to talk to him?

"Mom...he..."

"I know, sweetie. I know I've said it before, but I am so proud of you for taking the step to heal by contacting him. I know it didn't end the way you would have liked it to, but at least you tried. Now, it's my turn. There's been so much I have wanted to tell him since our split and after. I realized I don't want to go to my grave without getting it all out."

"What if he doesn't respond?"

"Then, like you, at least I'll know that I tried."

Kara doesn't know how to feel. There are so many emotions going on in her head right now she thinks she might fall over. Aaron instinctively wraps his arm around her waist and pulls her to him. She rests her head on him again. They all look over at the kids. AJ and Amaya don't look like they're going to stop any time soon.

"Did you tell them?" Kara asks Evelyn.

"No. I think we all should."

Aaron, Evie, and Kara retake their seats at the table.

"Guys, get off the trampoline and come here," Aaron says.

"Five more minutes, Daddy," Amaya says.

"Yeah, just five more," AJ agrees.

"No, get down and come here. We have something we need to tell you."

They get down and take a seat. Amaya continues to bounce in her seat.

"Amaya, settle down," Aaron says.

Amaya sits still. Kara, Aaron, and Evelyn all look at each other. No one knows what to say or who should go first.

Kara takes a deep breath. "Kids, Grandma Evie is sick."

"Like with a cold?" AJ asks.

"No, it's more serious than a cold, buddy," Kara replies. "She's very sick, and the doctors don't think..." Kara cries. She knows this must be so confusing for the kids, but she just can't bring herself to say the words.

Evelyn takes over, "Babies, grandma has cancer. Do you guys know what cancer is?"

"No," says Amaya.

"Kind of. My friend Henry's uncle, had it. He died," says AJ.

Amaya looks alarmed. "Granny, are you going to die?"

Evelyn musters up the strength to respond. "Yes,

baby. The doctors say I'm going to Heaven in a few months."

Amaya cries and hugs Evelyn. "Don't die, Granny. I'll be good. I swear," Amaya cries.

Evelyn holds Amaya close. "You're already good, sweetie. And that won't change anything, unfortunately."

Tears pour out of AJ's eyes. Aaron puts his arm around AJ as Kara holds each child's hand. Soon, everyone is crying.

Later, Aaron and Kara drive home. The kids are asleep in the back seat. They spent the whole day and a good part of the night with Evelyn. She told them that she's made an appointment to update her living trust, given the circumstances. She also told Kara and Aaron where she wants to be buried, the outfit she wants to wear, that she wants soul food served and R&B from every decade played at the repass.

When they arrive home, Kara takes AJ into his room and wakes him up to put on his pajamas. He snuggles up in his blankets and promptly falls back to sleep. The same occurs when Kara gets Amaya and helps her get ready for bed. Today must have been so exhausting for them. It's been a hell of a day for her. Kara feels like she's cried out all the tears in her body.

Aaron gets his and Kara's pajamas ready. He goes out to the kitchen and makes them both a strong drink. Kara comes into their room and accepts the drink from Aaron. She gulps it down in one sip. It's smooth going down but burns in her belly. Kara puts the glass on the nightstand not giving a fuck about the ring the glass will leave. She climbs into bed and reaches out to Aaron. He immediately wraps his arms around her. They look at each other. She clings to him, knowing that he's in pain too. Aaron loves Evelyn, but he's putting his own grief aside to be there for her. A tear escapes from Kara's eye. She cries due to sadness and for how grateful she is for the man holding her. Aaron wipes away the tear. Their foreheads touch. They close their eyes and drift off to sleep.

Twenty-Four

Aaron and AJ are playing a video game in the living room when his phone buzzes. It's Kara. She said she'd call when she and the other ladies arrived in Vegas. They must be having a great time because according to Denise, they arrived four hours ago.

"Hold on, Buddy. Your mom is on the phone."

"Okay, Dad."

"Hi, baby. You guys get in okay?" There's silence on the other end. "Kara? Baby, are you there?"

"Aaron," Kara whispers.

"Yeah?"

"Aaron," She whispers again.

"Kara, are you okay?" Aaron is beyond confused. She sounds like she's hiding in a closet.

"Aaron, you are so fine." Kara's tone is still hushed, but she's a tad bit louder, "And your dick is huge."

Okay. What the hell did those women give his wife?

"Um...thank you."

Kara giggles like a schoolgirl.

"Baby, are you okay?"

"Yeah, I'm good. Aaron, I love you so much."

"I love you, too."

"Aaron."

"Why do you keep saying my name like that?"

"Like what?"

"Like Gollum when he says 'precious.'"

Kara giggles for a solid thirty seconds. "I do not."

"Yes, you do," Aaron chuckles.

Whatever they gave her, she is gone.

"Aaron, I'm so high," Kara giggles.

Aaron looks over at AJ, who is too enthralled in the comic book he started reading to pay attention to his parents' conversation. Aaron walks out to the backyard and sits on his weight bench.

"What exactly are you high on?" he asks.

Kara giggles some more. Aaron hears a brief exchange between Kara and Janae. Janae gets on the phone.

"Hey, Smoke."

"Hey, would you like to explain to me why my wife is high?"

"Okay, so Momma Evic brought edibles and convinced Kara to try one, and Kara's goofy ass took two. They're ten milligrams each."

"Oh," Aaron replies. That explains it. Kara has never gotten high in her life. Aaron still occasionally smokes weed but not around the kids. He often tried to get Kara to try it when they were dating, but she was worried about paranoia. Kara takes the phone back from Janae. Aaron hears a door close.

"I'm hiding in the bathroom," she whispers. This is followed by a series of more giggles. "Aaron?"

"Yes, baby."

"Would you think it was corny if I started talking in a British accent?"

"No, why would I think that's corny? You talk in accents all the time."

"I do?"

"Yes. You do silly voices whenever you read Amaya a bedtime story. You've done that since they were babies and when you and I watch TV and the characters have accents, you talk like them for days."

"Really?" Kara laughs. "Oh my God, I thought I toned my silliness down."

"Naw, baby. You're the silliest person I know. Hell, you and Janae are always doing the goofy ass happy dance. You're always making me laugh."

"Thank you, Aaron," Kara sings.

Aaron can hear the smile in her voice. No doubt, it's bright and beautiful as always.

Aaron smiles back. "You're welcome, my love." He chuckles, "where did Evie get edibles, anyway?"

"Aunt Geri gave them to her to help her relax."

Aaron laughs. He's not at all surprised. Geri is a sweetheart, but she's also trouble.

"Aaron, I'm a little nervous. I can hear my heart beating."

"Just drink some water. You'll be fine. And I hate to say I told you so, but if you had tried weed when I offered it to you numerous times, your body would be used to it by now."

"And I told you, you sexy, trifling ass negro, that I was scared. And from the way my heart is beating, I was right to be."

This makes Aaron laugh so hard AJ looks up and stares at him like he's nuts.

"Where are you guys?"

"We're at the hotel trying to decide what to do for dinner before the concert."

Evie has a bucket list. They're in Vegas to knock off two of the items. One is a girl's trip—something Evie's been trying to organize for years—and the other is seeing some of her favorite artists in concert. Tonight, they're seeing SWV, Mint Condition, Chante Moore, En Vogue, and New Edition perform.

"Is everyone high?"

"Yeah, pretty much."

Kara hums into the phone. Aaron smiles at the idea of all the ladies in his family being high as fuck.

"Aaron?" Kara sings.

"Yes," Aaron sings back.

"Send me a picture of your dick."

"Naw, I'm not going to do that."

Aaron knows he's going to do it; he just likes fucking with her. Hell, if this is how Kara acts when she's high, then he's going to have to add edibles to their monthly budget.

"Do it," Kara whispers loudly.

"No."

"If you loved me, you'd do it."

"What kind of manipulative..." Aaron shakes his head and laughs some more. "Fine. Give me a minute. I'll call you back."

He gets up and goes into the house. AJ is still focused on his comic book. Aaron grabs his wallet and takes out a twenty.

"AJ."

AJ looks up. Aaron hands him the twenty, and he happily takes it.

"Go down to the taco place down the street and get us some lunch. Order whatever you want."

"Really?" AJ's eyes light up.

"Really, buddy."

"Cool. I hope mom goes out of town again."

"Don't say that. Now go."

AJ runs out the door.

Aaron just bought himself twenty minutes. He goes into the bathroom, locks the door, and takes out his dick. He strokes it slowly while filming himself.

"Is this what you want to see, my queen?" he asks in a husky voice.

His strokes become faster. Thinking about Kara's reaction makes him harder.

"Ugh, oh fuck. Kara. I love you so much, baby."

He grips his dick tighter. After a few more strokes he comes. "Shit," he whispers.

Aaron cleans himself up and sends the clip to Kara. He heads to the kitchen to get something to drink when his phone buzzes. He smiles anticipating Kara's reaction. It's Janae.

"What the fuck did you do Smoke?"

"What are you talking about?"

"Kara came bursting out the bathroom talking about 'I gotta go home and fuck Aaron. I'll come back tomorrow.'"

Aaron laughs so hard he falls to the floor. He is most definitely getting her some edibles before she comes home.

A few hours later, Aaron is fixing a plate for AJ and himself. They're having roast chicken, green beans, and roasted potatoes. They're about to eat when someone knocks on the door. Aaron answers it and sees Red, one of his old rapper friends. They shake hands and hug.

"Red, what's up, man? It's been a minute."

"What up, Smoke? Can I come in?"

"Yeah."

Red enters and can't believe his eyes. "The house looks good, nigga, almost like when Louella and Duke was alive."

Red sees AJ. "What's up, Little Man?"

"Hi," AJ says shyly.

Red points to AJ. "This your seed, Smoke?"

"Yep. That's AJ. He has a little sister, too, Amaya, but she's at a sleepover."

"That's cool, man. You got your shit on lock."

"What's going on, Red?"

"It's Tone, man. Look, I know shit went sideways the last time y'all saw each other, but he's in the hospital. Got into a real bad car wreck. I think you should go see him."

"I'm sorry to hear that." Aaron is genuinely sorry to hear about Tone. It's crazy to think they were once so close, but he's barely entered Aaron's mind since their falling out.

"Yeah, shit ain't been going well for him for a while. I think seeing an old friend might help."

Aaron thinks it over. "Okay. I'll go see him later."

"Cool." Red heads for the door.

"It's good to see you, Smoke."

"You, too, man."

They give each other another handshake and hug, then Red leaves.

Aaron turns his attention to AJ. "Make sure you eat those vegetables."

AJ giggles and puts them back on his plate after hiding them in his hand. Aaron wipes off AJ's hands and shakes his head. Aaron was a lot sneakier as a kid, which led to more trouble for him. He thanks God that AJ didn't inherit that from him.

~

Aaron takes AJ to Guillermo and Denise's place the next day. When Guillermo answers the door, he has on a princess tiara, fairy wings, a tutu, a feather boa, blush, and lip gloss. Aaron tries not to laugh. AJ doesn't even try to hide it.

"Guillermo, man. What is going on?" Aaron gestures at Guillermo's costume.

"What's going on is your daughter and my daughter are having a princess-themed tea party, and I am Princess Griselda of the gumdrop kingdom."

"Queendom!" Birdie and Amaya yell from the other room.

"Right Queendom. Sorry girls," Guillermo yells back.

"I'm sorry, man. I have to do this." Aaron takes out his phone and takes a picture of him.

This is too funny. Guillermo basically looks like an El Salvadorian version of the Rock with Jason Momoa's hair, so seeing him dressed like a fairy princess is hilarious.

Amaya and Birdie run up to the door. They're dressed similarly to Guillermo.

"Hi, daddy!" Amaya reaches up. Aaron picks her up and gives her a hug.

"Hi, Uncle Smoke," Birdie says.

Aaron puts down Amaya and hugs Birdie.

"Hello your royal highnesses," Aaron jokes.

Both girls giggle. Silly little sweethearts.

"Y'all are not dressing me up like that," AJ announces.

"Fine." Amaya rolls her eyes.

"You're no fun, AJ," Birdie adds.

"Thanks for doing this again, man. I shouldn't be too long. I'm just going to pop in and see him and leave."

"No worries, Smoke."

Guillermo puts his arm around AJ.

"We're going to have fun, right, AJ?"

"Are you going to teach me a new wrestling move?"

"Sure. But what is the rule?"

"Be careful and don't play too rough."

"My man." Guillermo high fives AJ.

Aaron addresses AJ. "I'll be back to get you in a bit. Listen to your Uncle Guillermo, alright?"

"Okay, Daddy."

Aaron enters the hospital. He approaches the nurse's station. There's an older Latina nurse behind the desk.

"Excuse me, could you tell me which room Antonio Nelson is in?"

She looks it up on the computer. "Room 412."

"Thank you." Aaron takes the elevator to the 4th floor.

He hears Tone and a woman arguing as he gets closer to his room. Aaron knocks on the door, more determined to make this visit as quick as possible.

"Who is it?" Tone yells.

"Smoke," Aaron replies.

The door opens. It's Reynisha. "Smoke, what are you doing here?"

"Red told me about Tone's accident. I came by to see him."

"Come in," she says.

Aaron comes in. Tone sits up slightly in surprise but says nothing. The awkwardness is thick.

Reynisha breaks the silence. "You still fine as hell, Smoke. How you been?"

"Thank you. I'm good."

Reynisha remembers something and giggles. "Remember that time we were at your house, and we spent the whole day fucking?"

Aaron looks around the room uncomfortably. Jesus Christ! Aaron shouldn't be surprised. Reynisha has never been subtle.

"Really, bitch?" Tone says. "You gone flirt with the nigga right in front of me?"

"Yeah, so? We are not a couple, Tone. We fucked a few times, and you got me pregnant—that's it," Reynisha spits more venom Tone's way. "Shit, the only reason I'm here is to make sure you get me your son's child support."

"How the fuck am I supposed to do that? I'm in the fucking hospital!"

"I don't fucking care. Your dumbass should have thought of that before you had some bitch sucking your dick while you were driving." Aaron looks appalled, and Reynisha notices. "Yep, that's right. Your boy here was getting his dick sucked by a twenty-year-old when he crashed his car into a tree. The girl's in a coma, and her parents are suing his dumbass."

Tone becomes silent. He's clearly embarrassed.

Reynisha gets close to Aaron and strokes his face. "Remember when you texted me and told me you couldn't fuck me anymore because you were seeing someone?"

She laughs. Hard.

"Yes." Aaron doesn't crack a smile. He simply removes her hand from his face.

"Whatever happened with the chick you tossed me aside for?"

"I married her, and we have two kids together."

"For real? How long did that last?"

"We've been together thirteen years and have been married for six."

Reynisha's smile fades. "You're still together?"

"Yes."

"You must be happy."

Aaron gives her a self-satisfied smirk. "I am. Very happy."

"I gotta go." She turns her attention to Tone. "You better call your momma or something because I will be back for that money tomorrow."

Reynisha storms out before Tone can respond. There's an uncomfortable silence between him and Aaron. He takes a seat next to Tone's bed.

Tone breaks the silence. "You married the uppity chick?"

"Tone, do not call my wife uppity again." Aaron looks Tone right in the eye.

Tone mockingly chuckles and shakes his head. "Can't believe you went out like that."

"Excuse me?"

"Smoke, we had a plan. Get a record deal, make some money, buy houses and cars, and fuck bitches. What happened?"

"I grew up and developed enough common sense to know that we had no talent and that dream we had would never happen. Shit, man, I was lucky. When my mom kicked me out, I already had steady work. I used the skill I was best at and parlayed that into a long-lasting career. I may not be rich and famous, but I'm fulfilled and happy. Can you say the same, Tone?"

"Hell, yeah. Nigga, before this accident, I was fucking bitches left and right. Shit, man, those hos was giving me money."

"So, you're happy with the direction your life has taken?" Aaron continues. "From what I can see, Tone, you don't seem like you are. You're thirty-four years old, chasing twenty-year-old girls, pursuing a pipe dream we had in high school that's going nowhere. You have a baby momma who hates you, no discernible skills and you rely on your mom or the foolish girls you sleep with for money." Aaron shrugs. "You can't possibly be satisfied with that."

Tone's smart-ass smiles is long gone. Aaron can tell that his words hit him like a ton of bricks.

"Two baby mommas," Tone says just above a whisper. He looks up at Aaron. "I got some other girl pregnant a year after Reynisha had our son. She had a girl I've never even met. I barely see my son, too." Tone takes some deep breaths. "The girl from the car accident, her parents are suing me for medical expenses and emotional distress. I can't afford a lawyer, and I have no idea what's going to happen." Tone sits up. "It's seems like I kept pursuing the rap thing to me get out of the jams my dick got me into. I figured if I made it, I could get away with whatever bullshit I created. I kept telling myself if I kept trying, some shit would pop off. Remember the talent show we did in high school?"

"Yeah."

"We got so much love after that performance, and I've been chasing that high ever since. I told myself that every record label that turned me down just didn't get my talent. How could the very first audience I ever performed for be wrong?"

"Tone, only a few of the folks in that audience clapped. The rest of the people clowned us. Even Niecey booed."

Tone gives a self-deprecating chuckle. "Even back then, I couldn't see it. I figured anyone who clowned us was just jealous. Hell, I thought you niggas was jealous. Each of you quit to do other shit, and I thought y'all was just jealous that I was better than you."

Aaron stifles his laugh. This nigga must have a concussion. He doesn't want to kick Tone while he's down, so instead of laughing in his face, he offers him an olive branch.

"Look, Kara and I have a personal thing happening in our family involving her mother, so that takes precedence, but I think I can talk her into letting you borrow a couple thousand dollars to get a lawyer. Everything else, you're on your own."

"You have to ask your woman permission for your own money?"

Aaron stands to leave. "Bye, Tone."

"Wait!" Tone calls out. "I'm sorry. Thanks, Smoke."

"No problem. If Kara's cool with it, then I'll drop off the money with your mom."

"Cool. Thanks again."

Aaron nods and heads out of the door hoping Tone doesn't blow it. He's always been his own worst enemy.

Three months later, Kara, Aaron and the kids are at the cemetery making final arrangements for Evelyn. Kara is a wreck. Six months went by too fast. Her phone buzzes. She looks and sees a message from Richard.

She doesn't have a lot of time left. Bring the kids and come say goodbye <3.

"I can't do this Aaron."

"Yes, you can. Baby, if you don't, you'll regret not saying goodbye."

Kara and Aaron arrive at Richard's place with the kids in tow. Richard lets them in. He's crying. Kara, Aaron, and the kids all embrace him. Trixie comes up behind him. Excited to see them, she sniffs and licks everyone. Richard leads them to the guest room where he and Evelyn have been sleeping at her insistence. It offers a vast view of Downtown L.A. that she loves. She lies in the bed and looks out the window. Trixie hops in bed and lays by her feet. There are flower arrangements everywhere.

"For the past few days, friends have been coming to say their goodbyes. That's why it looks like a flower shop in here," Richard jokes. He's trying his best to keep it together.

Kara takes his hands. "Thank you..." her voice cracks, "Thank you for taking care of my mother."

"I'm not dead yet, y'all," Evelyn says.

Kara looks over at her mom. She looks weak. Her cheeks are sunken in, and her skin is paler than usual. Kara walks over and sits next to her. Evelyn turns her head, sees her Kara, and smiles.

"Hi, sweetheart."

Kara cries, "Hi, Mom."

"Kara, don't cry. I'll be fine, and so will you. You are strong, stronger than I have ever been. You're an amazing mother, a wonderful wife, and a one-of-a-kind daughter.

I asked a lot of you all those years ago, and you rose to the occasion. I am so sorry for everything I cost you. I am so proud of you, honey. You amaze me every day."

Kara holds her mother's hand to her face and squeezes it. AJ and Amaya each hold Aaron's hands.

Evelyn sees them and motions for them to come to her. "Come over here and lay by grandma."

The kids carefully climb into the bed and lay down next to Evelyn on either side. She wraps her arms around them as they snuggle up to her.

Evelyn smiles at Aaron. "Aaron, could you please play me something?" she asks.

"Of course." He walks over and kisses her on the forehead before heading over to the piano.

Richard bought the piano so Aaron could play songs for Evie. She always requested something when he and Kara visited with the kids. Aaron takes a seat behind it and plays "Blue Rondo a la Turk" by Dave Brubeck as everyone listens. Kara lays next to her mom like she used to when she was little and had a bad dream. That's exactly what this feels like, a bad dream. She keeps hoping she'll wake up and Evelyn will be fine. It's crazy how quickly her health deteriorated. Just months ago, they were all in Vegas, and it was like Evelyn wasn't even sick. Granted, she wasn't able to drink, but she still had a great time. And now she looks like a shell of her former self. Still vibrant and beautiful—that will never go away—but tired. Like she's ready to go. Kara knows it's selfish, but she's not ready to say goodbye. She cuddles up to Evelyn.

Evelyn smiles and kisses Kara on top of her head. She whispers to the kids.

"Go over to your daddy and help him play."

The kids run over to Aaron and try to mimic him. Aaron and Richard laugh.

"I love you so much, mom," Kara weeps.

"I love you, too, my baby."

Kara calms herself and just enjoys her mother for however long she still has her while Evelyn requests song after song from Aaron, and he happily plays each one. The kids start to dance. Evelyn tells Kara to join them. Kara dances with her babies and soon, everyone's spirits are up.

Three hours pass, and Aaron finishes playing yet another song.

"Any more requests, Evie?" Aaron asks.

When she doesn't respond, everyone turns and looks at her. Evelyn lies still, with her eyes closed and a slight smile on her face. Richard checks her pulse. He looks at Kara and shakes his head. Aaron gets up from behind the piano and wraps his arms around Kara. She collapses in Aaron's arms. The kids hug her and Aaron's legs. Richard stares at Evelyn with immense sadness. Kara offers him her hand. He clutches it. They all hold each other tightly, almost as if they'll float away if any of them let go.

Twenty-Five

The day of Evelyn's funeral, Kara helps Amaya buckle her little black Mary Jane shoes, while Aaron helps fix the knot in AJ's tie. Pauline, Sheila, Denise, Guillermo, Birdie, Janae, and Rod are in the living room. They're joined by Aunt Geri and Richard. There's a knock on the door, and Aaron answers it. It's the limo driver. Everyone piles into the limo and heads to the funeral home.

They arrive at the Forest Lawn in Cypress and enter the chapel. Evelyn's body lies in a pink open casket. Everything has been done the way she specified it to a T. Friends and family fill the chapel. Kara greets each of them and thanks them for being there.

Kara makes her way to the coffin and looks at her mother. She looks peaceful but unnatural. The mortician overdid it with the makeup.

Janae approaches her and gives her a long hug. Tears stream down her cheeks.

"Kara…"

"I know," Kara cries, too.

"That woman was my everything. She was my role model, my mother, and my friend. God, I miss her so much."

Janae leans down and cries on Kara's shoulder.

"I do, too, J."

The two sisters hold each other, and they take another look at their mother.

Kara lets out a deep breath. "I'm not a fan of the makeup they put on her."

"Really? I think she looks great. She almost looks younger." Janae dabs her eyes with a tissue.

"You think? I don't know."

"She was a beautiful woman, Kare Bear. She looks amazing. Trust me."

Kara rests her head on Janae's shoulder. Janae kisses the top of her head, and Kara smiles. It's the first real smile she's had today.

The door in the back of the chapel opens and Stephen enters. Kara looks up and sees him. He looks at her with tears in his eyes. She storms over to him.

"What are you doing here?" Kara demands.

"Evie reached out to me. Listen Kara…"

"You need to leave!" Kara yells. She looks and sees the crowd of mourners looking at her.

"Kara, sweetheart, please let me explain…" Stephen begs.

"Explain what? How you dumped my mother leaving her heart broken? Or how when I finally tried to reach out, you ignored me?"

Aaron rushes over to Kara's side. She sees Janae take the kids out of the chapel through a side door. Good. Her babies don't need to see this. The only thing Kara is sorry about is that they saw her raise her voice. She swore after her fight with Aaron years ago she wouldn't do that in front of them again.

"Sweetheart…" Stephen begs.

"Don't, don't. You need to leave." Kara snaps.

"Kara, I knew your mother since we were fourteen," Stephen cries. "Please let me say goodbye. You can hate me all you want, but your mother wanted me here."

Stephen takes out a piece of paper and hands it to Kara. She takes it and opens it up.

It's a handwritten letter from Evelyn.

Stephen,

I'm dying of cancer. I don't have much time left. I loved you, and you broke me. It took me years to piece myself back together, but thanks to our daughter, I did. I even met a wonderful man and built a life with him. I have forgiven you for your infidelity and your betrayal, but I can't move past the hurt you inflicted on our daughter. Kara saw

*firsthand what you're leaving did to me. That's
why she resisted reaching out to you for so long. You
cost her so much, and so did I. We both owe it to her
to make things right, that's why I'm writing to you.*

*After so many years of ignoring you, Kara's
husband, who is a wonderful man named Aaron,
managed to get her to contact you. And what did
you do? You ignored her. You need to fix this!
Richard and Kara love each other, but you are her
father. She needs you as well. If you don't take care
of this, I swear to God I will haunt your Black ass.*

Kara chuckles. Her mom rarely showed her feisty side
but when she did, she did not hold back.

"I'm guessing you got to the part where she said she
was going to haunt me. Knowing Evie, she would do it,"
Stephen says.

Kara looks at him, hoping Evelyn makes good on her
promise. She continues reading.

*You need to come to my funeral and make peace
with our child, and for the love of God, don't bring
your wife and kids. Kara's not ready for that.*

Amen. Thank you!

*Be there for her. Get to know her now as the
woman she's become, meet your amazing grand-*

children, AJ and Amaya. Become a part of her family. You both need this. I did a damn good job raising her. The rest is up to you.

~Evie

Kara looks at her father. He looks so sad and old. Not geriatric but like he's aged from stress and pain. Not knowing what to say, she just stares at him. Aaron has his hands on her shoulders as he stands behind her. He gives them a squeeze before extending a hand to Stephen.

"Hi, I'm Aaron."

Traitor! Kara shoots Aaron a look that tells him he's going to be sleeping on the couch tonight.

"Stephen. It's so nice to meet you."

Stephen shakes Aaron's hand and looks at Kara.

"I am sorry for everything, sweetheart, but please... your mom and I married when we were eighteen, we had you when we were twenty-two. We were still kids. Honestly, as much as I love you, I had no business being anyone's father for at least another decade. Years passed, and your mom and I grew apart. Then I met Paige, and I felt alive again, and I know it's no excuse..."

"Your damn right it's not. Do you want to know what I remember? Holding my mother while she cried herself to sleep. Hearing her on the phone with Aunt Geri, 'What did I do wrong? I thought I was a good wife. Why did he cheat? Why did he leave me?'"

Angry tears fall down Kara's face.

"You were a fucking coward! What? You thought sending me an occasional present and constantly calling me and emailing me was going to change anything? You left. You left and went and made a new family. Me and my mother weren't good enough for you, so you went and got yourself a new younger wife and brand-new kids. And I bet you told yourself that you were a good dad because even if you didn't get to speak to me, you could sleep at night knowing you at least tried."

Kara sees the pain in her father's eyes, but she doesn't care. He deserves to be hurt for all the pain and suffering he caused. He clears his throat and opens his mouth.

"I...um...Paige and I are estranged right now. Turns out the email you sent me three years ago, she saw it first and deleted it. According to her, I was obsessing over you and not paying enough attention to her. Between my trying to reach out to you and me doing most of the child rearing, she felt neglected. So, when she saw that you contacted me back. She 'took care of it'. Her words."

Kara now hates the bitch even more than she did before, and she didn't think that was even possible.

"When I got your mother's letter—as luck would have it, I checked the mail that day—I reached out to her, and we talked for a long time. It was like when we were kids. It felt easy. There was no pressure. Over the years, we'd only really talk when it came to things that concerned you. Like buying your first car or helping with other expenses. But after the talk, she started sending me things. Photos, videos, things I had missed. I am a fucking coward, Kara. You're right about that. I should have fought for you. I thought if I sent a gift or shot you an email or tried to call, you'd know I was still trying, but I did not try hard enough. I missed out on over a decade of your life because I was too scared. I thought that if I pushed too hard, I'd lose you for good, and that was foolish because I had already lost you. I am so sorry, Kara. Please..."

Kara wants to keep hating him, but she can't help but feel sorry for him. She looks away so she doesn't have to see him cry.

"What did she send you?"

"Videos of your track meets, photos from AJ and Amaya's births and their subsequent birthdays. Videos of AJ's soccer games and photos from your wedding...I should have been there. I should have given you away. I missed everything. And now Evie gone. She's gone." Stephen breaks down and fully weeps.

Going against every fiber of her being and her better judgment Kara reaches out and takes Stephen's hand. He looks up at her. There's so much pain and anguish between them, if they tried to rebuild and start new, how would they even do that?

"You can stay," Kara says softly.

Stephen wipes his eyes and squeezes Kara's hand. "Thank you, sweetheart."

Aaron and Kara take their seats. Pauline brings Janae and the kids back inside. The babies sit next to Kara. She wraps an arm around each child. Kara will explain everything to them later. Right now, she doesn't want to think about the man sitting in the back. She just wants to celebrate her mother's life.

Aaron and Kara lie in bed. They still have their funeral clothes on. Pauline is asleep with AJ and Amaya in AJ's room. Pauline and Amaya sleep in AJ's bed while he sleeps in a sleeping bag on the floor. Aaron holds Kara close. She rests her head on his shoulder while his arms are wrapped around her waist. Aaron kisses the top of Kara's head as she traces her fingers over his most recent tattoos. They are AJ, Amaya, and Kara's names on his inner right forearm. She looks at the one dedicated to Duke. He sees her eyeing it.

"He...um...shit. Never mind, I shouldn't talk about him anyway."

Kara looks up at him. "Aaron, if you want to tell me something, please do."

Aaron clears his throat. He needs to do this before he loses his nerve.

"Duke died about six years before I met you. Had an aneurysm in his sleep. He was only forty. I'm the one who found him," Aaron says softly.

"Jesus. I'm so sorry, Aaron."

Aaron feels a lump growing in his throat. He gets it whenever horrible memories surface. Especially about Duke. Aaron tries not to think about him. It hurts too badly, but he's been avoiding painful topics long enough. He swallows a lump and begins Duke's story.

"Seeing you with your dad today made me think of him, and all the time he and I lost, too. Duke was the closest thing I had to a father figure, and he deteriorated right before my eyes."

"I don't want this to sound cruel, but this whole time I thought he killed himself."

"He might as well have. It was like his body just gave up. Duke had a sad life. He made and sold furniture and did repairs but with his talent and his natural teaching skills, he could have done so much more."

"Why didn't he?"

"Grandma Lou. She kept him dependent on her by telling him that he'd never make it on his own. Being her favorite meant her keeping him on a tight leash so another man wouldn't leave her. She'd tear down his dreams but would otherwise be soft on him. Meanwhile, she was always hard on my mom and Sheila."

"Pauline and Sheila's attitude toward Duke makes sense now. They both seem really chill about having a dead sibling."

"Don't get me wrong, Ma and Aunt Sheila miss him, but growing up with him and Grandma Lou was a lot. She outwardly favored him. Nothing Ma or Aunt Sheila did was ever good enough. Meanwhile, the sun rose and set on him. And it wasn't just because he was the youngest. He reminded Louella of my Grandpa Hyman; she missed him desperately. All that love and affection got redirected to her son and she smothered him."

"That's weirdly Oedipal."

"It was."

Aaron takes a breath and swallows again. Kara rests her head on Aaron's shoulder.

"You don't have to talk about this if it's too hard." She rubs his chest.

"No, you're my wife. You should know." He kisses her then continues, "Duke didn't have a lot of girlfriends. He had tons of women he slept with, but no one he was in relationship with. Grandma Lou would usually run them off. He stayed up under her for a long time until one day, he realized that his life had no meaning without his mother. Aimless and scared, he started drinking. Grandma Lou would make my mom and Sheila go out and find him whenever he'd go on a bender and be missing for days. They'd find him, he'd promise Grandma never to leave her again, and the cycle would continue. He remained active in mine and Niecey's life after he started drinking, but it was never the same."

Kara scratches Aaron's beard and kisses his face. "How did you find him?"

"Grandma asked that we go look for him again and I remembered a motel he would meet some of the married women he would entertain at. I drove my mom, Sheila, and grandma there. I insisted on going in first. Something told me it would be bad. I saw him, and he didn't even look like himself anymore. He had to have been dead for at least a week. I called an ambulance, came out, and told them he was gone. My grandmother immediately started yelling and screaming. She told Aunt Sheila and my mom that if they had found him sooner, he wouldn't have died."

"Good lord. That is awful. No wonder you never wanted to talk about it. I'm so sorry I tried to push you."

"It's okay. I know you only did that because you care."

"That's such a damn shame. She ruined his life and made sure his sisters resented him."

"Yeah, Lou was a real piece of work. When she died a year after Duke, Ma and Sheila organized the funeral, the repass, everything. Gave Louella a good homegoing. You would never have known how they really felt about each other. You know, it's strange getting all of this out does feel better. Maybe we should each talk to someone," Aaron suggests.

"Like a shrink?"

"Yeah. You're dealing with grief from losing your mom and trauma from your dad leaving, and I have so many issues concerning Duke. I think we should consider it."

"Yeah, we should."

They lie still for a while. Snuggled together, they allow themselves to breathe.

Aaron squeezes Kara's waist. "You know, he was the one who nicknamed me Smoke."

"Really?"

"Yep. I had gotten into a fight..."

"Of course, you did."

"Shut up." Aaron kisses her forehead. "Like I was saying, I had gotten into a fight when I was twelve, and Duke was supposed to be watching me. When the fight was over, the other kid ran home crying, and Duke said, 'Nephew, you smoked that little nigga.' From that day on, I was little Smoke until it just finally became Smoke."

"Good origin story. Nice to find out more about the man behind the legend."

"Your goofy ass always got to talk shit."

"You love it."

She's right. He does and he loves her.

Twenty-Six

I t's been four months since the funeral. Kara and Aaron have both been seeing therapists and have been making progress. Aaron talks about his feelings more with Kara. This has made their communication better and has even made their sex life more intimate. Kara didn't think that was even possible. Meanwhile, she has been using the tools her therapist, Nicole, has taught her to mend fences with her dad. For now, the two of them do Zoom calls once a week. She's even met her half-brothers, Jase and Cameron, and they're great kids. Turns out, Jase isn't such a stupid name after all. Stephen has bonded with AJ and Amaya as much as you can bond on Zoom—the next step is inviting them over for a family dinner. Kara's going to bring it up the next time they talk.

Kara sits in the conference room at Hinton's Southern Eats. Michelle and her husband, Dexter, sit on the same side as Kara while Gretchen and Jonathan sit on the other side. Each side has a lawyer representing them. They're hammering out the final details of the Hinton's acquisition of Nancy's catering business. Seeing Gretchen and Jonathan with their tails between their legs feels victorious. Kara's phone buzzes, and she looks down and sees a text from Aaron.

Show those motherfuckers no mercy. I love you.

Kara smiles at her phone and sends him a quick text back.

Aaron is currently in the car by himself on his way to Rod and Janae's place for dinner. Kara will be joining them later. Janae and Rod have been living together for five years. She moved into his condo almost immediately after they got serious. Kara keeps bugging them about getting married, and they keep telling her to mind her business.

Aaron parks the minivan and approaches the front door when his phone buzzes. It's Kara.

I love you too, my king.

Aaron grins as he rings the doorbell. Janae answers.

"Hey Smoke." Janae smiles. "What are you so happy about?"

"I love my wife."

"Baby, what else is new?"

Aaron smiles back. Janae looks vibrant and fun like usual. The only exception was the funeral, where she ditched the fun fake glasses and wig. She wore a modest black dress and wore her hair in a long braid extension. Today, she's back to looking like a cute nerdy librarian. She's wearing red rimmed glasses, a red button-down ruffle blouse, and black capri pants. Aaron is almost taken aback at her height. She's her normal six feet, no heels. He looks down and sees that she's barefoot with red painted toes. They give each other a big tight hug.

"I'm guessing Kare Bear is still at work?"

"Yes. The deal is being finalized, and since it was Kara's idea, they wanted her to obviously be there when the papers were signed."

"Yes! That's my girl," Janae cheers.

"I know. I'm so proud of her. They're talking about giving her a promotion to go along with the recent raise."

"That's what I'm talking about."

Aaron takes a seat on the couch, and Janae joins him.

"Where's Rod?"

"He went to the store to get some champagne. He figured we should celebrate Kara's good news."

"That's cool of him. She'll love that."

"Yeah, he's a good one."

Aaron looks at Janae sweetly and takes her hand.

"I'm glad you two found each other, J. I saw something between the two of you when we brought AJ home from the hospital. I'm happy I was right."

Janae smiles sweetly at Aaron before playfully rolling her eyes.

"Your trifling ass would give yourself credit for our relationship."

"Hey, usually Kara's the one who notices this type of shit first. She knew that Niecey and Guillermo would be a thing before anybody. Let me have this."

Janae burst out laughing and slaps Aaron's shoulder.

"You stupid, Smoke. First, we all knew Guillermo and Niecey were going to be a thing. She was so hung up on him. And second...thank you."

"For noticing you and Rod liked each other first?"

"For talking to him. He told me a couple years back that he was apprehensive about asking me out, but he said you talked to him and made him realize that if we liked each other, that's all that mattered."

"You're welcome, J."

An hour later, Kara and Rod join them, and they all enjoy good food, good wine, and some laughs. Rod made his famous seafood gumbo. Aaron has three bowls, and Kara and Janae each have two. Rod brings out a bottle of champagne and makes an announcement.

"I want to thank you guys for coming, but I must come clean. I had an ulterior motive for inviting all of you. It wasn't just to spend time with family and congratulate Kara, though I am happy for you."

"Thanks Rod." Kara smiles.

"I asked you two to be here because I want to ask Janae something, and I wanted to share this moment with Smoke and Kara since they are family, and they played a huge role in me and Janae meeting."

Janae is taken aback. "What did you want to ask me?"

Rod takes Janae's hand and looks into her eyes. He takes a ring box out of his pocket and gets down on one knee. Aaron and Kara look intently, with a mix of anticipation and excitement.

"Janae, will you marry me?"

"Rod," Janae sighs. Her eyes fill with tears.

"We have known each other for eight years. And we have been together for five. I have been in love with you since the day I met you. Please say that you'll spend the rest of your life with me?"

"Do it, girl. Do it!" Kara cheers.

This is so romantic! It's like a movie. Aaron tugs Kara's arm. She knows this is the cue to be quiet and let them have their moment, but she's excited to see her sister say yes to the man of her dreams.

"Yes," Janae says softly.

Rod takes Janae's face in his hands and kisses her. Squee!

"Aww." Kara smiles. "This is so beautiful. I love it."

Rod and Janae look at her. She knows she is disrupting their moment, but c'mon, this is so sweet. The two lovebirds join their friends.

"Congratulations." Aaron hugs Rod.

"Thanks, man."

Janae and Kara crash into each other and hold each other tightly. The two sisters squeal, jumping up and down with excitement before breaking into their happy dance. Kara now gets to be Janae's maid of honor. She just wishes their mother was here to see it. Evelyn thought the world of Rod. Kara and Janae have tears in their eyes as each one of them think about how happy Evie would be that both her girls found true love with such amazing men.

Twenty-Seven

2022

AJ and Amaya help Kara clear the table after lunch. AJ is about to be ten and is almost as tall as Kara and looks more and more like Aaron every day. He's the star soccer player at his school and is determined to become the next Cristiano Ronaldo, at least the Black American version. Word has spread about how great AJ is, and a few coaches from some of the best private schools have been showing up at his games. While they're both proud as hell of their son, Kara and Aaron want him to enjoy being a kid, so they often team up to get the coaches to back off. Kara plays good cop, and Aaron introduces them to Smoke while playing the bad cop.

The kids bring the dishes to the kitchen. Seven-year-old Amaya places them in the sink, then runs up behind Kara and hugs her.

"What do you want, My My?" Kara says, a hint of playful suspicion in her tone.

"Nothing, mommy," Amaya says sweetly. Her Cheshire cat grin and doe eyes remind Kara of when she would try to pull a fast one on Evelyn. It never worked.

"Amaya, you know how important tonight is, and I have a ton of stuff to do. Out with it."

"Can you or daddy take me to buy more makeup for my costume?"

Kara lets out an annoyed huff. "Jesus Christ, girl! How much makeup do you need?"

"Please mommy, this is important. First prize gets a pizza party. My zombie look needs to be perfect."

Kara could strangle Janae. During one of her many nights babysitting, Janae decided to introduce Amaya to some classic movies. It was close to Halloween, so she included *Night of the Living Dead*. After seeing the film, Amaya became obsessed with all things horror. Her current passion is monster makeup. It's gotten so that Aaron has had to warn Amaya more than once about leaving makeup rings in the sink when she washes it off. She signed up for a children's cosplay contest for a film expo happening in a couple of weeks. Every other day, she comes up with something more to add to her costume. Kara smiles and shakes her head. AJ is the competitive athlete like her, and Amaya is the creative one, making art like her dad, albeit a different kind of art.

The similarities between them and their kids never cease to amuse her.

"I'll talk to your father about it, okay?"

"Thanks, mommy!" Amaya squeals.

Kara might as well have said yes. Amaya is Aaron's princess. He bends over backward for his kids.

Amaya's excitement dies down and she looks worried.

"What's wrong, baby?" Kara asks.

"I just hope that I win. I'm going up against a lot of older kids who have done this longer. I don't want to look silly."

"Come with me," Kara says, holding out her hand.

Amaya takes her mother's hand and Kara leads her into the bathroom. Kara stands behind her as they both look into the mirror.

"Okay now, repeat after me," Kara says. "I am Amaya Evelyn Tompkins."

"I am Amaya Evelyn Tompkins," Amaya giggles.

Kara gives her a loving but stern look. "Get serious now."

Amaya stops giggling and stands up straight. "Sorry, mommy."

Kara nods and continues, "I am smart."

"I am smart."

"I am capable."

"I am capable."

"And I am strong."

"And I am strong."

Kara wraps her arms around Amaya and holds her. "Go get 'em, baby girl."

Amaya smiles a mile wide. "Grandma Evie said this to you before all of your races?"

"Yep, before each one, and I never lost."

Having lost three races, Kara's bending the truth a little bit, but so what. Her daughter needs to feel like the winner she already is.

"I miss her, momma."

"I do too, baby." Kara kisses Amaya on the top of her head. "Go on and help your brother."

"Okay."

Amaya runs out and joins AJ. The two of them clear off the dishes. Kara takes a deep breath and heads to the kitchen. She grabs herself a bottle of water. Glimpsing the refrigerator door, she smiles. It's practically covered in Amaya and AJ's most recent tests and certificates. They all have high scores. Both know that if their grades slip considerably, then soccer and zombies will be on ice. There's a knock at the door. AJ opens it and sees a UPS delivery man with a large box for Kara.

"Mom, there's a package for you."

"Finally," Kara replies as she heads to the door. "Could you please place it over there?" Kara asks the driver, pointing to the couch.

He sets it down and leaves.

"Is this your present for daddy? Can we see it?" Amaya asks.

"Yes, it is, and no, you may not. It's a surprise. I want

your dad eyes to be the first to see it."

"When is dad going to be home?" AJ asks. "I wanted to practice my soccer drills with him later."

"Him and Grandpa Rick are out running errands. It might be a while, kiddo."

Aaron and Richard walk through the hardware store looking for supplies. Richard wants to do some home renovations to his home and asked Aaron to help.

"What do you think of this color for the bedroom?" Richard asks, holding up a paint sample.

Aaron nods his approval. It's a pale-yellow color. He knows why Richard is picking that color. Evie always liked light, soft colors. He wants to change things but still have little reminders of her.

"I like it. I think she would like it, too."

Richard gives Aaron a warm smile. "I think you're right."

The pair leave the hardware store and are heading towards Aaron's truck when...

"Hey, yo Smoke!"

Aaron turns around and sees Tone. He looks much better than the last time Aaron saw him. He has a little boy and girl with him holding each other's hand. His demeanor seems calmer, a lot less aggressive. It looks good on him.

"Tone! How are you man?"

The two old friends hug. Aaron notes how happy Tone looks. This makes him smile. He sees the kids, and they look happy too.

"Hi there," Aaron says to the smiling children.

"Hi," the boy says.

The little girl gives a small demure wave.

"Anthony, Sierra. This is your Uncle Smoke, he's the man who helped daddy. The one I've been telling you about."

"Did you really punch daddy in the face?" Anthony asks.

"How did you know about that?" Tone asks.

"Momma told me."

"Reynisha and that mouth of hers, I swear," Tone grumbles.

Aaron laughs. "I did, but we're cool now." Aaron turns to Richard. "Tone. Kids. This is Richard. He's my stepfather-in-law. We were just doing some shopping. I'm helping Rick with some renovations."

"It's cool you still doing that shit, man. Duke would be proud."

"Thanks, man. Appreciate you."

"We better be off. I promised these two some ice cream. But we should hang out sometime, Smoke. We got a lot to catch up on."

"Yeah, that sounds good. You know, Rick, me, and my boy Rod got a poker game coming up at the house, you should join us."

"Okay, that sounds good." Tone's expression becomes serious. "Thanks again for helping me out back in day, Smoke. I got a job and have been stacking my coins, and I swear I will pay you back. I'm sorry I haven't reached out. Took me a minute to get my shit together."

"It's no problem. Good seeing you, Tone."

"You too, Smoke. Nice meeting you, sir."

"You, too." Richard smiles.

"Guys say bye to Uncle Smoke."

"Bye, Uncle Smoke," Anthony says.

"Bye," Sierra says.

Tone walks away. Aaron watches and a lump form in his throat. His boy finally got his shit together, and he couldn't be prouder.

"Alright, young blood. Let's get you back home to your woman."

That gets Aaron's attention. He can't wait to see Kara. Tonight's going to be incredible.

aron comes home after dropping off Richard. He's greeted by what appears to be an empty house.

"Kara!" he calls out.

"Be right out," she says.

"Mom got the kids already?" Aaron asks.

"Yeah. Sheila, Denise, Guillermo, and Birdie are there

too. She sent me pictures of them looking through old photo albums."

"That's sweet."

Kara enters. She has on a gorgeous knee-length, figure-hugging, sleeveless black dress with a plunging neckline. Her hair is done in loose ringlets, and she is wearing red lipstick, smoky eye shadow, and mascara.

"Holy shit," Aaron says.

"Aaron, do you know what today is?"

He takes her by the hips and pulls her to him. "My lucky day?"

Kara giggles. "Kind of. Fifteen years ago today, you and I started seeing each other."

Aaron smiles. "That explains it."

"What?"

"Why Richard suddenly needed a bunch of shit to redo his house. I've been offering to help him for years and this morning he calls me with a laundry list errands. You and your stepdad played me." Aaron smirks.

"Just a little." Kara indicates with her index finger and thumb just how little.

"Oh, just a little, huh?" Aaron chuckles, imitating her.

Aaron loves Kara's playful side. She's managed to throw him a surprise party every year for his birthday. And even though he begs her not to every year, he always has an amazing time. He's curious about what she has cooked up tonight.

He rubs his hands down her back and grabs her ass.

"And you weren't the only one scheming. Of course, I remembered what today is, and I made some plans myself."

"What kind?" Kara purrs as she scratches his beard. Aaron's happy he grew it years ago. Kara loves playing with it.

"You'll have to wait and see."

The two of them arrive at McCalister's, an upscale, five-star restaurant located downtown. He has on a finely tailored black suit with a charcoal gray tie. He and Kara walk arm and arm into the restaurant. A few people turn, look at them, and smile. Aaron catches a couple of dudes checking out Kara. He doesn't blame them. She's fine as hell. They're seated by the window with a great view of Downtown L.A.

The waitress comes by. "Hello, welcome to McCalister's. My name is Stephanie. Can I get you both something to drink?"

Aaron replies, "I'll have a seven and seven, and the lady will have a cosmopolitan."

"Coming right up." Stephanie goes to get their drinks.

Kara and Aaron stare at one another like they can't wait to devour each other. Stephanie comes back with their drinks and asks if they're ready to order. They order the three-course meal. She comes back with some caviar as their first course and a bottle of champagne. "Courtesy of McCalister's in celebration of your anniversary," Stephanie says as she pours them each a glass.

"Thank you," Aaron and Kara say in unison.

She leaves them.

"To us," Kara says as she raises her champagne flute.

"To us," Aaron replies.

They clink glasses and take a sip.

Aaron chuckles.

"What's so funny?" Kara stares at Aaron with a dreamy look in her eyes.

Aaron takes her hand and kisses it. "I'm just thinking about us and all that we've been through."

"It has been a wonderful journey."

"Yeah, it has." Aaron smiles. "Remember when AJ was two and he ran out of the house naked?"

Kara cracks up. "Oh, my God. I have never been so scared in my life. That little runt ran right into the street."

"And you took off like a gunshot, right after him. I have never seen you move that fast, not even during our 'race.'"

Kara giggles. "That wasn't a race. That was you watching me run."

"I do like watching you." Aaron stares at his wife. Taking in her beautiful face. Kara bites her bottom lip and blushes.

"You know what that does to me, Kara."

"You're right, I do."

The two of them lean across the table at the same time. When their lips are only inches apart, Kara's eyes light up.

"I got one," Kara says.

"Got what?" Aaron says as she snaps out of the trance, she put him under.

"A memory."

"You were never going to kiss me, were you?"

"No." Kara sticks out her tongue.

"I don't like you," Aaron jokingly sneers.

"Yeah, you do." Kara kisses his nose and sits back down.

Aaron rolls his eyes at his goofy ass wife and takes a seat. "I guess. So, what's the memory that was so important, you disrupted us."

"Remember the first time you showed up at my house?"

"Oh, shit." Aaron claps his hands as he laughs. "Yo, I thought Trixie was going to fucking eat me or Evie was going to wake up and have me arrested. That was before she even met me."

Aaron playfully cringes at the memory. This was when he was trying to prove his love to Kara after their talk at the diner and before he started walking Trixie each morning.

He decided to surprise Kara by standing outside her bedroom window and throwing pebbles at it to wake her up. Trixie barked and chased him, waking up Evie. That was the day Aaron and Trixie met.

"If memory serves correctly, after Trixie started chasing you, you ran to your car and hid," Kara laughs.

Aaron looks at Kara with a mocking frown. "That

wasn't my fault. Who names a pitbull Trixie? I was expecting a cute little beagle or something. And leave me alone. I was trying to be romantic."

Kara laughs even harder. She quickly composes herself and holds Aaron's hand across the table. "I think I'm closer to convincing Richard to move closer to us. Did you two get around to talking about that?"

"No, not at all."

"Aaron, I hinted all week that I wanted you to mention it to him."

"Yeah, I caught that. I'm sorry, baby. Rick and I got so caught up with the errands it must have slipped my mind."

It didn't. The renovations Richard needs Aaron to do were so he could rent out the current house and buy one closer to them.

He continues after taking a sip of his seven and seven. "That's not a bad idea, though. With Trixie on her last legs, he'll be alone soon. He should be closer to us. The kids would love that."

"I was hoping you could convince him."

"I'll see what I can do. Me, him, and Rod are having a card game in a couple of weeks."

"That's good. If he's still reluctant, we'll pull out the big guns and use the kids."

"Smart thinking. He can't say no to them. Speaking of the card game, guess who me and Richard ran into?"

"Who?"

"Tone. We caught up briefly, and I invited him to

join us."

"Really? How's he doing? It's been a minute since you saw him in the hospital."

"Kara, baby he's doing great. He has a job, and he had his kids with him. He looked happy."

"That's so great to hear."

Stephanie brings out their second course. They both have duck confit terrine. The two of them thank her, and she smiles and nods before making her exit.

Kara's phone buzzes at the same time Aaron's does. They both check them thinking something may have happened with the kids. They got the same message. Aaron's is from Rod and Kara's is from Janae.

Having fun in Barbados! Do not wish you were here ☺

The message is accompanied by a picture of the two of them kissing while on the beach, holding frozen drinks. They're celebrating their one-year anniversary as husband and wife. They didn't get to have a honeymoon. Before the wedding, Janae had top surgery and had to recover. That ate up her sick time and a huge chunk of her vacation time. The remaining vacation time went to all the celebrations leading up to the wedding and the ceremony itself. Leaving them with no time for a honeymoon. They finally embarked on their anniversary/honeymoon trip, arriving in Barbados three days ago.

Aaron and Kara laugh out loud and draw stares.

"I'm so glad they're having such a good time," Kara says.

"Me too." Aaron smiles.

"We need to go on a trip. Just the two of us."

"I know, we ain't been anywhere since...shit I don't even remember."

It's crazy that they haven't gone anywhere together in such a long time. Most of their trips are family ones and always include the kids.

"Okay, so this year, we are going on a trip. Just you and me. We are going to make this happen," Kara says. She holds out her pinky, and Aaron hooks it with his. "Maybe we can make it into our own second honeymoon, go somewhere out of the country. New Orleans was fun, but I'd like to use my passport."

Aaron kisses her hand. "We can make that happen."

"And you can have a bachelor party, too. I know you had quite a time at Rod's."

"Please, I was so busy organizing it and keeping his crazy ass brothers in line I didn't even have a chance to enjoy anything. Besides, I don't want one."

"Seriously? I know you have your card games, but you really don't want to have like a boy's weekend to just wild out and have fun?"

Aaron clears his throat and looks away. That's his tell that he wants to talk but can't quite come up with the words.

"Smoke?" Kara sings.

Aaron looks at her and grins. She rarely calls him

that. "Yes," he sings back.

"Why didn't *you* have a bachelor party?"

Aaron shrugs again. "I didn't want one and I still don't."

"But why?"

Aaron sighs and avoids eye contact. "I didn't trust myself not to hurt you again."

"What do you mean?"

Aaron has a pained look on his face. "The thing with that chick at the party years ago. Ever since that happened, I've made sure to keep myself away from situations like that."

Kara looks at him warmly. "Aaron, that was almost twenty years ago."

"I know, but I never forgave myself. I came really close to...I can't hurt you like that again. And it's not like I even want to. I just don't want to put myself in a situation like that."

"Aaron, you can be around as many smart, attractive, sexy women as you want, and I won't be worried. I trust you. I know you would never do that to me."

He looks down in shame. "Again," he says, barely above a whisper.

Kara warmly rolls her eyes. "We were kids. It was your first relationship, and Reynisha got in your head. You're a grown-ass, mature man now. You have nothing to be worried about. I know how much you love me."

Aaron looks back up at her. "More than anything."

Kara smiles. "Exactly." She takes his hand. "You love

me. And I know you would never cheat, no matter how much thicker I've gotten."

Now Aaron rolls his eyes. "Not this shit again."

"What?"

"This insane obsession you've been having with your weight lately. Kara, baby, stop tripping."

Stephanie brings them their third course. Kara has roasted chicken, and Aaron has Wagyu beef. They smile at her as she places their food down.

Stephanie leaves, and Kara responds. "That's easy for you to say. Your body basically looks the same," Kara says.

"Uh, no, it does not. And it certainly doesn't feel the same. Remember last week? My dumbass picked Birdie up, and I had to soak in the tub for damn near an hour."

Kara giggles at the memory. He and Guillermo were talking shit about how much they lift, and Aaron—who was being extra—decided it would be a good idea to try and pick up nine-year-old Birdie. Next thing Kara knew, she was taking care of him for two days while he recuperated.

"And so, you have a little more thickness to you, so what?" Aaron continues.

Aaron cuts a piece of beef and places it on Kara's plate. She does the same with her chicken.

"So? I have been trying to get rid of the extra weight from the kids for years, and nothing I have done has made it go away. I was an athlete. I should be able to shed pounds like that." Kara snaps her fingers.

"I don't see the issue. Your ass, titties, and thighs got thicker. You should consider yourself blessed. I know I do." Aaron winks.

Kara laughs. "You're so stupid."

He joins in her laughter.

Kara gets serious, though her expression is full of love. "And you, my dear husband, need to stop tripping over something that happened so long ago. Hell, you told me that when you last saw Reynisha, you didn't even flinch when she hit on you."

"That's different. After she talked all that shit, there's no way I'd fuck with her ass."

"Aaron, if any woman hit on you, you wouldn't fuck with her. You would politely tell her you're married, and if she kept going, you'd introduce her to Smoke."

"I'm not going to hit a woman, Kara." Aaron playfully looks at her like she's insane.

Kara laughs and throws a green bean at him. "You know what I mean. You'd make sure she got the picture."

"You're right. I would." He pops the green bean in his mouth and grins at her.

"Can you please give yourself some grace and stop beating yourself up? For me?"

"For you, I will try."

Stephanie brings them dessert. Kara has lemon custard with strawberry sorbet, and Aaron has chocolate almond lava cake with brown butter ice cream.

They take a bite of one another's dessert.

"That ice cream is good," Kara says.

"So is your custard."

"This and my gift I'm saving for later was my contribution to today. What do you have planned?" Kara says.

"It's at the house."

Kara gives Aaron a seductive smile. "Let's go."

They arrive at home. Aaron walks ahead of Kara and turns on the lights. The living room is filled with rose petals, and early 2000s R&B plays throughout the house. Fake candles are lit on the dining table. Aaron takes Kara's hand and leads her into the house.

"This is beautiful, Aaron."

"Thanks. I thought about getting us a suite at a hotel..."

"No, this is perfect. This house is where we fell in love and built a life together."

Kara hugs him. Soon they're swaying back and forth in each other's arms to "Can't Let Go" by Anthony Hamilton.

Aaron notices the large flat package against the couch. "What's that?" he asks.

"It's your present. Open it."

Aaron lets go of Kara and walks over to the couch. She takes a seat next to him. He opens the package and is speechless. It's a portrait of her, Aaron, and the kids when they were younger. He has tears in his eyes. Kara takes his hand.

"For years we've talked about what to put on the wall by the dining table. I think this is perfect. Right above the bookcase."

AJ's Library is now called AJ and Amaya's Library and it's filled with graphic novels and Percy Jackson books.

Aaron looks at her lovingly. "Thank you." He wipes his tears. "I love it."

He takes her in his arms and kisses her. Their kisses become more urgent and passionate. Kara cups Aaron's face in her hands while his hands travel all over her body. He lifts her up and takes her into the bedroom.

"Careful now. You don't want to fuck up your back again," Kara teases.

"Very funny." Aaron smacks Kara's ass.

Aaron lays her on the bed while "All That I Can Say" by Mary J. Blige plays. He carefully takes off every stitch of her clothing. He takes her by her hands and leads her to the mirror on their closet door, standing behind her. She turns her head away, but he gently forces her to look in the mirror.

"I'm not going to take you slandering my wife much longer," he whispers in her ear.

Aaron kisses her shoulder and slowly traces his tongue up her neck. Kara lets out a moan, and he cups her breasts.

"Goddamn, you're beautiful," he whispers in her ear.

Aaron turns her around so she's facing him. He takes her by the hand, leading her back to the bed. He slowly kisses her down her neck, chest, and stomach. She smells intoxicating. Especially between her legs. Aaron stops in front of her pussy. He raises her right leg over his shoulder and takes a lick.

"Mmmm," Aaron moans. "I love tasting you when you're nice and wet."

"Then stop talking and keep licking."

"Yes, ma'am."

Kara rubs her hand over Aaron's head. He laps up her wetness before looking up and wiping his mouth and beard. Without saying a word, she summons him. He knows what she wants, and he happily obliges. Aaron climbs on top of Kara and kisses her. They gaze at each other as he pushes his dick inside of her. She lets out a desperate moan causing him to take a deep breath. She feels way too good, but he needs to chill. He can't have this be over before it starts. He moves faster and faster. They wrap their arms around each other. Their bed slams against the wall with each thrust. They roll over, and Kara is now on top. She leans up and rides Aaron with fervor.

"Aww, shit," Aaron says as he grabs hold of her ass and squeezes. He picks Kara up and presses her against the bedroom door. Her legs are wrapped around his hips. They don't break their rhythm. Kara has her arms around his neck. His hands still cup her ass.

"Still think I can't pick you up?" Aaron asks with a Cheshire cat grin.

"Shut up," Kara chuckles. Her laughter quickly turns into moans. "Oh, shit. Aaron, Aaron. Oh, fuck!" Kara cries out as she orgasms.

"Ohhh, Kara, Kara," Aaron moans as he comes inside of her. His knees give out and they collapse on the floor laughing.

Minutes later, they lie in bed. Aaron plays with Kara's nipples. He rubs them, licks them and sucks them. "Mmmmm," she moans. They smile and face each other, tracing their fingers along each other's faces.

He chuckles. "I'm glad you got that IUD."

Kara giggles. "Me too. I love our kids but…"

"No way in hell are we having more."

"Nope."

They laugh and continue to caress one another.

"I remember watching footage of one of your track meets with Evie and Janae. As we watched you go, Evie said to me, 'That girl moves as fast as fire,'" Aaron says.

Kara releases a mournful sigh at the memory of her mother. Aaron kisses her forehead. "I didn't mean to… I know thinking about her is still raw."

"It's okay."

He gathers her in his arms. "I was trying to make a point; not make you cry."

Kara giggles again and rubs Aaron's nose with hers. "I'm okay. I swear."

Aaron smiles and continues. "I got called Smoke because I'm a fighter, and so are you. That's why we work. Just like there's no smoke without fire, there's no me without you. You're my fire, Kara. I love you."

Kara has tears in her eyes, and she smiles. "I love you, too, Smoke."

Acknowledgments

There are so many people who made this book possible. First and foremost I want to thank my husband and my kids. I know my not being able to spend a lot of time with you this past year was hard but thanks to your patience, I made one of my biggest dreams come true and I am now a published author.

I want to give a big shout out to my Black author Twitter friends including Presh aka Bella Jay, Tia Love, Kema B and so many more. I want to thank my Sunday writers group for their encouragement. I want to thank Black Girls Who Write, Smut U and the Melanin Library as well for their support.

And to everyone at Word Makers, special shout out to the Write Owls! Thank you for making me laugh during this sometimes very arduous journey.

Lastly, I want to thank everyone who helped be make this book possible:

Jessica thank you for your editing genius, Meka, thank you for making this book better with your wonderful, thorough notes . Mia, thank you for your constant support and help, Gabby thank you for being patient with me and for your amazing proofreading skills,

Brynn thank you for your amazing help throughout all of this, Leni thank you! You are the greatest and Jazelle James, thank you for making Janae into the amazing lovable nerd she is. Your help was invaluable.

Thank you to all who have read this book and to all that will read it. I hope you love these characters as much as I do!